ADAM CLAYTON
DEATH MIST

AETHON THRILLS

aethonbooks.com

DEATH MIST
©2025 ADAM CLAYTON

This book is protected under the copyright laws of the United States of America. No part of this publication may be reproduced, stored in a retrieval system, or transmitted, in any form or by any means, without the prior permission in writing of the publisher, nor be otherwise circulated in any form of binding or cover other than that in which it is published and without a similar condition including this condition being imposed on the subsequent purchaser. Any reproduction or unauthorized use of the material or artwork contained herein is prohibited without the express written permission of the authors.

Aethon Books supports the right to free expression and the value of copyright. The purpose of copyright is to encourage writers and artists to produce the creative works that enrich our culture.

The scanning, uploading, and distribution of this book without permission is a theft of the author's intellectual property. If you would like to use material from the book (other than for review purposes), please contact editor@aethonbooks.com. Thank you for your support of the author's rights.

Aethon Books
www.aethonbooks.com

Print and eBook layout, design, and formatting by Josh Hayes. Cover by Steve Beaulieu.

Published by Aethon Books LLC.

Aethon Books is not responsible for websites (or their content) that are not owned by the publisher.

This book is a work of fiction. Names, characters, places, and incidents are the product of the author's imagination or are used fictitiously. Any resemblance to actual events, locales, or persons, living or dead is coincidental.

All rights reserved.

ALSO BY ADAM CLAYTON

HANNAH AHEMD THRILLERS

Shadow Agenda

Janus Curse

Death Mist

You can also join our non-spam mailing list by visiting Thriller Books: https://aethonbooks.com/thriller-newsletter/ and never miss out on future releases. You'll also receive five full books completely free as our thanks to you.

CHAPTER 1

The last train to Brixton came to a squealing stop at London's Highbury & Islington underground station. Curved subway-tiled walls amplified the harsh screeching of train wheels in the empty station, and fluorescent lighting made the station feel cold and lonely.

There were only two people on the train at this late hour: an elderly man in a threadbare overcoat carrying a package under one arm, and a cloaked figure in an oversized rain slicker with the hood drawn tight. Thus masked, the latter passenger's identity was hidden.

Exiting the carriage car, the cloaked passenger swayed while standing and grabbed the edged of the train door for support. Even with the additional support the figure still stumbled slightly while stepping out, despite the *Mind the Gap* sign on the wall. The old man buttoned his coat and held his package tight, then stepped onto the escalator. The hooded person, lagging behind, stopped and looked around as if making certain the station was empty.

The cloaked figure moved slowly, almost painfully approaching the escalator. There was a sudden halt, as if moving stairs were a strange phenomenon that needed observation before continuing. Grasping the running handrail, the person stumbled and then steadied.

By the time the top was reached, the old man had disappeared into the night. The cloaked figure stopped and scanned the street. There was no one around, not even traffic. Even the moon was absent, creating a dark world that kept most Londoners inside.

Stepping out of the building's entry, the hooded figure looked up. A thick, heavy fog was rolling in, almost obscuring a sign atop the red brick façade proclaiming the station's date of construction: 1904. The thick mist moved like some gigantic amoeba, swallowing buildings, homes, and streets alike.

With a shrug, the hooded figure set out.

A nondescript sedan crept along the silent streets through the fog. Two men were inside, both dressed in gray suits. Their car was followed closely by a plain white cargo van. The van's dark-tinted windows obscured the interior.

The thickening fog soon made it impossible to see more than a few feet ahead. The sedan driver leaned over the steering wheel, wiping condensation off the windscreen while trying to hold a steady course. On his left, the passenger was checking the side-view mirror to be certain the van was still with them. He was also listening to a police scanner mounted under the dash.

"Nothin' yet," said the passenger. They were waiting for a bulletin regarding their fugitive.

The small radio issued an almost constant chatter, mostly inconsequential small talk. Bored cops trying to get through a dull night shift.

"Can't see a damn thing," said the driver.

His passenger fiddled with the radio's squelch knob. "There

was only one train headed for London when the escape was reported."

"Yeah, to Brixton. We just gotta follow that line."

"Don't worry," said the passenger, "no one's gonna get past us."

"Just keep your ears peeled... we don't want to miss an alert."

Leaving the Islington underground station, the hooded figure struggled to walk along empty sidewalks. The fog looked like an enormous wave breaking over the city. It descended noiselessly and obscured everything. Even street lamps became dim, diffused blobs that looked like fireflies bobbing in the fog.

The air was clammy and wet and smelled like soggy wool. The thick atmosphere made breathing difficult. Each labored step the figure took splashed water onto the slicker, causing the person to stop frequently to shake off the excess.

The howl of a lone dog, like some kind of demon hound, echoed in the night air. The figure froze and tilted an ear in the direction of the baying.

Big Ben tolled twice. It seemed far away, and the bells sounded muffled and flat.

The figure reached a streetlamp and grabbed it for support. The dog howled again. This time it sounded closer. The figure pushed back the hood in order to listen more closely.

The hooded figure was a woman.

I have to make it...

She shivered, the heavy moisture plastering her short blonde hair. Lifting her right hand, she checked the shoulder bag strapped across her chest. She pulled out a scrap of paper, looked around at street signs, and then set off anew.

Fog-shrouded storefronts appeared and disappeared in the

thick mist, tilted at crazy angles like horror movie houses. The baleful openings seemed to groan out sinister, frightening warnings. In her confused state, the entire world was askew.

Distorted perspectives caused missteps and stumbles. It was a scary, insane world where anything could happen.

Shuffling through the night, she came to the Islington Green.

Close now...

At Upper Street, Islington's main shopping area, she stumbled again, grabbing a bench for support.

Can't go on...

After a long moment, she regained some measure of strength and stood erect.

Must reach Hannah...

The sound of the baying dog echoing through the gray mist caused her skin to crawl. The howling definitely sounded closer now. She knew her altered condition was detectable by dogs. It was something they reacted to—aggressively.

After re-checking the scrap of paper, she took a deep breath and moved on, fear driving every step.

The distance between street lamps seemed to grow as each step became more difficult to muster. She was forced to hold on to each lamp before continuing. After a seemingly endless trek, she reached the street she sought.

This is where I'll find my friend.

Climbing the stairs, her only thought was to reach Hannah.

Standing before the door, she silently apologized for the hour and knocked. Wobbling as she waited, she hoped she could hang on.

After what could have been an eternity, a light came on. Locking tumblers turned and the door opened.

Hannah Ahmed was a light sleeper. A rap at the front door pierced through her slumber. Her eyes flew open, mind instantly alert. "A knock on my door in the middle of the night? That can't be good." She heard howling in the distance. It stirred something visceral, an ancient human response to danger: flee, hide, and escape.

Opening a nightstand drawer, she grabbed her SIS service weapon, a Beretta Nano. Smoothing her nightgown and tossing back her long, dark hair, she went into the front room.

Standing beside the door, not in front, she held her weapon at the ready. Taking a deep steadying breath, she unlatched the security lock and cracked the door open.

In a gestalt blink, she took in the intruder's appearance: a woman about her own age... face haggard... oversized rain slicker, wet and dripping. The woman swayed almost drunkenly, yet she judged it to be an injury or illness, not intoxication.

The moment passed and her eyes went wide in surprise and recognition. Before she could say anything, the woman fell forward, collapsing against the door and into her arms.

Carrying the woman inside, she removed the rain-soaked cape, put the shoulder bag in a closet, and laid her on the couch. "Amy? Amy Perry... is it you?"

There was only a groan.

"Amy, what's happened? I got your text message. It was disturbing." She looked questioningly at one of the few friends she'd kept in touch with from her university days. "You said you were in trouble and couldn't trust anyone. You said you needed sanctuary..."

Her friend groaned while thrashing her head from side to side.

"I didn't expect you to turn up in the middle of the night."

Amy's eyes fluttered and she tried to sit up. Holding her shoulders lightly, Hannah eased Amy down on the couch.

"Stay right there. I'll get you some hot tea."

While she was busy in the kitchen, Hannah heard a noise. Amy was sitting up. Her eyes were vacant, yet fear was written on her face.

Hannah stopped what she was doing and rushed to her friend's side. Amy's eyes were clouded over. The pupils were dilated and the whites of her eyes bloodshot. Amy's breathing was quick, shallow, and irregular. Whatever was wrong with her friend, it wasn't good.

"You. Must. Stop it," Amy croaked, her voice all but gone.

"Stop what? What do you mean?"

"The mist… stop the mist…"

"What mist is that? The fog outside? How do I stop it?"

"My notes… they'll lead you."

Hannah had an uncomprehending look.

"Notes tell everything…"

Amy went limp and fell back onto the couch. Alarmed, Hannah grabbed her friend.

"Amy!"

There was no response. Amy Perry was dead.

CHAPTER 2

The sedan came to an abrupt stop. Both men inside listened intently to a notification coming over the police radio. *This is a 10-78 for Islington. Is anyone in the area?* The passenger lifted the microphone and keyed it.

"10-8. This is Detective Walters. We can provide assistance. What's the address?"

The passenger looked over to the driver and smirked. "See? I told you. This little freelance gig is going to turn out fine."

Walters wrote down the street address. They set off as quickly as the thick fog would allow. The chase van followed.

Hannah was no stranger to death. She acted immediately and contacted the authorities. The arrival of the police surprised Hannah. First, because of the remarkably quick response time, and then, the officers' attire: they wore suits, not uniforms.

These aren't beat cops.

Presenting badges, they identified themselves as Detectives Walters and Smith. As they entered her flat, she was unsure which

7

was which. She also wondered why detectives were responding to her call. That wasn't normal procedure.

The detectives examined but didn't touch Amy's body, still lying on the couch. She noticed neither man took notes. One of the detectives—she thought it was Walters—took out a mobile and made a call. Almost immediately, two EMTs wheeled a gurney into the flat. After a swift, muted conversation with the detectives, they placed Amy's body on the wheeled stretcher.

As the EMTs moved Amy's body out, the detectives turned to Hannah. She'd been sitting patiently at her kitchen table. "This looks suspicious," Detective Walters said. "Maybe a homicide."

Hannah was taken aback. "You don't suspect me…?"

"Certainly not. This location looks to be entirely coincidental."

The detectives' continuing questioning was cursory and lacked curiosity about the circumstances surrounding Amy's death. But she said nothing. This was their show.

As they left, the detectives announced they may have more questions later.

She felt… what did she feel? Disappointed? Let down?

In and out in what… ten, fifteen minutes? And they didn't even leave a card.

She had a strong feeling there wouldn't be any meaningful follow-up.

The detectives had gone, Amy's body had been taken off by the EMTs, and Hannah was left alone in her living room. Her head spun with the evening's events.

With all the activity, she hadn't had time to think about Amy's appearance in the middle of the night or the things she'd said before dying. She wandered to the hall closet.

I didn't tell the policemen about Amy's bag. It must have slipped my mind.

Opening the door, the bag still laid where it was dropped. Closing the closet door, she headed to her bedroom.

I've had quite enough excitement for one night. I'll deal with the bag tomorrow.

CHAPTER 3

The Applied Science Research Institute, or ASRI, was located outside London. It was a modern building but easy to miss in the countryside, as it was positioned behind tall trees lining the roadway. The only indication of ASRI's presence was a small sign at a turnoff. The road led through a stand of woods and opened onto the institute, a long, sleek building standing alone, like an island in a sea of trees.

Dawn was breaking when the sedan and panel van turned up the drive. Passing through the woods, they emerged in an open field surrounding the ASRI building. The vehicles passed around the building to the rear, coming to a stop at a set of double doors.

Two men got out of each vehicle. The gray-suited men emerged from the sedan and made their way to the building's rear doors. The others got out of the van. They were dressed in white coveralls embellished with various medical-looking patches. They looked like legitimate EMTs.

Opening the van's rear door, one of the EMTs leaned around the open door and called out, "Hey! You wanna give us a hand here?"

"That's not our job," Walters called back.

Death Mist

With a murmured curse, the EMTs pulled out the gurney. A shrouded body lay atop the wheeled stretcher. They struggled a bit, rolling it across the pebbled parking area until finally reaching the rear doors. Walters and his partner held them open. One EMT gave a *thanks-for-nothing* look to the unhelpful pair. Their duty now complete, Walters and Smith left the EMTs to complete their task.

The EMTs wheeled the gurney down a sterile, white-tiled hallway. The wheels clacked an off-beat rhythm as the gurney passed over each floor seam. Overhead, lights automatically blinked on as they passed from one to the next.

Reaching the hallway's end, the EMTs rolled the gurney into a room resembling an operating theater. There were medical machines, monitors, blinking lights, and glowing displays. A lamp mounted to a large, gimbaled arm hung from the ceiling over a stainless-steel examination table. A smell of disinfectant hung in the air.

A man wearing a green surgical gown and latex gloves stood by the examination table. He wore a head covering with a clear mask that flipped down over his face. He reeked of anxiousness.

"Where've you been? Don't you know time's critical?"

The EMTs shrugged as they wheeled the gurney over and lifted the body onto the table.

"She's all yours, doc," said one of the men, and they left the room.

The begowned doctor looked up at the clock on the wall. "I hope we're in time."

The postmortem was rushed. There was no time to waste, no time for normal procedures. The body was stripped and lay face up, the eyes still open in horror. Ignoring the look of terror on the dead woman's face, Dr. Hughes made a long incision down the sternum to the pubic arch. It was more like a hasty butchering than a professional autopsy.

The body opened to reveal a mass of gray particles filling the body cavity. It resembled dust with the appearance of a clinging mist.

Moving carefully so as not to disturb the particles, Dr. Hughes reached for a vacuum standing nearby. The machine wasn't a consumer-style shop-vac; it was made from stainless-steel with an air-tight lid held in place by several large bolts. The hose, curled around the top, was made from a special polymer. There was a cap inserted over the open end of the hose.

Flipping a switch, a soft hum announced the canister was operating. The doctor removed the hose cap and tested the suction with his palm. A squelching sound assured him the vacuum was working properly. He bent over the body and began sucking up the gray particles.

Most were soon gathered in the canister, however, reaching all the dust specks lodged around organs would take special care. Dr. Hughes changed to a nozzle attachment that was long and flat on one end, allowing him to reach in and around the body cavity.

When he was satisfied everything had been extracted, Dr. Hughes was ready to sew up the cadaver. He checked the time. The wall clock read ten o'clock in the morning.

As he was closing the body, a wall-mounted video monitor came to life. The screen was filled with the face of a stern-looking, middle-aged woman. Large, thick glasses magnified her eyes and made the pupils appear unnaturally large.

"Have you finished?" The barked question filled the room and caused Hughes to jump.

At first annoyed, his demeanor changed as he recognized the woman in the monitor, and he became more conciliatory. "Just finishing up. I've transferred the specimens to the storage canister."

"Did you recover it all? Are they still viable?" The woman's face leaned closer, distorting her features even more.

"Yes, yes, I captured them all. I haven't tested them yet, but it looks like most survived."

CHAPTER 4

Margret Corbyn had excelled in school, graduating with an advanced degree in biology, specializing in biochemistry. That led her to the Applied Science Research Institute, a start-up company in California. Once hired, she soon gained a reputation as a capable—if aloof—manager. She had to fight to get ahead, but it paid off. She was now the Operations Manager for ASRI-Great Britain.

Her medium-length hair, once brown, was now invaded by gray. Not an attractive gray. It was dark and streaked. She wasn't heavy, though her solid frame made her feel eternally fat. That body image was an irritating grievance her entire life, one that manifested in her interactions with others.

Corbyn was dressed in her customary medium gray pantsuit, her "uniform." It was her practice never to run, but she did walk briskly, often leaving others behind. That didn't bother Director Corbyn—behind is where she liked her subordinates.

When she wasn't in earshot, the staff called her "Maisie." It was a childish British nickname for Margaret. She hated it. It set off deep-seated feelings of anger and bitterness that had begun as a child in America...

Dreams of greatness and success filled her young mind. She imagined herself a hero, breaking down walls of inequity, trampling the unworthy, and finally reaching the pinnacle of success. But that was not to be.

She felt trapped by fate and rebelled against adversity with grim determination. Her ambition had, in gradual steps, become greed—not for money, but for power. She craved dominion over others and the respect she was owed.

Dreams of ambition, success, and domination became the driving force in her life. It kept her isolated and lonely, though determined. Then, by pure chance, she stumbled onto a project she believed would bring her closer to realizing her dreams—a project that would make her feel complete.

This afternoon she'd assembled her "special project" staff, each a senior technician. She hadn't told them they were going to work on an off-the-books project. Only Dr. Hughes and Callum Robertson, ASRI's head of security, knew the truth.

The technicians, two men and a woman, sat at polite attention.

Tipping heavy-framed glasses down the bridge of her nose, she glared at the techs. It pleased her when they squirmed. She wasn't going to let this current complication stop her program. There were rivals within the institute's organization just waiting for her to slip up. She was determined not to let this present setback torpedo her career.

"The problem of the escaped traitor has been resolved," Corbyn said, looking over the three technicians.

This announcement generated a murmur of relief.

She pushed the glasses back into place. "I want to know how much Dr. Perry found out. More importantly, how she managed to get away."

Alarmed looks passed among the three. They knew about the body in the morgue. It was an earlier test subject, and they'd been sworn to secrecy. They were well aware of Director Corbyn's solution for loose lips and traitors: the end of their careers. None were anxious to be singled out as responsible for Amy Perry's escape.

Oliver Bouy finally mustered the courage to speak, "We think…" he turned to include the others, "Dr. Perry happened into the cold storage room and found the body."

Another technician, Myra Shipman, chimed in, "Dr. Perry's been acting suspicious lately. Asking lots of questions, poking around. She must have found something that led her to the cold room—and the remains."

"A body is easily explained," Corbyn said.

Myra cleared her throat. "Yes, ma'am, but in this case, she found the nanites."

Oliver jumped back in, "It wouldn't take a great leap for Dr. Perry to understand what had happened."

The second man, George Kraft, spoke up, "By the time we found out about Perry's discovery, she was gone—snuck out before anyone knew. I called Dr. Hughes and we both went to the cold room. We found the body out of the locker. Dr. Hughes put a mask on and inspected the open cavity. After poking around, he said that Dr. Perry most probably had inhaled nanites."

Corbyn turned to Dr. Hughes, who nodded slightly, acknowledging the veracity of the technician's statement.

Callum Robertson had come to ASRI in the early start-up days, taking a job as a security officer. It was humbling, but the baggage of his past made this lowly position a necessity. He'd been hired because of his background in the US Army. The circumstances of his separation from the service were murky; a time in his life he refused to talk about.

Because of Corbyn's influence, when the company opened a

satellite facility in Great Britain, he was assigned as Chief of Security. In this new position, he enjoyed autonomy and power. As he watched the interchange between Corbyn and the three technicians, his mind wandered back to the early days of ASRI—and how he and Corbyn first met.

It was night. I was on my regular rounds and saw a figure through an office window. I knew the office. It belonged to Margaret Corbyn, a bright star on the ASRI team. But it wasn't Corbyn that I saw. It was a man.

When I opened the office door, I saw the man sitting at Corbyn's desk, going through her computer. I recognized him as one of the department heads. When I entered, the man quickly shut down the computer. There was guilt on the man's face—like a kid caught with his hand in the cookie jar.

The man rushed out, mumbling excuses as he passed, but the whole episode was suspicious. The next day, I came back to Corbyn's office and told her what I'd seen. She was shocked at first and then angry. She asked who the intruder was. I told her. A dark look came over her face. "Thief," she'd said.

Two days later, Corbyn stopped me in the hall.

"I want to thank you for alerting me to the snooping on my computer. I checked the logs and found someone has been accessing my account over the last month. Always after hours. I had no idea."

"He was a supervisor," I replied. "Isn't he entitled?"

"Absolutely not! My research is private. When it's ready for presentation to senior management, I'm the one who will make it."

I asked her if she was going to report the man.

"Oh, no," she'd said. "He'd just get off, and it would be business as usual. I'm going to lay a trap. I'll change some key data points that will result in total failure. He won't dare try to present

it to senior management, and he won't take the risk of invading my office again."

From that time on, we became allies. I watched out for Corbyn and she helped me advance. It paid off. Now I'm chief of security in the UK office.

His attention returned to the meeting. He'd been quiet to this point, but when he stood, he got Corbyn's attention. His six-foot stature and muscular frame were concealed by a windbreaker. A company patch decorated one breast. The paratrooper-style boots he wore were in contrast to the other men's loafers, not to mention the low heels of the woman, Myra Shipman.

Clearing his throat to get everyone's attention, he began, "As soon as my office was made aware of the escape, we initiated pursuit. The subject was on foot, so the logical escape route was the train station. At that time of night, only one train operates—to Brixton."

Oliver Bouy broke in, trying to justify himself to Corbyn, "Dr. Hughes believed Amy Perry was infected... that turned out to be true!"

The security man gave the tech a withering look. Oliver backed off and looked around for support from his colleagues. The others avoided eye contact.

Robertson returned his attention to Corbyn.

"As luck would have it, a call was made to the Islington police reporting a death. I had a team in the area searching for the escaped woman. They were able to retrieve the body before anyone else arrived. The body was delivered back here just after dawn."

He sat down with a self-satisfied look.

Death Mist

After the meeting, Director Corbyn asked Robertson to her office. The room was sizable and strictly utilitarian. All the walls were vanilla-white and the carpet a plain beige. A large desk dominated the space, with two uncomfortable-looking side chairs. A heavy wooden credenza backed the desk. A small incense burner on the corner of the credenza released a pungent aroma that filled the room. The intense smoke practically adhered to the tongue.

The office walls were bare, except for a long rectangular multi-faced clock. Each clock was set to a different time zone around the world.

When Robertson entered, Corbyn wasted no time with small talk, launching into the topic on her mind, "There's more to this episode, Callum. Questions that need answering. For example, who lives in the home Dr. Perry felt compelled to visit in her last moments of life?"

"The flat belongs to a woman who lives alone. I believe it was a random selection—pure chance."

"You're saying that Perry, infected and growing increasingly delirious, went to the city and just stumbled into that particular flat?"

Robertson stood in silence, his stoic features offering no hint that the rebuke had any effect.

Frustrated by the security chief's seeming lack of analytical skills, she continued, "There's nothing more? No other connection?"

"Not that we know of. Running away was an instinctive reaction, like a wounded animal. Where the subject ended up was coincidental."

"I don't believe in coincidences, Callum. Dr. Perry just happens onto our project and then disappears. It wouldn't have taken much for her to put the pieces together. You call that coincidence?"

Robertson stood stock still, at attention.

"Whatever you may think of her instinctual reactions, she was still a highly intelligent woman. She escaped with secret information vital to our project. She went specifically to Islington. For what purpose? The address was important to Perry. She had to know she was dying... I think she was determined to expose us."

Director Corbyn sat alone in her office. She turned to the credenza behind her desk and lit a new incense stick. Inhaling deeply, she reveled in the almost intoxicating aroma. Next, she pulled out a worn charm and began rubbing. The distraction calmed her.

After mulling over recent events, she picked up the telephone and punched in Dr. Hughes' extension. It rang several times. The delay was annoying. *Why do I always have to keep tabs on him?*

Finally, the call was answered.

"Tell me about the Perry autopsy." There was irritation in her voice and she could almost see Hughes sitting up at attention. "Has gain-of-function been satisfied?"

"Yes, it has. The nanites are intact, and combining them with the previous experiment, I think we're ready for the next phase."

The report pleased her. Inhaling the rich incense sent, she closed her eyes in quiet meditation.

CHAPTER 5

Hannah hadn't gotten much sleep since the incident with Amy, and she felt it. Getting up and shuffling into the living room, she passed a decorative wall mirror. Stopping to inspect herself, she cringed and hastily tied back her long, dark hair. A few strands hung over her ears and cheeks.

"You need some serious help, my girl," she said to her reflection.

Her normally bright blue eyes were dimmed. The stress of Amy's death, combined with the interruption of her sleep, had taken its toll. Straightening up to her full five-foot, nine-inch height, she set off for the bathroom.

After a hot shower and a bit of makeup, she felt revived. Peering into the steam-covered mirror, she was satisfied with what she saw. Her hair now cascaded over her shoulders, framing her alabaster complexion and blue eyes. After dressing, she checked the time. It was almost noon. With a shrug, she straightened her lapels and set off.

Secret Intelligence Service headquarters was an imposing postmodern structure on the banks of the River Thames. Some people called the building *Legoland*, a reference to its stacked-block architecture; others called it *The Ziggurat*, the classical reference obvious. Regardless, she thought, it's an unmistakable London landmark.

The chief's office was on the top floor. His view of the River Thames was spectacular. She stopped to admire the panoramic vista. She had no such riverscape view from her small office in the rear of the building, which didn't bother her. She was mostly abroad on assignment.

She found Emily Fallon, C's administrative assistant, sitting as usual at her desk. Emily was middle-aged, impeccably dressed, with hair coiffed in a style that reminded Hannah of a helmet. Emily was stern with most people seeking access to her boss, but she had a soft spot for Hannah.

"What in the world…? Hannah, you look absolutely haggard. I thought you were on leave."

"I am, Em, but something happened that was most upsetting."

"My heavens! What?"

"Someone died. An old friend." Emily put her hand to her mouth, then Hannah added, "In my flat."

Emily gave a shocked look.

"That's what I've come to discuss with C."

Hannah opened one side of the double walnut doors and entered C's inner office. She found him engaged in a telephone conversation. Noticing her entry, he motioned her to one of the chairs before his desk.

Ending the call, C looked closely at her. "You're supposed to be on leave, Agent Ahmed." He made it sound like an accusation.

"Yes, sir. I am. But something happened that I think may be important."

"Go on."

"An old friend from university came to my door very late last night. She was disoriented, ill, and frightened. She quite literally collapsed in my arms. After laying her on my sofa, I went to make her a cup of tea. When I returned, she was almost hysterical, talking crazy." She paused. "Then she died."

"You called for help, of course."

"Yes, I contacted the police. Oddly, a pair of detectives came. They didn't really interview me, just asked for my name and the time of Amy's death. They never asked my occupation—isn't that odd? In fact, they seemed anxious to get out of there."

"Could she have died from some natural cause? A heart attack or something."

"I don't think so. Amy was my age. She was fit and strong. No, it wasn't a heart attack. In fact, her dying words were 'stop the mist.' That's odd, too, isn't it? Amy said the mist would kill us all."

C inspected his operative. "What is it you want?"

"I'd like your authorization to look into this."

C gave her a closer look, the kind that made most people squirm. "Fine. But you'll do it on your leave time."

"That's agreeable, sir." She gave him her best pleading look. "But I'd also like an autopsy performed. I can't ask for that, but you can order it."

"What do you hope to find?"

"I'm not sure."

The next day, Hannah received a call from C's admin. Emily had disturbing news. "I called to tell you that C contacted the ME in your district. They've no record of a body being delivered."

"What do you mean, no record?"

"Just that. C was going to ask for an autopsy, but they told him there've been no recent deliveries. I'm sorry, but there's nothing more he can do."

Hannah wanted to ask if he'd checked the other districts, but Emily had already hung up. She stared at the phone. *Something's very wrong...* She tried hard to remember the two EMTs who joined the detectives in her flat. *What were their names? Neither man wore a name tag, but then, I'm not sure their occupation requires name badges.*

They did have proper looking jumpsuits, patches, and a gurney... I never saw an ambulance or flashing lights. And they arrived so quickly, it was like they were waiting outside.

She dug deeper into her memory, focusing again on the two detectives. There was no reason to think they were anything other than what they claimed, was there? She remembered again how cursory their questioning had been. She was surprised they were in and out so fast. Like they were in a rush to leave.

Her suspicions wouldn't let her alone.

CHAPTER 6

Callum Robertson, ASRI-Great Britain's chief of security, had spent the night watching the Islington apartment building. He knew the flat number; it was on the first floor and registered to woman with an Arab-sounding name. *Surely, no connection to Dr. Perry.* Nevertheless, he had to be certain.

Based on the description given by his phony police detectives, he had a good description of the woman.

She shouldn't be hard to spot. They said she's tall and very attractive. Long dark hair, blue eyes, and an alabaster complexion.

He was having difficulty squaring that description with his preconceived notion of what Arab women looked like.

It was fortunate there was an all-night café on the street. He occupied a window table where he could observe the building without being obvious. He watched a number of strange characters come and go throughout the night. Night-crawlers, he called them. Still, the café was keeping him caffeinated while he watched and waited.

Morning came. No activity. Morning became noon. He was tired and beginning to worry the woman wouldn't leave the flat.

He ordered fish and chips and continued his surveillance. As he was finishing the meal, a woman emerged.

"That's her," he said with a grim smile.

The dark-haired woman drove out of a parking area behind the building. He had no idea what her destination might be, but it didn't matter. It gave him an opening.

He left the café and crossed the street.

Hannah sat alone in her flat, the memory of Amy's death fresh in her mind. Amy's warning about a mist continued to gnaw at the back of her mind. She finally decided what to do. Gathering her things, she set out for the police station.

It was a short drive down the A1 to Liverpool Road. A left turn onto Tolpuddle Street brought her to the Islington Police Station, a typical London structure of gray-brown brick. Three arches formed the entry, and lettering above identified the building. An arm extending over the sidewalk held a large blue lantern with *Police* emblazoned on all four sides.

Before leaving the car, she checked herself in the tiny visor mirror. She was pleased to see her eyes were now clear, and her complexion looked healthy.

She entered the police station and looked around to get her bearings. Spotting the information counter, she approached. A uniformed attendant at first paid no attention to her presence. He was busying himself with forms. The attendant must have felt her staring at him. He raised his head with a disinterested look.

"Good morning, officer. I'd like to speak with Detective Walters."

The officer looked weary. Clearly, it had already been a long day for him.

"One moment. Let me see if he's on duty."

As the officer searched his computer, she gazed around the busy lobby. Police officers were coming and going... people sat on uncomfortable-looking wooden benches, waiting to be called... angry shouts came from somewhere deep within the building... miscreants were being escorted toward the back in handcuffs.

The duty officer looked up, and she shifted her attention back to him. "Walters is upstairs. You'll find him in Investigations."

Thanking the officer, she took the stairway up to the first floor.

This must be where the real policing takes place.

There were a number of doors, each identifying a different department or squad. A little searching brought her to a door labeled *Investigations*. She opened the door and stepped into a large room filled with cubicles. Each workstation was occupied by a man or woman, and each was on the telephone. The room was filled with the sound of overlapping conversations. The hum and clack of printers and the occasional garbled sound from a police scanner filled the room. It wasn't as frantic as she expected, but there was still a sense of urgency in the air.

She walked through the cubicles until coming to one with a name plate reading *Det. M. Walters*. Peeking in, a man was hunched over his desk. One hand was held up to the side of his face, the other pressed a phone to his ear. Unable to make out the detective's features, she waited for him to finish his conversation.

The detective finally looked up. She put her hand to her mouth. *This isn't the man who was in my flat!*

"Yes?"

"Uh, I was looking for Detective Walters."

"You found him. What can I do for you?"

"Were you on duty two nights ago?"

"No. Had the night off. Why?"

"You came to my flat. But it wasn't *you*. Is there another Detective Walters?"

"Used to be, but he's not here now."

"What about Detective Smith?"

"Never heard of him, at least not in the Metropolitan Police. You might check the City of London Police, ma'am."

———

Callum Robertson had little difficulty finding the woman's flat inside the building. Looking around to be certain he wasn't being observed, he jimmied the lock.

The flat was clean and neat. There were a few frilly touches, like the curtains on the front windows and doilies on occasional tables, but fewer than he expected in a woman's home.

Where to start?

He began in the kitchen. Opening several drawers, he found only silverware. Dishes and various pots and pans were neatly stored in cupboards.

Nothing here connects her to Dr. Perry.

The living room was clear except for a laptop. It sat on an elegant Edwardian-style desk that seemed out of place in the flat. He opened the laptop. It was password protected. In order to get into the computer, he'd have to take it back to ASRI. That was out of the question. He closed the laptop and moved on, looking into the coat closet. A normal selection of coats and rain slickers. A large purse sat on the floor. Lifting the flap, he saw nothing of interest. Moving on, there was only the bedroom left to search.

He found it neat and tidy, like the rest of the flat. He began to believe his initial assessment was accurate: there was no connection between the two women.

He poked around until reaching the side table next to the bed. Opening the top drawer, he looked in confusion. *What's this?*

He lifted an empty holster from the drawer. *It looks like it's made for a small weapon.*

Replacing the holster in the drawer, he wondered why the woman would have such a thing. *Maybe she's just prudent, but then, where's the weapon?* He considered the implications of an empty holster. *Is she a police officer?* He searched around for credentials or a badge, finding none. Despite that, he was beginning to sense his belief that Dr. Perry showing up here wasn't a coincidence.

It would take more digging to confirm or refute his belief that this was a completely random act on Amy Perry's part.

After searching the Islington flat, Robertson returned to ASRI and went to his department. He avoided Corbyn's office. She'd want a report, and he wasn't ready to give her one. Not yet.

He brought his computer to life and began searching the name "Hannah Ahmed." To his surprise, there were no citations or links. He thought that remarkable. These days, virtually everyone left a digital trail.

Given her obvious Arabic heritage, he switched to different databases. Instead of Web searches, he accessed telephone directories, property records, school records, professional license records, and even driver's license records. Having no luck, he searched databases for North Africa and Middle Eastern countries. This was no small task, certainly not one he could accomplish alone. The good news was, he had a staff—and one of the most sophisticated computer systems in England.

Gathering his staff, he gave them search parameters, assigning each person a country or category.

CHAPTER 7

Hannah filed an investigation request before leaving the Islington Police Station. The inquiry allowed the police to search for the so-called detectives who'd come to her home. She didn't have much hope. Whoever they were, they were convincing. She didn't think they'd be found, much less brought to justice for impersonating a police officer.

Returning home, she sat down in frustration, angry that she'd been duped. She remembered Amy's last words. At the time, her attention was on Amy's warning about a mist and everyone dying, but there was something else... *She said something about notes.*

Remembering the shoulder bag she'd placed in the closet, she went to retrieve it. Finding it on the floor, she returned to the kitchen. There were a few personal items: a brush, a comb, a small mirror, a scrap of paper with her address scrawled on it, and a small booklet. Nothing out of the ordinary, except at the bottom of the bag, she found a high-capacity flash drive.

Picking up the booklet, she inspected its red leather cover. An empty pen loop was attached on one side; other than that, nothing notable. Putting the booklet aside, she examined the flash drive. There were no markings that might identify the contents.

Death Mist

Placing the bag on her kitchen table, she went back to the booklet, becoming confused. *What's this?*

The entries began a year ago. Fanning through the pages, she didn't pay much attention to the content. She closed the journal and set it aside, thinking about her many unanswered questions. *Why did Amy die? Where was Amy's body taken? What does it all mean?*

She went to her small desk, an Edwardian design made of lacewood and cherry inlays, arranged in a pleasing patchwork pattern. She was quite proud of the desk and the unique statement it made in her living room. She sat down in the small red velvet chair, also Edwardian, thinking about where to start.

Opening her laptop, she typed *Doctor Amy Perry* in the browser. A list of articles and citations came up. Hannah clicked on the first link. A biography. Some of Amy's accomplishments she knew, like her Ph.D. in biochemistry. However, Amy's recent work history was news to her. Especially the grant Amy had received. She clicked on a link to learn more.

The Feynman Foundation has awarded a grant of $50 million to Amy Perry, Ph.D.

The Foundation seeks those exceptional individuals in the field of nanotechnology who are paving the way to new applications and innovations in this exciting field.

A spokesman for the Foundation was quoted:

"Dr. Perry's grant allows her to expand the important work of integrating nanotechnology and biotechnology to achieve breakthroughs in nanomaterials and establish entirely new levels of tissue engineering."

The article continued on, but quickly became highly technical and hardly understandable to the lay person. Regardless, Amy was clearly an important figure in the field. Hannah was able to glean that Amy's work in nanotechnology was developing microscopic biological constructs that could be programmed for specific tasks. Amy appeared to be working toward a cure for certain cancers.

The article finished by identifying Richard Feynman as the father of nanotechnology. Before his death in 1988, Feynman established a foundation to ensure continued research in the field.

Hannah was impressed and said aloud, "Amy, you really distinguished yourself."

More digging and link-following brought her to a site for the National Institutes of Health in America. It was old. A 2008 Request for Application: "To Solicit Ideas for Common Fund/Roadmap Trans-NIH Strategic Initiatives."

"That's clear as mud," she mumbled.

Reading on, she found the agency was seeking ideas from the scientific, medical, and patient advocate communities about initiatives that might be supported by a fund created in the 2007 NIH Reform Act.

Remembering her friend's drive and ambition, it was no surprise that Amy had responded to this call for applications, and it clearly led to funding her project.

Looking through other articles, she found Amy had been highly sought after by leading research laboratories, finally accepting an offer from an American company, Applied Science Research Institute. She was assigned to their newest facility located outside London.

That's quite an organization. Who knew this nanotechnology stuff was so big? She sat back with a sigh. *I'm sorry not to have kept up with you, Amy.*

Hannah remained troubled by the loose ends surrounding her friend's death, especially what had happened to the body. She remembered Amy's appearance at her door in the middle of the night... her delirious state... the warnings...

Frustrated by her inability to find more information, she thought a fresh perspective would help. She sent a message to SpartanZ.

She smiled, remembering her two friends, Shadow and Davies, the principals of SpartanZ. They'd joined forces after the recent Interpol affair and turned their shadowy Dark Web Clan into a legitimate business operation. Her sometimes partner, Joel Braithwaite, was able to steer government work their way, and since then, they'd been flying high.

It didn't take long before Shadow responded to her message. He apologized, saying they were involved in something and they'd call her back.

Hannah returned to the laptop and accessed the Transport for London traffic site. TfL operated nine-hundred fifteen cameras across London, and with her SIS clearances, she would have access. She was sure some of them had recorded the ambulance at her flat.

She knew the time and place, which was a big help. Selecting the closest camera to her location, she got a hit. "There!" A white van followed a plain sedan. The video wasn't high-resolution, and the thick fog that night made identification impossible.

The ambulance wasn't like any she'd ever seen, at least not around London. It was a plain white cargo van, the sort typically used by tradesmen. She watched the video feed as the two vehicles turned down her street and disappeared from view. There was another camera in the vicinity. She moved her cursor to that point

33

and clicked on the icon. She got a gray screen with a message stating the camera was offline. "Damn!"

She returned to the first video feed and let it run. After about fifteen minutes, the van returned. This time, it turned left toward the camera. She leaned into her laptop screen to get a better look. She couldn't see any faces through the rain-soaked window. She noticed the van had no identifying numbers or Red Cross logos, and there was no hospital name on the van. Adding to these inconsistencies, there were no emergency lights on the roof.

Letting the video feed run, she followed the van's progress through London until it passed out of range at the M40.

"That settles it. Amy's body was hijacked."

CHAPTER 8

Hannah could do no more at the moment. She noticed Amy's bag and the journal sitting on her dining table. She opened the red leather book. This time, she wasn't distracted and began reading the entries with growing interest. These were notes on Amy's research, most of which was over her head. Then she came to an entry dated six months prior.

5 MAY
Received a most peculiar request for my latest research. I was reluctant to hand it over, but it's an order from Director Corbyn. Why do I feel uneasy about this? After all, we're working on the same team.

That does sound strange. How would she have given her research? It must have been voluminous...
After several intervening pages of scientific notes, she came to another entry that caught her interest.

12 JUNE
Just had a disturbing meeting with Director Corbyn. After

> *giving her a portable hard drive containing a copy of all my research to date, I asked why ASRI wanted this information. She was evasive. All I got was corporate doublespeak.*
>
> *Not sure what to think. I guess I'll just continue on. My first full-scale experiment is set for next month. This should prove my hypothesis is true.*

There were several pages of notes and formulae. *Must have been something Amy didn't want to forget.*

She continued to the next entry.

> **15 JULY**
> *Experiment a resounding success! Rats were infected with a brain virus. My nanites were injected. The nanites came to life, sought out and then eliminated the virus. My little ones worked perfectly. They accomplished the job and then, as programmed, became inert and passed out of the bodies.*

The entry continued...

> *It took five days for the programming to run its course. The rats all survived the procedure. The only odd thing was the unexpected (and unwanted) audience that came to observe.*
>
> *I knew Director Corbyn, but not the strangers with her. Corbyn told me not to worry. I didn't like their dark sunglasses, and their silence during the procedure was unnerving. Why were they there?*

I'm beginning to get a sense of Amy's growing unease. Maybe that's just the SIS operative in me.

She went through more pages of scientific notes until reaching the next entry of interest.

15 AUGUST
So much work... analysis... cross-checking... Haven't seen or heard from Corbyn or anyone else in a month. That's good. I was getting the feeling that someone was looking over my shoulder, like a teenager caught cheating on a school exam.

She seems to have gotten over her misgivings.
More pages of scribbled notes came before the next dated entry.

30 SEPTEMBER
Busy putting the final touches on my babies, my nanites. I know it's silly, but I feel like their mother. Not only have they worked perfectly in successive experiments, I think we're on the brink of having something revolutionary.

There'll have to be clinical trials, of course, but I don't think we'll have a problem finding subjects willing to go through this experimental procedure.

Several scribbled names and even something that looked like doodling.
What's she trying to figure out?

15 OCTOBER
I've been nicked! One of my colonies has gone missing.

What's going on? Only way to find out is to question Corbyn. I won't let her dodge me this time.

25 OCTOBER

Finally got an appointment with Corbyn. She wasn't helpful—said I was imagining it all. I'm not! I know how many colonies I have in development, and one of them is missing. I can't, for the life of me, figure out why someone would steal a colony of my nanites. To what end?

After more pointless discussion, I came away with a greatly diminished opinion of the director. I'm going to have to mount my own investigation. What is Corbyn doing with my research?

Hannah sensed there was trouble ahead for her friend. She read on.

31 OCTOBER

Probing has led me to the small morgue. Actually, it's just a converted room in the basement. It's right next to the kennel area where lab animals—rats, monkeys, dogs, and so forth—are caged.

The cold room's log showed only one body. I pulled out a cooler compartment drawer and stood in shock. It was a male cadaver. A rough autopsy had opened the chest cavity. It was filled with what looked like a mist. Leaning in with a magnifying glass to look, I saw my nanites! But they can't be my nanites, there are too many of them. And they're swirling around in a soft mist—something I've never seen before.

It took a moment to process what I was seeing. I was angry. Whoever had stolen my nanites made some sort of modification. Someone is clearly conducting a parallel experiment—one I know nothing about.

In my experiments, I used only a small quantity of nanites, and there was never a mist. It takes several hours before they populate and activate. The programming includes a shutdown process once their task is complete.

The body in the cooler drawer has far more nanites than I ever used, and it doesn't look like their programming includes a shutdown sequence. Could these nanites have continued to multiply and spread through the entire body?

Hannah made a mental note on how Amy's handwriting was getting hurried.

I disturbed the nanites. They puffed up like a small cloud in my face. I reacted instinctively, hastily brushing my face. In doing so, I disturbed more nanites. I was covered, head and shoulders. I ran out of the morgue in a panic, stripping off my lab coat.

Back in my office, I'm trying to calm down. Telling myself that the swarm must be inert—they'd been in that body for days. Without living tissue, there's no way for them to survive—is there? My mind doesn't convince my heart. I'm scared.

Am I infected? If so, will the nanites follow my original programming and become inert in five days? What are the symptoms? What is the prognosis?

Now the handwriting had grown frantic. It was almost a scrawl.

I don't know who to trust. Certainly no one in ASRI. I remember my school friend, Hannah. We've traded occasional messages over the years. I think she went to work with SIS a while back. I'll reach out to her. Maybe she can help me...

Thank God I have a backup.

That was the last entry. Hannah shut the journal and closed her eyes, offering up a silent prayer for Amy. She went back to the bag and inspected the flash drive.

"Amy's research."

CHAPTER 9

Another day passed. Hannah grew increasingly anxious, waiting for Shadow's return call. Pacing back and forth from front room to the kitchen was no help. Television didn't distract her. She tried reading a book.

Finally, the call came. It was a Zoom from SpartanZ. Smiling, she activated her screen. Two familiar faces appeared.

"Hello, boys. I'm awfully glad to see you."

Davies peered into the monitor, wearing his perennially rumpled, untucked shirt. His long brown hair still gathered in an untidy ponytail and glasses that looked like they needed cleaning. Behind the lenses she saw eyes that were quick and inquisitive, confirming what she already knew: Davies was highly intelligent and extraordinarily gifted.

"Hello, Miss Hannah. It's been a while."

Davies' partner, Shadow, whose given name was Dylan Farrell, crowded his way into the shot and greeted her as well.

Farrell, a.k.a. Shadow, was slightly younger than Davies. She liked his quirkiness. He was about six feet tall, average build, and casually dressed. His brown hair was lighter than Davies'. It was a bit long and hung down across his ears and the nape of his neck.

41

She thought his hair hadn't seen the business end of a comb in some time.

"I've been looking into my friend's death, but it's been frustrating. I went to the police station and discovered that no one knew the detectives who came here. I have to assume the EMTs were phonies as well."

"Good Lord," Davies exclaimed. "What have you gotten yourself into?"

"I'm not sure... She shared the information she had on Amy. "Sorry, it's mostly just bio information."

"I think we should take it to Shadow's Dark Web buddies," Davies said.

Shadow nodded. "Yeah. They're a great resource for esoteric information. One of the Clans I formerly associated with call themselves *Paynim*."

"Does that mean something?"

"It's an archaic term for pagan," Shadow said.

Confusion crossed Hannah's face. "What does this have to do with Amy?"

"Let me look into this and get back to you."

It took the better part of the day, but Shadow finally called back. "I contacted the Paynim Clan. They're as strange as I remember. Like I said, these Clans can get you pretty deep into the weeds. The Paynim revere a talisman. It's like a charm. They call it an Achlys. It has two ends, one with a snake-wrapped hand holding a bottle of poison, and the other a bottle with smoke billowing out —like it's releasing a genie."

"It sounds like the mist Amy mentioned," she said.

Davies took over, "The Paynim Clan call it a death mist."

Based on her recent experience with Amy, it seemed to fit.

"This is all starting to make sense." Hannah's expression turned serious. "I need answers. What's the connection with Amy's place of employment? Can you set up a meeting for me with this Paynim Clan?"

"What's the bait for this meeting?" Davies asked.

"Would they respond to money?" Hannah asked. "Money for information about Amy's death?"

"I guess it depends. How much are you talking about?"

"Do you think ten thousand pounds would be an enticement?"

Shadow's face grew grim. "Be careful. Those Paynim are a ruthless bunch."

"Thanks for the warning, but I can take care of myself." She gave them a stern look. "You both know that."

The pair looked embarrassed.

"Make the offer. I want a meeting with someone from Paynim."

Davies was uncomfortable with Hannah's plan. She'd told him she was working this case on her own time. *That means she doesn't necessarily have all the SIS resources.* After talking it over with Shadow, he put in a call to Joel Braithwaite.

The call was answered by his admin, a pretty young woman who didn't let that stand in the way of her professionalism. She told him that Mr. Braithwaite was away on an assignment. "Would you like to leave him a message?"

"I'd like to, please. Tell him SpartanZ called..."

"Can you spell that, please?"

Davies spelled it out for the admin. "Tell him we're concerned Hannah is going into a dicey situation with no real backup."

"Are you talking about the SIS agent, Hannah Ahmed?"

"Yes. When do you expect to hear from Joel?"

"Not for a couple of days, and then he's scheduled for leave."

"Do you know where he's going?"

"I believe he's going to visit his father in England."

Davies ended the call and could only hope his instincts were wrong.

Hannah's offer of money garnered the reaction she hoped for. Shadow argued against a meeting but she wouldn't relent. The meeting was set for two days hence. She was to meet with someone calling himself "Reaper." *No doubt a Web handle,* she thought.

She left in the morning, stopping by SIS to make certain arrangements. After meeting with the Finance Department, she had what she needed: a certified bank draft for £10,000, payable to bearer—upon countersignature. It was all bogus, of course, but it would serve her purpose.

Driving north out of London, she enjoyed the beautiful countryside. The sky was bright blue and the clouds billowy. Grass-covered hills alternated with open meadows. Forested areas were filled with orange, yellow, and red leaves.

She passed through a number of villages, like Kelvedon and Marks Tey. Each town had a village green, scenic churches, and several pubs. The experience was nostalgic and entirely enjoyable.

Remembering Shadow's admonition, she focused on the meeting ahead. She didn't think there would be trouble, but she would be prepared.

There's no reason for violence. It's a simple commercial transaction. Money for information.

The meeting site was outside Wakes Coine. The instructions from Shadow said she'd know the place by a small flag planted on a hill. She drove through the village, noting there was a good deal of activity: people in costumes, music playing and the like. "They must be preparing for some festival or fete."

Slowing as she left the village proper, she kept a sharp eye for a hill and a flag. After about ten minutes of driving, she spotted a rise over the trees. There was a slender stick and a triangular red flag on the hilltop. She pulled to the side.

This is a curious site for a meeting. Isolated.

A dirt road led in the direction of the flag. *This must be the way.*

Driving through thick forest, she emerged on open country—and the hill. There was nobody around. Only the flag atop the bare hill. Her suspicions were immediately aroused. She took the Beretta from her shoulder bag. Lifting the envelope with the fake bank draft, she thought, *Here's hoping you'll get me through.*

Getting out, she slid the weapon into a holster at the small of her back and the bank draft into the outer pocket of her tailored coat.

There was still nobody in sight. Nevertheless, the hairs on the back of her neck stood on end. As she stepped away from the car, her senses were on full alert.

Then she heard a sound from beyond the hilltop. An engine. As it came closer, a head and shoulders appeared over the crest that became a man riding a black ATV. She noticed he wore no helmet. The small four-wheel-drive vehicle crested the hilltop and came to a stop next to the flag.

The machine looked mean, almost carnivorous. Knobby wheels sat under mud flaps that flared up and out, like the wings of a bat. The fenders were shiny black and decorated with blood-red pin striping. The headlights could easily be mistaken for eyes, completing the impression of a predatory beast.

The man sat up in the seat but didn't get off.

I guess the next move's mine.

She stood her ground, evaluating the ominous-looking ATV and its rider. The man looked to be in his forties. He wore black jeans and boots, a black T-shirt, and a black biker-style leather jacket with lots of zippers. Dark glasses made it impossible to see his eyes. She didn't have a good feeling about this meeting.

She shouted, "Are you Reaper?"

The ATV rider gave a single nod, took off the sunglasses, and placed them in one of the many zippered pockets of the jacket.

"I'm told you have information about Dr. Amy Perry," she said.

The man leaned forward on his ATV. "You promised money. Where is it?"

"I've got it right here." She patted the envelope in her pocket. "It's a bank draft, only payable when I'm satisfied with your information."

"Show it to me."

She took the envelope and held up the bank draft.

"I can't see that. Come up here so I can verify it's real."

"First, you tell me what you know about Amy Perry."

The man on the ATV scowled but gave no reply.

"Where is Amy Perry's body?"

He drew a pistol from under the ATV's dashboard.

CHAPTER 10

Hannah spotted Reacher's move and reacted instinctively extracting her Beretta, stooping down, and searching for cover. There was none, only her car, and that was several paces behind.

A shot rang out, raising a puff of turf several feet in front of her.

Poorly aimed. This Reaper guy's no professional.

As she reached the relative cover of her MINI Cooper, there was another shot. This one struck the front bumper, harmlessly ricocheting away. She thought she might be able to drive Reaper off with a few well-placed shots of her own.

She was thinking through a counterstrike strategy when two more ATVs came racing over the hill. Reaper signaled them toward her. The two new attackers split, going for flanking positions. Before they could get into position, she fired a round at the closest attacker, the one going to her right. Because of the uneven turf, the ATV was bouncing, and her shot was slightly off. It struck the fender of the ATV and ricocheted at an oblique angle, causing the driver to swerve and tip over.

Okay. One down, two to go.

The left-flanking driver reached his position and dismounted.

He'd seen his partner go down and knew the woman was armed. He took shelter behind his machine, drew his weapon, and began firing.

The MINI Cooper was pelted by the burst of bullets, but she was unharmed. The firing allowed Reaper to drive down to provide backup.

"Get behind your vehicle!" Reaper ordered the man who'd dismounted and was now crouched behind his overturned ATV. "You—keep firing! I'm gonna circle around."

Reaper set off at a high rate of speed, kicking up sod as the knobby tires bit into the soft turf. He circled around, coming up the road Hannah had followed. Too late, the woman saw him—she was trapped and knew it. He gave a snarling smile as he watched the woman drop her weapon, stand, and raise her hands in surrender.

The flanking drivers moved from behind their ATVs and covered the woman from both sides. Reaper drove up and got off his machine. Brandishing his pistol, he stepped up to her and took the envelope from her coat pocket.

Taking a few steps back, he was able to take his eyes off the woman and inspect the bank draft. "This is no good. It requires another signature." He gave a hard stare. "Your signature."

The woman responded with a small smile.

"Which, it seems, you'll not willingly give." He gestured to his men. "Tie her up. This one's going to need some additional persuasion."

Hannah's hands were bound and she was put on the rear seat of one ATV. The three men drove to the top of the hill and down the grassy backside. The knobby wheels left deep ruts as they headed toward their destination: a cottage in the distance. As they came closer, she saw the cottage was a typical English country, storybook-scenic structure with a softly sloping thatch roof.

The building was two stories with white stucco walls trimmed in dark wood beams. A smaller building in the same style sat off to one side. She was escorted through the front door into the main room. There was aged wood plank flooring with white stucco walls that were punctuated by colorful drapery on the windows. Large age-darkened ceiling beams ran the length of the room.

The furniture was functional and appropriate to the setting: An antique flower-patterned sofa sat against one wall with another facing across the wood-planked floor. An upholstered ottoman sat in between.

The wall opposite the entry was dominated by a large but non-functional fireplace. Instead, a potbellied stove filled the firebox.

She thought, under different circumstances, the cottage would be considered quite homey.

With wrists still bound, she was placed on one sofa. Reaper stood in front of her. The other took up a position to her right.

He means to kill me. But he can't until he has the money. She wondered if he wanted more money.

Reaper paced while Hannah tried to find some way out of this. She needed a solution that wouldn't leave her dead.

"You're not the only one who responded to my offer, you know. There were other Clans besides yours."

"You're bluffing," Reaper said, pulling out his weapon and pointing it directly at her head.

Reaper held the upper hand. With her Beretta confiscated, a shootout was off the table. She couldn't see any course of action that would lead away from this present danger.

"You can't make me countersign."

"We'll see about that." He turned to the man on her right. "Take her to the storage cellar. A little alone time may change her mind."

The man gave an evil grin and grabbed her arm.

"Hey, ease up there." A nasty bruise was sure to appear. The man snorted in response.

Not much sympathy here.

The man said, "Come on… to the cellar," and led the way to the back of the cottage.

As they entered what looked like a kitchen, she heard Reaper make a call on his mobile. He was calling someone named "Quicksilver."

Reaper's man pulled a small table and two chairs aside to reveal a hatch set into the floorboards. Opening the hatch, he pushed her toward the dark hole. *This looks like a deprivation chamber.*

"Down you go," the man ordered.

As she climbed down the ladder into the dirt cellar, she heard Reaper say, "We've got the money, we just have to get a counter signature." There was a pause, then Reaper continued, "At least we've got some money, maybe more with her as a hostage."

The hatch was slammed shut and locked.

The cellar was cold but not completely dark—light seeped through the boards of the hatch. As her eyes became accustomed to the dim light, she noted shelves standing against the wall. They appeared to be stocked with a variety of canned goods. Two full smoked hams hung from the low ceiling rafters.

Sitting on the bottom step of the ladder, she put her fists under her chin. "Time to think outside the box."

Reaper was pleased with himself. "Maybe after marinating overnight, she'll be more compliant and willing to countersign." He looked at the confiscated banknote, imagining more to come when he leveraged this hostage.

"Whoever financed her will no doubt be willing to pay much more for the pretty lady."

He gave a mirthless laugh.

CHAPTER 11

Director Corbyn went to her home in Cherwell Valley in northern Oxfordshire, near ASRI. She had a private message from Robertson on her home computer.
I went back to the flat. I think the woman is somehow connected with law enforcement. She went to the local police station looking for my two officers.
Corbyn could only hope the money they'd paid those men would keep them quiet. The report went on.
A message board on the Dark Web caught my attention. It was offering money for information relating to the death of Amy Perry.
Neck veins beat a visible pulse beneath her skin. She read on.
A Clan group calling themselves Paynim took the offer.
She was worried her private deal for Dr. Perry's new nanotechnology would be compromised. She tapped out a response.
Locate Paynim and report back.
She was too distracted to go into ASRI, and spent the next day fretting. There was no word from Robertson. Then, a call—Robertson. "I have news of Paynim."

She almost jumped through the phone. "Give it to me!"

"They have a headquarters of sort, a cottage just outside Wakes Coine."

She relaxed. "Get a strike team together. I want them hit." It was harsh, but to her, a necessity. "Leave none alive."

Callum Robertson reacted to his director's harsh order. He'd never known her to be like this. He reluctantly contacted a mercenary group that he'd used to solve certain problems in the past. The team was transnational, and one member, his contact, was located in England.

After listening to a summary of the situation, the mercenary agreed to take the contract.

"How soon can you hit the cottage?" Robertson asked.

"I'll assemble the team and we'll be ready at sunrise tomorrow."

CHAPTER 12

Hannah fumbled around the dark root cellar, searching for a way out. There was none to be found. Neither were tools of any description, nothing she could use to pry open the ceiling hatch. She slid down the dirt wall in defeated futility.

It was difficult to determine the passage of time sitting in the dark. After a long period, she heard scraping feet overhead. It was followed by the front door opening, then closing. Greetings could be heard. She tilted her head, trying to listen more closely.

Someone else has come. I wonder if it's that Quicksilver person Reaper was talking to?

There was no answer to her question, so she returned to running through escape scenarios.

Having no success with her mental gymnastics, she tried to sleep, but it eluded her. *There's no way out of this pit. The walls are dirt, sure, but I'm ten feet down. How much dirt would I have to move...?*

Any calculation was futile since there was nothing down here, not even a spoon, that could be used to excavate a tunnel.

With my mobile taken, there's no way to contact anyone... Maybe there's a way to lure someone to the hatch. If I can

Death Mist

convince one of them to open up, conceivably I could reach the mobile.
Problem was, that plan sounded too far-fetched to work.
She continued running scenarios, every one equally implausible and unlikely to succeed. Finally, somewhere during the night, she fell asleep.

———

An hour before sunrise, the mercenary group hired by Robertson passed through Wakes Coine. They moved silently, like a mist that swirls up in silence and then dissipates.
The group of five found the Paynim cottage in an open field. No cover for a hundred yards. The leader thought it would have been better if the cottage were in a forested area. He let out a sigh. *We'll just have to make the best of this situation*
The leader divided his team: two men to approach the front, and the other two he sent to the rear to cover any escape. He would remain with the first team.
Since there weren't trees or other ground cover to conceal their movement, the first team was forced to approach the cottage in a belly crawl. It was slow going. Team Two had it easier—they were able to move around the perimeter under cover of trees and approach the cottage from the rear.
Dawn was spilling over the trees, spreading like a soft yellow tide across the field, until reaching the cottage. Team One was in position, waiting for movement inside. The leader motioned to the man on his left, who raised his assault rifle in response. Mounted under the rifle barrel was an M651 tactical grenade launcher. The operator slipped a tear gas canister into the launcher and waited for his commander's signal.
A light appeared in a window. The team leader motioned his man to fire.

55

Whoosh.

The sound of the canister's launch wasn't heard inside the cottage, nor was the second. There was only the sound of breaking glass as the 40mm canisters shattered the window—that, and the quiet of the morning.

Hannah awoke with a start. *What was that? It sounded like breaking glass.* She was up the ladder and pressed her ear to the ceiling door. Muffled shouts and curses could be heard through the trap door. *Something's wrong.*

A white mist began creeping around the edges of the hatch. She jumped down the ladder and scrambled to the rear of the root cellar, her attention fully on the ceiling hatch. More wisps of white smoke seeped around the edges of the cover.

Tear gas! Someone's attacking the cottage.

Footsteps raced back and forth on the floor above, and to her, it sounded like confusion—even a panic. Then Reaper's voice ordered an evacuation. Scurrying footsteps indicated the others were following Reaper's order.

Moments later, she heard the susurration of automatic gunfire.

CHAPTER 13

Reaper was the first up that morning and turned on a light in the kitchen area. It was quickly followed by crashing glass. First confusion, and then chaos. He stood against a wall and watched two projectiles that looked like shaving cream cans skitter across the floor. His confusion turned to understanding as smoke began billowing from the canisters.

The new arrival from the night before, Quicksilver, was the first out. A questioning look turned to surprise then fear as the tear gas canisters billowed impossible amounts of thick white smoke into the room. Reaper's other two companions, groggy with sleep, stumbled around and began shouting. They were unsure what was happening.

"It's an attack!" Reaper shouted.

All four men began to experience the effects of tear gas: throats swelling, noses running uncontrollably, eyes stinging and weeping to the point of blindness.

Each man, coughing uncontrollably, extracted weapons and looked for targets. But the tear gas in the enclosed space had reduced visibility to zero.

"Get out of here!" Even though Reaper's shout was garbled

by phlegm, the others understood well enough. The men burst out the front door, coughing and wheezing. They didn't expect the fusillade of bullets that met them.

Team Two came running around the cottage and found their leader, along with their two other comrades, standing over four bodies. Feathery tendrils of smoke trailed from the barrels of Team One's assault rifles.

The leader ordered both teams inside. "The order said there'd be four, but make certain."

Each man put on a gas mask before entering.

With the tear gas now dispersing, the mercenaries could see the chaos in the cottage. Much of the furniture had been upended during the former residents' panic. Each team took a search area.

The leader shouted, "Anyone else here?"

"All clear," responded one.

"I found a mobile phone," said another, "and an envelope."

He handed the manila envelope to the leader, who looked inside. "A check for ten thousand pounds... worthless unless countersigned." He looked around. "You're certain no one else is here?"

"Negative. It's clear."

"Smash the phone and let's get out of here."

Hannah got up from the floor. The tear gas hadn't penetrated any farther than the hatch in the ceiling.

Careful not to make a sound, she listened closely. People were reentering the cottage. There was some conversation, but it was mostly unintelligible.

Not Reaper's group. Someone else. Four, maybe five? They must have ambushed Reaper and the others. Who are the attackers? A rival Clan?

The bits of conversation she could hear confirmed what she surmised: the attackers didn't expect to find anyone in the cottage.

"All clear," she heard and let out a sigh of relief.

Looking around the dark cellar, she wondered if this dungeon would be discovered. She had no illusions about her fate should she be found. The alternative, not being discovered, was equally bleak. It would mean a long and tortured death. "There's no good way out of this," she groaned.

Then came an order to clear out. Soon, the cottage was quiet. Even so, she was careful to make no sound. She stared at the ceiling door, expecting it to fly open at any moment. After what seemed a very long time, she climbed the ladder again and listened at the hatch.

Nothing. It's dead quiet up there. She climbed back down.

Standing at the bottom of the ladder in the dark, she thought, *I guess I should start looking for a way to open that hatch.*

CHAPTER 14

Joel Braithwaite looked again at Davies' message. He put in a call to SpartanZ, and Davies answered. "Mr. B, you're back." Davies sounded anxious and that concerned him.

"What's the situation?"

Davies told him how he and Shadow planted a request on the Dark Web for Hannah. "She thought it was the only way she would find out what happened to her friend."

"Back up a minute," Joel said. "What friend, and why is she going to the Dark Web to find her?"

"I forgot—you weren't in at the beginning of all this…"

Davies recounted Hannah's description of the death of her college friend, Amy Perry. He described the visit by fake police detectives and how the presumably fake EMTs took Amy's body away.

"She wasn't successful in finding Amy's body, so she turned to us for help."

"Hannah put up a bounty… who bit on that?"

"A Clan called Paynim. She asked Shadow to set up a meeting. That's when we called you. I can't believe this would be a SIS case because it's domestic. She knows better."

"Do you know where she was meeting this Paynim group?"

"Wakes Coine, a small village in the country. She was to look for a flag on a hilltop."

"As it happens, I was going to take some time off to visit home." He looked at his watch. "I can't possibly make it to London before midday tomorrow."

Joel flew into London the next morning, rented a car, and set out to find Wakes Coine. It took some doing, and after a couple of wrong turns, he finally arrived.

Wakes Coine was the very picture of a rural English village: tidy buildings lining the main street, people coming and going, some on foot and others by car or small lorry. A village green occupied the middle of town with a clock tower as its centerpiece. A church that looked a little tired but still much used faced the green. An ever-present pub, the *Thirsty Toad*, was visible down the road.

As he drove on, he noticed rooms above the public house. He took note since he wasn't sure how long he would be in the area. Driving on, he passed out of the village into the open country. He looked left and right, seeing hills but no flags. He drove on for about thirty minutes before thinking, *I must have missed something.*

Backtracking toward Wakes Coine, he noticed a small road on the right that seemed to go in the direction of a hill. "Looks more like a path than a road." He gave a *why-not* shrug and took the turn.

The narrow road turned out to be in better shape than he expected. As he came around a corner, the thick woods ended, revealing the open hill. More importantly, he saw a classic MINI Cooper—Hannah's.

He got out and inspected the vehicle. There were bullet holes along the right side. A feeling of unease grew as he looked inside, trying to tease out what had happened, putting himself in Hannah's mind.

Davies said Hannah was meeting with a Dark Web group to buy information...

Reasoning that Hannah would be cautious when meeting with people of that sort, he didn't think she would show the money until a deal was struck.

The fact that her car was riddled with bullet holes meant the deal must have gone sour. Looking around, he feared the worst. Evidence of off-road vehicles was everywhere: torn-up turf, deep tire tracks, and, most ominously, spent ammunition cartridges.

"9mm," he said, picking one up. He tried to follow the flow of action. "Looks like she was ambushed."

He followed the tire tracks to the top of the hill, and once there, found a slender pole lying in the grass. "This has to be the signal flag." He tried to work through the sequence of events, stooping to inspect the turf. The tracks led down the back side of the hill.

Standing on the hilltop, he surveyed the surrounding countryside. He stopped when he saw a cottage in the distance.

A mile or so. If she was taken, that's where she'll be.

Joel returned to the main road and looked for a cutoff that would take him to the cottage. Now that he knew what to look for, it was simple. Driving up to the cottage, he noted how the front door was ajar, as if there'd been a hasty evacuation. Then he spotted bullet holes in a blood-splattered stucco wall. *What the hell happened here? Judging from the bullet holes and all this blood, I'd say it was an ambush.*

He looked around—no bodies in sight. There were drag marks on the ground. He followed the trail of blood It led to a smaller building adjacent to the cottage. In the rear of the small building, he found four large garbage bags. Flies swarmed and thousands of ants marched around the bags. Joel knew what this was: a body dump.

Something forced them out of the cottage. They were ambushed and then dumped here.

Going back to the cottage, he stepped through the open front door and announced his presence. It felt very empty.

The place was a complete mess. Overturned furniture, chairs carelessly tossed aside, kitchen drawers hanging open, a crunched-up mobile phone on a counter, and two spent tear gas canisters on the floor.

This was a coordinated, military-style attack.

He could smell the lingering odor of tear gas as he looked at the devastation around him.

Moving into the kitchen area, he called out again. This time, he heard something. A muffled shout, followed by soft knocking.

It's coming from the floor.

He looked around, trying to locate the source of the shout and knocking.

Calling out again, he repeated his name and organization. More return shouts—a woman's voice—muffled, but definitely female.

He searched around the kitchen for a door to another room. Nothing, only a small rug with a table and four chairs. They were positioned toward the back wall. Dragging the rug and dining table to one side, he found a hatch in the floor.

The voice called out again, and he could now tell it was from below.

He grabbed an inset handle and pulled.

The hatch wouldn't open. Looking more closely at the inset

metal casing, it was pointed to the "Lock" position. He moved it to "Open" and pulled up the hatch. The dirty face of a very relieved Hannah looked up at him.

He gave Hannah a big smile. "Does madam need a hand up?"

"Joel! This is no time to be cute! Help me out of here."

After being extracted from the pit, Hannah threw her arms around Joel's neck and held on for a long moment. She said nothing, just held on with her eyes closed. Finally releasing him, she pushed back and said, "Thank you." Only then did she notice the destruction all around.

She was taken aback. "I heard all the commotion up here but had no idea... I had to give them the money, but I refused to countersign. They tossed me down there..." She glanced at the still-open hatch to the cellar. "I guess they figured to hold me as a hostage and get more."

She stepped toward the front door. "Whoever attacked the Paynim didn't know I was down there. Otherwise, I'm certain I'd be dead."

CHAPTER 15

"I'm afraid your car was damaged," Joel said sympathetically.
"Many bullet holes."
"Yes, I know." He could see a look of sadness on Hannah's face.
"No worries. We'll have it taken to a garage and repaired in no time. Meanwhile, let me drive you back to London."
He could see Hannah was spent by her ordeal. "You're exhausted. There's a public house in Wakes Coine. Let's see if we can get rooms. Tomorrow, after you've slept, we'll decide our next steps."
Hannah was visibly relieved. "I wasn't looking forward to driving all the way home. The first thing I'm going to do is soak in a hot bath."

Joel made arrangements for Hannah's car to be towed to a local garage. That settled, he turned his attention to arranging accommodations at the *Thirsty Toad*, a warm and welcoming public house with low ceilings and aged wood planking on the floor. A long bar that looked to be a hundred years old was flanked by a well-used dart board. Several tables were scattered around. It was the very picture of a classic British pub.

It was well after noon before Joel was joined by the recent prisoner. He was waiting for her at a table under a small window.

"Sorry it's so late, but I just got up," Hannah said.

"No worries. I didn't expect you to rise with the sun. You went through a pretty harrowing experience."

"I'm famished," Hannah said.

Joel motioned to the proprietor, who came over and took her order.

"When was the last time you ate?" Joel asked.

"Breakfast yesterday."

Her meal was delivered and, in short order, polished off.

"Now, I believe we're ready to get to work," Joel said. "All I know about this situation comes from Davies. But first, I'd like you to tell me how this all began."

Hannah told him about her friend, Amy Perry. Joel was most interested in Amy's research specialty, nanotechnology. He asked questions about the company Amy worked for, Applied Science Research Institute.

"Did you get any background on ASRI?" Joel asked.

Hannah shook her head. "Beyond the basics of a multinational operation, there wasn't much."

Joel looked thoughtful. "You said Amy showed up unexpectedly."

"Yes, and she was ill."

"Where do you suppose she contracted whatever she had? Could it have been at ASRI?"

"Now that you mention it, that seems the most likely place to become infected."

"Let's put a bookmark on this place. We'll come back to it. Please, continue with your story."

Hannah described Amy's death and the subsequent visit from the police and EMTs, all of whom turned out to be imposters—or at least, untraceable. She recounted her unsuccessful search for Amy's body. She went on to describe her plan to buy information, followed by a meeting that Shadow had set up with the Paynim Clan. "One thing led to another, and I was taken and then thrown into that root cellar."

"You heard no sounds of a struggle while you were down there?"

"Oh my, yes," she said. "But I wasn't in a position to see anything, much less take action. I heard what sounded like an attack on the cottage—breaking glass, lots of running, furniture being turned over, and shouting. And then, tear gas. It seeped into the cellar but didn't penetrate any further than the ceiling. Probably because it's below ground level—the cool air was a barrier.

"After the assault, I heard the attackers enter the cottage. They were looking for survivors. When none were found, they left."

Joel sat back, trying to make sense of this series of events. She remained quiet until he was ready to offer his observations. When he did, it wasn't at all what Hannah expected.

"There's a company—no, it's more like a family enterprise—they've been in high-level politics, licensing deals, influence peddling, and the like. They came on our radar a couple of years ago. One of the Baltic States, Latvia, had launched an investigation of the managing director of their national energy company, alleging corruption. On the eve of bringing charges, the prosecutor disappeared. It was a big scandal. The prosecutor was never found, and the case fell apart.

"The UN Terrorism Prevention Bureau became involved because it was suspicious. Was it terrorism? Was it blackmail? We tried to find out but came up empty-handed. The only thing we discovered was a mention that there had been a meeting days before with this family's representative. The subject listed in the visitor's log was natural gas exploration. There were no meeting notes, so we can't know what was actually discussed, but a few days later, the corruption case disappeared."

"What's the family name?" Hannah asked.

"Buchanan—an American connection."

"I've heard of them. I was never directly involved in a case, but they are certainly known to SIS. How does Senator Buchanan figure into the hit on the cottage?"

"I don't know yet, but I think there's something going on at ASRI. I think your doctor friend found out, and they killed her for it."

"Hold on. We don't know ASRI actually killed Amy," Hannah said and then thought about it. "But, you're right. It's awfully coincidental."

"Before we go off chasing around the countryside," Joel said, "I'd like to go back through my notes on the Buchanans."

CHAPTER 16

Joel left Hannah in the pub. Back in his room, he was thankful Wakes Coine had good internet service. He was able to access his UN files and search for those relating to Buchanan. At first glance, there was nothing suspicious. Just a note on the Latvian meeting he'd remembered. More searching didn't add too much to the Buchanan story. *They're pretty good at keeping their name out of the spotlight.* Then he found a photo on a newspaper society page. He inspected the picture. It showed two men holding drinks, smiling at the camera, and looking very much like bezzies. The caption read:

Kurt Buchanan, eldest son of Senator Jack Buchanan, at a White House reception for technology leaders. With Mr. Buchanan is Michael Roark, a government relations consultant for Applied Science Research Institute, a leader in the field of nanotechnology.

That gave Joel a new direction to search.
A knock at the door interrupted him. It was Hannah. "I'm glad you're here. I may be onto something."

"I was concerned," she said. "I thought you were coming back down."

"Sit down." He gestured to a comfortable overstuffed chair.

After taking a seat, she said, "Okay, regale me."

"There may be a connection between Buchanan and ASRI." He told her of finding the article. "On the society page, of all places."

"May I help? My laptop survived the assault. It was still in my shoulder bag."

Joel and Hannah spent the rest of the afternoon digging up every scrap of information available on Senator Buchanan and ASRI. When Joel stopped to look at the time, he was surprised. "Do you know what time it is?"

Hannah looked up. "I hadn't noticed."

"Well, it's almost eight o'clock." Joel stood. "I saw an interesting-looking Indian restaurant in town. How about dinner?"

"That sounds wonderful," she said. "I'm up for tandoori."

They left everything and walked into Wakes Coine, locating the Indian restaurant. After ordering a round of drinks, they fell into a light, collegial conversation. After a time, Joel brought the discussion back to the mission at hand.

"There are a couple of things that have bearing on our present situation: ASRI and an outside group, the Buchanan family. I couldn't find a registered corporation in that name, and it's not in any business directory, either in America or Europe. But it seems that in certain circles, Buchanan is a well-known name.

"Their primary business seems to be influence peddling. Jack Buchanan, a long-standing US senator, has been at the center of it all—like a Mafia godfather.

"The senator's been the Chair of the Senate Appropriations Committee for decades. It's one of the most powerful government committees in Washington. And Senator Buchanan has built a reputation as an avaricious, unscrupulous bully who uses the power of the committee to make certain that things go his way.

"Using his position, he's been able to quietly amass wealth and influence. His reach today goes far beyond the United States. In fact, no one publicly disagrees, much less attacks the senator. He's considered untouchable. Politicians avoid conflict with Buchanan, and corporate leaders simply get out of his way—or give him what he wants."

Hannah asked, "The Buchanan family's business is providing political influence for cash and favors?"

"Yes," Joel said. "It started small, but in the last few years that's changed. I had a hard time finding more. As I said, there are no articles of incorporation, no partnerships, and certainly no taxes paid. It was only through oblique references that we can infer there is, in fact, an enterprise."

Hannah looked thoughtful. "So... Buchanan built a Neo-Mafia style operation that relies on secrecy and loyalty."

"And the only loyalty Senator Buchanan trusts is family," Joel added. "He's enlisted only family members to take key positions in the growing business: his wife, his brother, and his son. As the enterprise prospers, so does the family.

"Buchanan's conquests include controlling elected US officials, dominating unelected government officers, influencing foreign governments, and intimidating business leaders with the threat of new regulations or costly law suits. Those who cooperate are rewarded with lucrative contracts from the US government."

"And kickbacks," Hannah said.

"That goes without saying. With power and influence comes money. Lots of money."

"Where do we go from here?" Hannah asked.

"We should pay a visit to the ASRI facility. It's not too far from here."

CHAPTER 17

Kurt Buchanan, the eldest son and the family's connection to ASRI, discovered someone in the senior bioengineering ranks who was in need of money. A female. He was certain she could be easily manipulated because of her past history with drugs. She never would have been hired by ASRI had they known of her arrest, and that was just the leverage he needed.

He approached the woman, threatened her with exposure, the loss of her job and livelihood, and possibly jail time. The woman caved.

It wasn't long before she began feeding Kurt intelligence on ASRIs nanotechnology activities. The mole provided almost immediate results. He learned that Director Corbyn, managing director of ASRI-Great Britain, was conducting a secret project unknown to ASRI senior management. His mole reported that the project was a secret experiment in nanotechnology, a tidbit that pleased Kurt. He contacted his father, the senator, reporting his success.

Reports from his mole continued, and it was soon clear that the project was not only off-the-books but highly secret—and deadly. Such projects were of interest to the Buchanans. Whatever this nanotechnology project was, it was bound to be something they could sell.

Director Corbyn was relieved that her security man, Callum Robertson, was back. Standing before her, Robertson offered a debrief on the operation to eliminate the Paynim Clan.

She stopped him. "I don't need to know the particulars. Just tell me the Paynim are taken care of."

"They're no longer a problem," Robertson said. "They were the last connection to Amy Perry—and us."

"Then we can consider the Perry incident closed?"

"Yes."

"On to new priorities. We're ready for a proof of concept. I want to expose a larger, more diverse group. Now that gain-of-function is established, the nanites can go into full production."

Robertson furled his eyebrows. "Where do you suggest we find a large population of 'participants' that won't be missed?"

She gave a stern look. "I'll leave that to you."

Robertson looked confused. "Does it have to be here, in England?"

"No. As a matter of fact, after this Perry incident, I think we'd be safer somewhere else."

CHAPTER 18

Using GPS, Joel found the ASRI building. They were surprised. It was modern, sleek, and long. To Hannah, it looked like it belonged in a high-tech industrial park, not the English countryside. She mentioned her observation to Joel.

"Yeah, it does look strange out here in the country." He looked around. "At least it's behind that line of trees."

Pulling into a visitor's parking space, Hannah focused on the polished surface of the building. It looked almost like stainless-steel and reflected a warm glow in the afternoon sunlight. Oddly, there were no windows, only a front entry of tinted glass doors. She wondered if they would find Margaret Corbyn in the office.

Inside, the lobby was as sleek as the exterior. Walls were crisp white. Lighting was so cleverly hidden it was difficult to determine if it was coming from the ceiling or the floor. Regardless, the walls were bathed in pastel colors that shimmered and changed as Hannah and Joel moved through the lobby.

The reception area was generous, and in keeping with the minimalist style of the building, it was sparsely decorated. A seating area with very low, black leather chairs sat in a circle to one side. It looked more like a bullpen than a visitors' waiting area. Three of the chairs were occupied by men in dress shirts and ties—none wore suit coats. The men were leaning over a round glass table, passing around documents.

Hannah noticed the floor was a combination of light wood planks and white marble tiles. Two long trough-like planters ran down the opposing walls. The planters were filled with alternating ferns and palm trees, and pastel backlighting made the branches and leaves shimmer and glow.

The receptionist, sitting behind a large polished marble reception station, had watched the pair from the moment they entered the lobby. Hannah asked to see Margaret Corbyn, and no, she didn't have an appointment.

"That may be a problem, ma'am. Director Corbyn is a very busy woman."

"Would you mind checking?" Hannah presented her SIS credentials.

The receptionist's eyes went wide, and there was a slight flush in her cheeks. "Of course." She turned to a touch-screen telephone console, and with her back to the pair, she spoke in low tones.

Completing the call, she turned back to the visitors. "If you'll wait here, someone will be out shortly."

The meeting in the bullpen seemed to be breaking up. "Why don't we wait over there?" Hannah asked, gesturing to the seating area. Joel was happy to follow along.

The men leaving the seating area couldn't help but notice Hannah. She watched them try to hide their obvious stares. It was interesting how predictable men were, how easily distracted.

She and Joel waited only a short time before a man came out. Hannah made mental notes as he approached.

Not the typical corporate drone. He's wearing a windbreaker with a company logo. Tall and muscular, not like the men who just left. He looks like a soldier. His stern look suggests he's wondering why a government agent is here. I don't expect him to be helpful.

Stepping into the circle of chairs, the man introduced himself without shaking hands, "I'm Callum Robertson, Chief of Security. You've asked to see Director Corbyn."

Hannah and Joel exchanged looks. Their unspoken question was, why is the chief of security meeting us?

"That's correct," Hannah said.

"I'm afraid the director's unavailable."

"How unfortunate," she said. Neither she nor Joel made a move to leave.

"You can make an appointment for another day," Robertson offered.

Joel, eyeing the man carefully, said, "You don't look like an appointment secretary."

"I'm not," Robertson responded, giving them a stony look. "I meant, make an appointment with the receptionist."

"Does Ms. Corbyn have a superior we might see?" Joel continued.

"Not here. She reports to headquarters."

"And where is that?"

"In America." Hannah gave a questioning look, and Robertson added, "San Francisco, to be precise."

Sitting in the car outside ASRI, Joel had become resigned. "It's to be expected... our dropping in uninvited would get us nowhere."

"I can think of a dozen different ways to handle our unexpected appearance," Hannah said. "Sending out the chief of security isn't one of them. Do you suppose our visit spooked them?"

"Clearly, it did."

"Would you say they've got something to hide?"

"I can't imagine a multi-national business like ASRI would be put off by a visit from the government," Joel said. "They must get inspections and official visits all the time."

"Let's get back to London. We need to dig a little deeper into this company."

CHAPTER 19

At four o'clock, Corbyn's three senior technicians, accompanied by Dr. Hughes, filed into her office. The technicians, Oliver Buoy, George Kraft, and Myra Shipman, sat in the chairs arranged before her desk. Dr. Hughes took another chair off to one side. The three techs all crinkled their noses at the aroma of incense drifting around. Myra even rubbed her nose to avoid sneezing.

Corbyn began, "With the late Dr. Perry's exposure to the nanites, I've decided our project is ready to move forward." She looked at each of them—questioning stares looked back. "The first subject, already dead, was our breeding ground—a petri dish, if you will. Perry's unexpected exposure has given us a unique opportunity. We now know this technology works and we're ready for proof of concept. We need to show that the nanites can be programmed to target specific groups."

She noticed some shuffling in seats and a few glances between the technicians.

"To that end," she continued, "we need a larger number of subjects—diverse in age, gender, and ethnicity. We, and by that, I mean *you*, will alter the programming to reach specifically targeted groups. I have tasked Mr. Robertson to give recommendations for sourcing the subject pool."

One of the men, Oliver Buoy, looked a little sheepish. "Madam Director, we were wondering if this is moving a little too quickly. Perhaps we should hold back and consider all the data to this point." The other two technicians nodded agreement. Dr. Hughes, sitting a little apart, remained expressionless.

"Out of the question."

At that moment, her office door opened, and Robertson entered. Corbyn saw concern on his face. It was unsettling. Her security chief wasn't easily disturbed. Robertson looked at the people in the director's office. "Madam Director, may I speak with you—privately?"

Corbyn dismissed everyone, "I'll let you know when we'll reconvene."

Robertson stood before her desk. She could see he'd managed to get himself under control.

"What is it?"

"We've just had a visit from SIS. They were asking for you. I told them you were unavailable."

She knew about SIS, of course. They were an international investigative agency, not domestic. She'd dealt with local authorities, even MI-5. But never SIS.

"What did they want?"

"Unknown."

"I have an uneasy feeling about this. Do you suppose they know about Paynim?"

"Uncertain."

"Could they be investigating the Perry affair?"

"Possibly."

She began rubbing her temples. "In either case, we don't need government spies poking around. Especially when we're on the cusp of completing our project."

"Do you think it's safe to proceed?" Robertson asked. "Maybe we should stop, just temporarily, see what SIS is really after."

"Absolutely not. I haven't come this far to just drop it. We just need a change of venue, that's all. Something out of the government's line of sight, but it can't look like we're running away."

"What about headquarters?" Robertson offered.

"Headquarters... yes. And it occurs to me that San Francisco may offer a solution to our participant problem as well. I want you to go there, see what can be done. We need to move quickly."

———

The technicians, along with Dr. Hughes, returned to Corbyn's office, taking their respective seats.

"There's been a development," Corbyn began. "One that necessitates our moving forward immediately."

The technicians traded looks, not certain how to respond.

"You will pack up the necessary laboratory tools and supplies that you'll need."

Oliver Buoy cleared his throat. "Where are we going?"

"I have dispatched Mr. Robertson to handle that detail."

"What about equipment?" George Kraft asked. "If we're moving to a new location, won't we have to take all the lab equipment?"

"I'll deal with that when we decide on a location." She gave the trio a stern look. "Since we don't want to risk exposure, I suggest the proof of concept should take place outside the UK."

Myra Shipman leaned forward. "Where is a location with the capacity to supply the equipment and the number of subjects you want?"

"I believe we have that covered," Corbyn said. "The United States—corporate headquarters. More importantly, we have a friend who can help clear the way: Senator Jack Buchanan, the man who was instrumental in passing several pieces of legislation that were beneficial to ASRI."

Myra closed her eyes slowly, pleased that Director Corbyn had come to this conclusion.

CHAPTER 20

Hannah and Joel decided an offsite meeting place would be more appropriate for their inquiry. "I'm supposed to be on leave," Hannah said. "C will blow a gasket if I show up at headquarters."

"This is no way to spend your holiday," Joel said.

"Nor is it yours," she replied.

They chose the business center in Joel's hotel. "Now, let's see if we can find out more about ASRI," Joel said.

"And their security man, Callum Robertson," Hannah added.

They spent the afternoon in focused silence, each working separately. Occasionally, one would utter an exclamation, but otherwise, there was quiet concentration.

By the end of the day, they were ready to stop. Joel suggested a drink in the hotel's lounge. Hannah agreed.

Taking a corner table away from other patrons, they placed drink orders with a young waiter. Joel began, "Everything I found was just a rehash of what I already knew."

"Then I think you'll be interested in my research," Hannah said. "It concerns the Buchanans. They found themselves in the peculiar position of having too much wealth. It was becoming too visible, too noticeable. They needed to diversify."

"And how'd they do that?" Joel asked.

"They set up a series of shell corporations. It was a way to shuffle around large amounts of cash without alerting regulatory agencies."

"Money laundering," Joel said.

"More to the point of our present inquiries, I found a newspaper article with a picture of Kurt Buchanan, the senator's son. He was rubbing elbows with a government relations flack for Applied Science Research Institute."

"Yes, I saw that picture as well," Joel said.

Hannah continued, "And wouldn't you know, with gifts, grants, and donations, they insinuated themselves into ASRI."

"What was their interest?" Joel asked.

"ASRI was working on some pretty cool biotechnology stuff, among other things, developing new ways to deal with inoperable illnesses."

Joel asked, "What is the most promising area of ASRI's research?"

"Nanotechnology."

Joel nodded. "You know the old saying, 'He who gets there first, profits most.'"

"The Buchanans made certain that ASRI received favorable legislative decisions, not only in the United States but in all the countries they operate. In return, regular 'royalty' payments were made, always to the shell companies."

Joel, now keen on the subject, added, "They were hiding their connection... and in typical fashion, the Buchanans always found a way to coerce someone on the inside to act as their spy. There's no reason to think they haven't cultivated a spy within ASRI, someone able to provide intelligence leading to insider knowledge."

"How about Robertson? Did you find anything on him?" Hannah asked.

"Yes. I used UN resources to access Interpol. They had a record on Robertson. He was a US special operator in the Middle East. But something happened—he was abruptly separated from the service. That's where Interpol's records end."

"It looks like he landed at ASRI," Hannah said.

They sipped their drinks in silent contemplation before Hannah had a new thought. "In all the commotion, I almost forgot about Corbyn."

Joel snapped back to the here-and-now. "You found something on her?"

"Oh, yes. Those guys that captured me, the Paynim, turned out to be real opportunists. They kidnapped me with the intention to demand more. And whether they shot me outright or just held me in that locked root cellar, they meant for me to die."

"There's a happy thought," Joel said. "Who do you think killed the Paynim?"

"I'm not sure. Such a brutal attack wasn't the work of a bunch of internet geeks. It was professional."

"Contract killers," Joel said. "Who were they, and who gave the orders?"

Hannah sat back. "My money's on Corbyn. She must have seen my offer. I'll bet she gave the order."

Pleading exhaustion, Hannah left Joel and took a taxi to her Islington flat. Opening the door reminded her that she still hadn't solved the mystery of Amy Perry's death or the location of her body.

"It'll have to wait. I'm too tired to think."

The next morning, she was up, rested, and ready to go. Returning to the hotel, she went to the dining room and was pleasantly surprised to find Joel there.

"Good morning," she said.

Joel stood and pulled out a chair for her. As she sat, she noticed Joel had finished his breakfast and was sipping coffee.

"It looks like you're ready for a full day of sleuthing."

Joel put down his coffee cup and wiped his lips with a napkin. "As I see it, there are two avenues to pursue. The first is digging into Corbyn and her involvement with the attack. Then, there's the question of what part ASRI plays in all this."

Hannah said, "I need to find out what happened to Amy Perry's body. Somehow, Amy's death is key to this mystery. I need to get to the bottom of it."

Joel sat back in his chair. "Let's go back to ASRI and press for an interview with Director Corbyn."

CHAPTER 21

On their return visit to ASRI, Hannah and Joel did finally meet Margaret Corbyn. The director stood when they entered her office but didn't offer to shake hands. Hannah immediately noticed the pungent aroma of incense. Corbyn's unfriendly demeanor and obvious suspicion signaled this was not going to be an easy interview. "I should take the lead on this," Hannah whispered.

Corbyn kept her hands out of sight below the desk. At first, Hannah didn't give it much thought, except she couldn't help noticing Corbyn's hands were constantly *moving* beneath the desk.

"Director Corbyn," Hannah began, "we don't mean to alarm you with our visit—"

Corbyn interrupted, "Why are you here? What is the government's interest in my company? And who are you?" She looked directly at Joel. "This doesn't feel like a casual visit."

"My name is Joel Braithwaite. I'm with the UN Terrorism Prevention Bureau."

Surprise flashed on Corbyn's face as she looked between them. But there was more. Fear plagued Corbyn.

Joel continued, "This isn't an official investigation. We're gathering background on a case. We hoped you might be able to help us."

That did nothing to win over the director. Corbyn's shoulders relaxed a little, but a look of suspicion remained.

"Go on," Corbyn said.

Hannah took over, "It's about one of your employees, Amy Perry."

Corbyn's gaze became sharp. "Dr. Perry... yes." Corbyn looked directly at Hannah. "She disappeared a while ago. There was some concern here. She didn't leave word or even a note. Why do you ask? Her disappearance certainly doesn't rise to the level of a national incident."

"Amy Perry died in my flat," Hannah said. She watched Corbyn's face turn pallid. "And her body was stolen. Our only lead is her position here at ASRI. Who was her supervisor?"

Corbyn stood. "I won't be answering anymore questions, not without a court order and a lawyer present."

Hannah looked at Joel. They were taken by surprise. They hadn't expected this aggressively negative response. As they left the office, Hannah turned. "One more thing. Do you know anything about an internet Clan called Paynim?"

"Absolutely not. Now, please leave."

Once outside, Joel said, "I'd say you touched a nerve back there."

"More than that," Hannah said. "Did you see her? She was frightened."

"Especially when you mentioned Paynim."

"What do you say we park off the road under the trees? Let's see if she's spooked enough to run."

Corbyn felt like a trap was closing around her. The whole Amy Perry incident was very much *not resolved*. "So, Dr. Perry's destination that night wasn't coincidental," she lectured to the empty office. "Damn that Callum Robertson! He got it all wrong, and now it's led here, to me! How much do those people know, or think they know? And why that off-handed question about Paynim? Was it connected to the Dark Web post?"

She was looking for answers that wouldn't come. Dropping into her office chair, she put clutched fists to her forehead. After a time of silence, her mind going through doubts, self-recriminations, and anger, she left.

The sky was darkening when a late model Land Rover pulled out of the ASRI entry. "There she is!" Joel exclaimed. They watched it turn. "And she's *not* heading to London."

"Let's follow her," Hannah said.

"Hold on a moment. We've seen where she's headed—I don't want to give us away."

"Do you have any idea where she's going though?" Hannah asked, still strapping on her seatbelt.

"Wherever it is, it's not in London, so it shouldn't be hard to find her."

"Still, at least follow at a distance. I don't want to lose this lead."

Joel relented and after a few miles, Corbyn's Rover turned onto a road that headed into the open country. Joel and Hannah followed. It was twilight and they still had to hang back. They wondered where Corbyn could be headed.

"She's making a turn," Joel commented. "Going into a community."

CHAPTER 22

Returning to her home in a tidy condominium community, Corbyn went directly to a computer. She was glad that some years ago, she'd taken the precaution to keep a separate computer that wasn't connected to her work. It was where she could access the Dark Web and find people willing to work outside the law. A few years ago, she found a group, a Clan as they called themselves, who became her private research unit. She paid well and in Bitcoin. That was always an enticement to the Dark Web types.

For her, the Dark Web offered anonymity. This was a state she preferred. A solitary existence had shaped her life, made her what she'd become.

Sixteen years old... Even at that age, I was heavy. All the girls in school let me know it. But I learned how to manage the teasing and harassment. After all, they couldn't torment me if I wasn't around. So, I avoided contact and kept to myself.

I was surprised when a boy asked me to a school dance. It was my first date. I was nervous and excited at the same time. I bought a new dress and had my hair done.

At the dance, it all went wrong. Instead of being nice to me, the boy criticized my dress and mocked my hairstyle. He paraded me in front of his friends. I didn't know they'd put the boy up to this date. He'd done it on a dare. He didn't care about me; only wanted to win whatever wager he'd made.

The gang of boys cat-called and hooted at me. Their girlfriends joined in on the fun. I was humiliated. I called my father to come for me—that was even more embarrassing.

After that, I stayed in my room.

My only friends were books. I read—a lot. It must have helped, because getting into college was easy.

I hoped college would be different, but the girls there were no better than high school. I had to shower in the middle of the night to avoid whispers and giggles. I had a roommate, but she moved out before the first semester ended. I was alone, which was fine with me.

I finished college in three years and went to graduate school, received a Master's in microbiology. From there, I was recruited to a start-up company focusing on bioengineering—right up my alley.

That's where I met the only person who seemed to understand me: Callum Robertson. He was a security officer for the company, but seemed to be more than that. It would be some time before I found out his background. In any event, Robertson was stern, though kind. He seemed to understand my deep-seated anxiety, my suspicion that everyone was watching me, judging me, out to get me. Even within the company, I had no friends—only enemies. Except Callum.

She refocused on the computer and sent a message to her private team, telling them she would be away for some time and not to attempt contact.

She had much bigger issues to deal with.

———

After watching Corbyn's home for an hour, they agreed she was in for the night. Hannah and Joel headed back to London.

"It's time I get back to Brussels," Joel said. "I can get the late flight."

"Do you mind stopping by my flat? There's something I want to give you."

When they arrived at Hannah's flat, she went to her bedroom and returned with a USB drive.

"Since you're going back to Brussels, I wonder if you wouldn't mind giving this to Davies." She handed him the drive. He gave a questioning look. "This was in Amy's bag. I believe it's a copy of the research she gave to Corbyn. I'm going to need someone with greater computer skills than I have to figure out exactly what Amy was doing."

Joel pocketed the drive. "Sure. I'll get it to the boys right away."

"I'm going to follow the Buchanan angle," Hannah said. "I have a feeling there's something strange going on with ASRI—and Amy's death is only part of it."

"Agreed," Joel said. "I'll work with Davies and Shadow, see what more we can find about your friend's research. I'll leave ASRI to you."

CHAPTER 23

Joel returned to Brussels and delivered the USB drive to Davies. There were other duties waiting for his attention, and he made certain Davies understood Hannah's request. Davies promised to report when he'd analyzed the drive.

Two days later, Joel received a call from Davies. "What've you boys found?"

"Plenty. I think you may want to come over. It's easier to show than to tell."

Arriving at the SpartanZ office in an unremarkable, semi-rundown industrial park, Joel was ushered to a task chair set before a large computer monitor. Davies, anxious to begin, was jumping around like he was walking on hot coals.

"We've spent the last two days—and I do mean forty-eight straight hours—analyzing Dr. Perry's research."

Joel leaned into a screen full of scientific notations. He didn't understand any of it and told the boys so.

"Not to worry, Mr. B.," Shadow chimed in, "we'll walk you through this." He hit the spacebar and the screen changed. It was a series of animations demonstrating a process Joel didn't understand.

Davies began, "Let's start with a primer on nanotechnology. I'm sure you're aware of what it is but probably don't know how it works."

"My ignorance is that obvious?" Joel asked.

"In simplest terms, it's all about nanites—tiny little machines that can be programmed for a specific purpose."

"You mean, like a robot in a factory," Joel said.

"Exactly, except these robots are microscopic. Nanites are programmed for specific tasks. In the case of this research—which, by the way, is very cutting edge—it requires building biological robots. Dr. Perry grew a specific group of viruses and then modified their DNA structure. That's what the video animation is showing you."

"That sounds easy enough," Joel said.

"Oh, no, it's anything but easy. It's not like building a physical machine. It requires the alteration of the virus' DNA. It's painstaking, meticulous work that has to be done using all sorts of exotic equipment. It's easy to screw it up, but Dr. Perry seemed to have mastered the technique.

"Once learning how to manipulate the viruses, she needed to isolate a target illness. In her case, Dr. Perry was focused on inoperable brain lesions. After mapping the subject's brain, she could program her modified viruses to attack only the lesions. Voilà! Lesions shrivel up and the patient is cured, and all without invasive brain surgery."

"This sounds important," Joel said.

"You bet it is. The company that brings this kind of technology to the world of medicine will make billions."

"So, why isn't it out there?"

"This is cutting edge experimental biomechanical medicine. They have to go through years of trials before anything is approved for general use. This particular application of nanotechnology was ready to move to the next level, but it stopped."

"Stopped? Why?"

"Because Amy Perry disappeared. It brought the project to a halt," Davies said.

"Couldn't someone pick up where she left off?"

"If they had what you gave us on this USB drive, yes."

Joel understood. "There wasn't any record of her research..."

"Until you handed us this drive, yes."

"Hannah told me Dr. Perry's logbook mentioned giving her work to the operations director, Margaret Corbyn, but there was no mention of what was done with it."

"Until Dr. Perry showed up at Hannah's door and dropped dead," Davies said.

Joel pushed back in the rolling chair. "Let me see if I understand what you're saying... Hannah told me that Perry's log indicated she was successful in creating this pioneering technology. After that, she was ordered to turn over her research. Later, she found one of her seed colonies was missing. Then she found a body in the company's cold room. It occurs to Amy that someone's been altering her process behind her back, but she accidentally becomes infected. Perry goes to an old friend—someone she considers safe and not connected to ASRI." Joel looked at Davies and Shadow. "The question is, what was Dr. Perry's original process changed into?"

Neither could answer that question.

"On to another topic," Joel said, "the people that captured Hannah. Whoever attacked the cottage was professional."

"Who would have the resources to mount such an attack?" Davies asked. "Assassins?"

"How do you find guns for hire? It's not like they're listed in a directory," Shadow added.

"Corbyn has resources," Davies said.

"You think Corbyn arranged the hit?" Joel asked

"Yes. Maybe not directly, but she gave the order."

"Is ASRI complicit?"

"There's something strange going on there," Davies said. "Why would an international company order the killing of one of their employees? Firing would work just as well."

"This goes to something Hannah was talking about," Joel said. "Somehow, this began with the death of her friend. Maybe we should start there, too."

CHAPTER 24

Hannah had to wait two days for a meeting with C. She finally received a text message from Emily Fallon telling her that C would see her at ten the next morning. She presented herself at precisely ten o'clock.

Emily looked her over as she entered the waiting area. "I can see something's going on with you," Emily said. "What's been happening on your leave?"

"That's what I'm here to discuss with C. Things have gotten a little out of hand."

The intercom on Emily's desk buzzed. "It looks like he's ready for you."

"Thanks, Em."

It didn't seem to matter what time of day she entered the director's office, he was always on the phone. She stood just inside the door, waiting for C to acknowledge her presence. Ending his call, C called her over, "Sit, Agent Ahmed." He looked at his agent with a discerning eye. "I can tell there's something disturbing you."

"Yes, sir. I would like to open a new investigation." She gave a summary of events up to that point. C sat back in his chair, listening.

"Very well, I'll authorize an inquiry. You'll have to coordinate with MI5 if you intend to look into ASRI's operations here in Great Britain."

"It's not so much the company. There's one person I'm interested in: Margaret Corbyn, the operations director. I think she may be up to something the company knows nothing about."

"Is she British?"

"No, she's American, sent here from company headquarters when they set up their local operation."

"Are your suspicions solely with the British division, or is it broader?"

"I don't know. My feeling is that whatever is happening doesn't involve ASRI as a whole."

"Very well. You're back on duty. Now, if you don't mind..."

C picked up the telephone, and Hannah left. Her next stop would be ASRI.

This time, Hannah didn't ask to see Director Corbyn. Based on her last visit, Corbyn wouldn't be cooperative. There were lots of pieces to this puzzle, and how they fit together was still a mystery to her. So, instead of Corbyn, she asked for Human Resources.

The HR director stiffened when she presented her credentials. He relaxed somewhat when she told him there was no problem with the company; she was simply following up on a missing person. "One of your employees—Amy Perry."

The HR director's face went pale. "We reported this to the police. Dr. Perry didn't show up for work as expected. After a couple of days, we became concerned. She just vanished."

"Can you tell me about her work?"

Death Mist

"Dr. Perry was heading up a project in bio-medicine using nanotechnology."

"Can you explain?"

"It's believed that nanotechnology can be used to reproduce or repair damaged tissue without surgery. It's ASRI's position that tissue engineering, if successful, may replace conventional treatments like organ transplants or artificial implants."

"Who did Dr. Perry report to?" Hannah asked.

"As a doctor and a Research Fellow, she worked autonomously. Her results were reviewed regularly by our operations director, Margaret Corbyn. As to her day-to-day activity, she was on her own."

"How close to a successful treatment was she?"

"That's way above my pay grade, but based on water cooler talk, I'd say she was on the verge of something big."

"May I see where she worked?"

With a visitor's badge and directions, Hannah went in search of Amy's office. It turned out to be a large room, complete with all manner of esoteric machines, test tubes, and other laboratory paraphernalia. It was a little daunting.

"Where to begin?" she asked aloud with an exasperated sigh.

Pulling Amy's journal from her shoulder bag, she reviewed the entries. *On October fifteenth it says one of her colonies was stolen.* She looked around the lab for evidence of other colonies, but she had no idea what she was looking for. *Are they in glass jars? Or maybe plastic baggies?*

She found several stainless-steel containers in a refrigerator. Inspecting one, she found it was empty. "It looks like someone cleared out this lab."

She returned to the journal and turned to October thirty-first.

"This is what I'm looking for... a morgue. I wonder where that is?"

A lab-coated woman happened to walk past Amy's door. "Can you help me?" Hannah called out. "I'm looking for the morgue."

The woman stopped, gave a quizzical look, then smiled. "You mean the cold room. 'Morgue' is a little grand. There's a door at the end of this hall. Follow the signs down that hallway. You can't miss it."

Hannah had no trouble finding the cold room. There was no one around, so she let herself in, flipping the light switch as she entered. The room was indeed cold. And was also small. *Then again, how many autopsies are performed in this place?*

Unlike the rest of the ASRI facility—contemporary, clean, upscale—the cold room was sterile. White subway tiles covered the walls, and the floor was a light gray linoleum. A single autopsy table sat in the center of the room with a gimbaled light fixture directly overhead. A bank of three mortuary cabinets were on one wall and took up the better part of the available floor space. A video monitor was mounted above a small desk that was pushed up to the wall. She thought it a singularly uninviting place to work.

Stepping up to the autopsy table, she noticed the floor sloped slightly. Looking under the table, there was a large drain at the bottom of the decline. The table itself was clean. A large glass cupboard holding all manner of medical supplies was positioned within easy reach. Testing the doors, she found the cupboard was locked.

Turning to the mortuary cabinets, she opened the top one. The body tray was empty. *Amy's journal said she found a body... I wonder where it is?*

The second drawer was empty as well. The third, however, wasn't. It was occupied not by a body, but by a small stainless-steel container. *Just like the empties in Amy's lab.*

She inspected the container carefully and found no identifying signs or notes. Placing the container on the autopsy table, she began unscrewing the top. She stopped, remembering Amy's warning. Looking around, she found a mask and put it on. There was a *hiss* as the seal was released. She pulled up the top.

Inside the container was a swirling mist. Not smoke, exactly, it looked heavier than that. *Opening it must have disturbed the contents.* Then she remembered Amy's warning about the mist and quickly replaced the top, screwing it down tightly. She was going to return it to the cabinet drawer but had second thoughts.

This may be valuable evidence.

Hannah beat a hasty retreat from ASRI. *What should I do with the canister?* As she returned to London, she believed this could prove that ASRI was responsible for Amy's death.

Back in her flat, she was still undecided how to proceed with the canister. *It was being stored in the cold, so maybe I should keep it in the refrigerator.* Exhausted, she went to the bedroom telling herself, "Tired minds don't plan well. Get some sleep and see what the morning brings."

She passed an unrestful night filled with disturbing dreams. When the sun came up, she'd reached a decision. After a light breakfast of tea and a croissant, she returned to her SIS office. *I need to find more about that managing director, Margaret Corbyn. It seems odd that her supervisor would be in America. There's no one in the UK facility to check on her activities.*

SIS had vast information resources. Navigating the sheer

volume of files, folders, videos, etc., made searching an art she didn't have time to master. *This is when I could use Davies!*

She finally got a useful search string. There was a casebook on Corbyn. It sketched out a complete background. *How about this? The report had been ordered by the Buchanans.*

That took her on a new track—following the Buchanan trail as it intersected ASRI.

She discovered that the Buchanans had become involved with ASRI-America when the company was beginning to get a foothold in the biotechnology field. There were, naturally, many regulations to navigate before the company could begin to operate, and a meeting with Senator Jack Buchanan and his son, Kurt, had been a turning point. Soon after, the regulation roadblocks just... disappeared.

When the company tried to open a facility in the UK, it ran into trouble. The Buchanans once again stepped in. Red tape gone... permits and licenses approved... and Kurt Buchanan was appointed to the Board of Directors.

What a cozy arrangement, she thought.

Hannah found a photograph in the New York Times society section. It was part of an article about the dashing young Kurt Buchanan, scion of the powerful senator. Amidst the details of Kurt Buchanan's nightclub forays, restaurant sightings, and rumored romances, she found a photo. It was Kurt looking very chummy with another man, identified in the caption as Michael Roark.

Looking up Roark, she found he was a government consultant for ASRI—a lobbyist. Going back to the photo, she noted how Kurt was shaking Roark's hand while placing his other hand on Roark's shoulder. That was her lead. She needed to get to Washington, DC.

CHAPTER 25

FBI headquarters in Washington, DC is a large, imposing building. Hannah looked up at the façade. *Not much style. At least our SIS building is architecturally interesting.* She thought about FBI Special Agent Rick Simmons. He'd been very helpful during a previous case and she felt comfortable conferring with him on this present investigation.

After passing through several layers of security, she came to the last security stop, where a uniformed officer asked her to wait. The officer made a call, presumably to Simmons. After getting directions to Simmons' office, she set off and found herself sitting in a small waiting room facing several office doors. There was no receptionist. Each door had a different nameplate, and one of them read *Special Agent Richard Simmons*.

The door opened, and Simmons greeted her. His broad smile signaled acknowledgment of their past shared experience.

He's just as I remember: six feet tall, clean-cut, attractive— but not movie star handsome. A good trait for an FBI Special Agent.

"Hannah, how great to see you again. Please come in."

Simmons held the door for her and motioned to a sitting area on one side of a surprisingly spacious office. After she settled into an upholstered leather chair, Simmons offered her something to drink.

"No, thank you."

Simmons sat across on a small couch. "This is an unexpected pleasure. But I think this isn't a social call."

"No. I'm into something, and I could use your help. But it's got to remain unofficial."

"I'm all ears..."

She ran through a digest version of Amy's sudden appearance in her flat, her death, and the subsequent hijacking of the body. She didn't tell him about the discovery of the canister. *That can wait until I know more.*

She described her research into ASRI and how it led to the Buchanans.

"Do you mean Senator Jack Buchanan?" Simmons asked with surprise.

"Yes. More specifically, his son, Kurt. I found the younger Buchanan had been appointed to the ASRI Board of Directors, even though he has no background in science, much less biotechnology."

"The Buchanans have a way of inserting themselves into things like that... Do you suspect Kurt Buchanan had something to do with the death of your friend?"

"Not directly, but he's a person of interest. Knowing how powerful his father is, I need to tread lightly—approach this from an oblique angle." She showed him the photograph of Kurt Buchanan. "I need to meet with the man shaking Kurt's hand."

"Yes... that's Michael Roark. He's a fixture in the Washington lobbyist fraternity. Been around for years."

"Do you know where to find him?"

"Sure. His office is on K Street. Let me get the address for you."

After handing her a slip of paper, Simmons asked, "Is there something that the FBI can officially do for you?"

"At this point, no. It's too early. But I may need help after I learn more."

Hannah took a taxi to the address Simmons scribbled down. It was a tall building that looked like a dozen others along K Street, stylishly modern, the kind of setting that evoked a sense of wealth and power. Checking a brass-enclosed building directory, she found Roark and Associates. Scanning the others listed, they all had *and Associates* attached to their names. She guessed they were mostly one-man operations—funded, of course, by larger interests outside the Capitol.

Taking the elevator to the fifth floor, she saw a long row of office doors, each with a different nameplate. Locating Roark's, she knocked and entered. The reception area was small and well-appointed. The walls were covered in flocked wallpaper and expensive carpet was underfoot. There was a hint of fragrance, not displeasing, but still noticeable. A polished wood reception station sat before a professionally lettered sign reading:

Roark & Associates—Government Relations

The receptionist was a pretty young woman with blonde hair trimmed to a conservative length; she was dressed in a tailored suit with a splash of color along the collar and cuffs. She couldn't see the receptionist's feet but assumed she wore designer shoes. She judged the receptionist to be in her late twenties. *Young enough to have coquettish appeal—the kind of attractiveness that's an allure to middle-aged men—and the source of the perfume in the air.*

She asked to see Mr. Roark, and no, she didn't have an appointment. She presented her SIS identification. "You may tell him it's a private matter."

The receptionist made a hushed call to her boss.

"Mr. Roark will be right with you."

Roark looked much like his photo in the newspaper—urbane, with a bespoke tailored suit, expensive dress shirt, and striped school tie. He stood with a practiced smile as she entered. Hannah read that smile as a well-crafted mask. She wondered who the man behind the mask really was.

The office was decorated in what might be called "corporate luxury." A fine grade of carpet filled out the space. Soft music drifted through the room but didn't dominate. The walls were paneled in rich walnut, polished to a soft shine. A bar was inset on one wall with sparkling glassware hanging above cut-crystal decanters filled with various liquors. A comfortable conversation area was across the room, but the focal point was the desk. Behind the desk, a "brag wall."

She was surprised Roark didn't have a traditionally styled desk, the typical symbol of an important man. Instead, his desk was a large, thick, asymmetrical piece of polished wood. The wood hadn't been milled, looking like it had come directly from the heart of a great tree and hand finished. Rich veining, ranging from light blond to dark walnut, made the four-inch-thick piece resemble a manufactured product; which she knew it wasn't. That piece was one-of-a-kind.

Solid Ironheart—an Amazon tropical hardwood. Impressive. Expensive.

The brag wall was covered with photographs of Roark meeting with world leaders, corporate chieftains, and other dignitaries. Citations scattered among the display attested to his lobbying skills. The message was clear: Roark was a man who got things done.

This man's the ultimate fixer, she thought.

"My assistant tells me you're from the British government." Roark paused to inspect his unusual guest. "How can this humble American be of service?"

The unexpected diffidence was, she knew, anything but humble. It was meant to throw her off. "You were recommended as someone who could help with something we're looking into. I understand you were instrumental in solving certain 'problems' for Applied Science Research Institute."

Roark looked up to the richly plastered ceiling. "What is the Special Investigative Service's interest in ASRI? You can't be investigating anything here. This is America."

The sharp rebuke was a complete departure from his smiling welcome.

"I'm looking for background information. It's not an investigation." She could see her response did little to satisfy Roark. "We were wondering why would someone like Kurt Buchanan be placed on the company's Board of Directors?"

"I couldn't tell you."

"You're close to the senator and his son, correct?"

"I've met with Senator Buchanan occasionally. I wouldn't say we're close. I've done some consulting work for the senator over the years, that's all."

She showed him the newspaper photo. "This looks like you've done more than a little consulting."

Roark stood. The meeting was over.

"I'm a busy man, and I resent your questions. You may leave."

———

The moment Hannah left his office, Roark called his assistant. "Get Kurt Buchanan on the phone." He didn't have to wait long. When Michael Roark called, people jumped.

"Kurt, I've just had a visit from a woman representing the British government. She wanted to know about my relationship with you and your father—and ASRI."

He listened to silence from Buchanan. "Are you there, Kurt? Did you hear what I said?"

"Yes. I'm sorry, I was momentarily startled. Who was she? Why did she come to you?"

"She identified herself as a representative of the Secret Intelligence Service."

"Isn't that like the British CIA?"

"Yes, it is. It made me very uncomfortable to have her sitting here, asking about my relationship with your family. I told her it was strictly business, that I'd done a little consulting for the senator—that's all."

"Should we be concerned?" Kurt asked.

"My instincts have served me well over the years, and my gut is signaling caution. I think you may want to look into this woman." He picked up the business card Hannah had left. "Her name is Hannah Ahmed."

CHAPTER 26

Kurt Buchanan called his father, Senator Jack Buchanan. "Dad, we may have a problem. A woman's been poking around ASRI and the nanotechnology project… She's a British agent."

"Well, shit, son. That's not good. How did this happen?"

"I'm not sure, but she's asking questions about me—and about our family."

"Okay then, we get rid of her."

"That would be a problem. It would be news, like killing some VIP. A larger investigation would begin. That's why I called. What do we do?"

"A British agent, you say… Is she a spook?"

"She's with the SIS—the Secret Intelligence Service."

"Administrative?"

"I don't think so, sir. I tried to look her up, but SIS is a hard nut to crack."

"What's her name?"

"Hannah Ahmed."

Kurt could almost hear his father's mind churning, calculating.

"I agree, she's much too visible to take out. I have another way to get her out of the picture. We'll have her discredited... get a buzz going, something that'll bury her."

"Great idea, Dad. How do we do that?"

"Leave it to me. We have someone in the British Secret Service. He'll finally start to earn the money I've been investing in him."

Soon thereafter, articles began to appear in the *Times of London*. The initial articles posed questions about SIS' control of its field agents. The story was soon picked up by other international news organizations. After several days of escalating scrutiny, SIS scheduled a press conference.

Journalists filled the small briefing room off the main floor in SIS headquarters. The briefing began civilly enough. The public affairs spokesman made opening remarks outlining SIS policy and procedures, and with that bit of housekeeping complete, the floor was opened to questions.

A reporter representing the *Times of London* began, "SIS is restricted to international investigations, yet we understand you've been probing into domestic companies. Can you explain?"

"Certainly. SIS works closely with its sister service, MI5. They, of course, handle domestic investigations."

"What about ASRI?" the reporter insisted. "Why is SIS making inquiries into a British company?"

"As you know, ASRI is a multi-national business. Our present activities are part of an ongoing investigation, so I'm afraid I can't comment."

This response caused an uproar among the reporters. Outside, a crowd of people assembled and began picketing and shouting, "Shut down SIS!" The disruption was heard by the press inside. With all the disruption, the unfortunate spokesman couldn't regain control.

By that evening, the raucous news conference and demonstration were all over television. BBC, Reuters, GB News, and ITV all had reports, and they were asking the same question: Why is SIS investigating a domestic company? Video clips even made it to international providers like CNN, Fox News, and Sky News.

A flood of interview requests came to C's office. The public clamor soon drove him to issue a written statement in which he apologized and promised to get to the bottom of the issue. The press wasn't satisfied. Increasingly critical articles and on-air reports continued, many calling for C's resignation.

The public relations battle was picked up all around the world. SIS was under attack. And it was something they were not equipped to combat.

Hannah sat in her Washington, DC hotel room, watching the spectacle on television. Her concern grew as her agency's PR crisis mounted. Sagging back in her chair, she had a premonition that it would all eventually fall on her. She wondered where this attack came from—more importantly, how to combat it. There seemed to be a malevolent force behind it all.

She sat up. "I think I know who's doing this."

Her probe of ASRI and the discovery that Kurt Buchanan was on the company's Board of Directors meant he was perfectly positioned to seize Amy Perry's research. To what end, she didn't know, but it became clear to her that Margaret Corbyn had to be involved.

She'd been faced with two paths of inquiry but could only pursue one at a time. She chose to begin at the top, the Buchanan angle. Now, with this growing PR problem, she wasn't so confident that was the right choice.

It wasn't long before her name began popping up. She believed this was a deliberate smear campaign; one she believed could only have originated internally. Reporters were being fed details of her private life. Hannah couldn't believe this was happening.

She looked at her notes on the Buchanans. *Their vile operation infects everything it touches.*

The SIS story grew in public interest. Even American news outlets began carrying regular reports. The local Washington, DC news stations, WRC-TV, WJLA, WUSA, and others, announced a special report was coming up, a statement from Senator Jack Buchanan.

"Oh, great." The senator was at the heart of the operation she'd uncovered. She didn't want to watch, but she had to. "Know your enemy," she whispered.

The news piece was an edit from a longer speech delivered earlier that day, but what was shown was enough to make her sick. The piece opened with the senator standing at a lectern overlooking the Senate chamber. All one hundred seats were occupied, as was the visitors' gallery. Expectant faces waited for Buchanan to begin.

Senator Buchanan was a tall man, well over six feet. At sixty-eight years of age, he looked fit. A full head of white hair bespoke wisdom. His smile was obsequious and decidedly unwelcoming. A finely tailored suit conveyed wealth and influence. She watched the senator's harangue, making claims that rogue SIS agents were being set loose in the world causing "who knows what kinds of havoc."

"One in particular," the senator said, lowering his voice almost to a whisper, "illustrates what I'm talking about." He stood back and boomed, "SIS agent, Hannah Ahmed. She's been involved in a number of destructive operations." The senator went on to enumerate details of several of her past missions.

How in the world did he get that information?

"In conclusion, I call on the British government to censure

SIS and immediately remove Hannah Ahmed from active service."

A thunderous applause filled the Senate chamber. Shouts of approval could be heard not only from the assembled senators but from the visitors' gallery as well.

That was enough. She flipped off the television. She was immobilized by total shock.

"I've been identified to the world. What do I do now?"

Hannah's answer came less than ten minutes later. It was Emily Fallon, C's assistant, asking her to return to headquarters as soon as possible. Her face went ashen, her stomach rock hard. She knew what was in store but didn't want to admit it.

Almost immediately, she received another call. It was Joel. "I saw Senator Buchanan's speech. Talk about being thrown to the wolves... I'm sorry. That crook has singled you out to be a sacrificial lamb."

"Yes, and I know why. Do you remember how he operates? This public crucifixion fits right in." She took a second to get her emotions under control. "I got a call a minute ago summoning me back to SIS. I'm expecting a public flogging."

CHAPTER 27

Hannah was pleased to find her MINI Cooper returned, good as new. On the other hand, her drive to headquarters filled her with dread. After parking, she took the lift to the top floor where Emily Fallon was waiting. A sad look marred Em's face.

"Go right in. He's expecting you."

This time, C wasn't on the telephone. He was sitting behind his desk with a serious look that didn't bode well for their meeting.

"Agent Ahmed, I have a problem. Everyone, from the PM on down, is climbing up my ass, asking questions, looking for answers, and looking for blood. Specifically, your blood."

"May I speak? There's much you should know." C grunted, his signal to proceed. "I've been digging into the Buchanan family. It seems they're involved in influence peddling on a breathtaking scale. Not just in America, but worldwide— including Great Britain. It's made them rich, and I'm sorry to say, powerful.

"I discovered that some years ago they approached ASRI with a promise of regulations relief and other political considerations.

Death Mist

When the company's new UK installation became stuck due to political resistance to their research, it became desperate. Buchanan stepped in, offering 'assistance.' ASRI jumped at the offer. I can only imagine how large a payment was made and who the recipient might be, but it wasn't long before the political roadblocks were pushed aside and ASRI could move forward with their British operations.

"I tracked down a government relations consultant in Washington, DC, who was helping ASRI. A man named Michael Roark. I asked about his relationship with the Buchanans. At first, he claimed ignorance. I shared a newspaper photo showing Kurt Buchanan and himself happily shaking hands. He hemmed and hawed, eventually admitting to a 'casual' relationship with the Buchanans. I pressed him—not only on Kurt, but for information about the father, Senator Jack Buchanan. My questioning must have hit close to home. The meeting was abruptly ended, and it wasn't too long before the senator made his big speech."

C went to the tall glass windows overlooking the River Thames, hands clasped behind his back.

"Agent Ahmed... Hannah," C said with uncharacteristic softness, "your work has been exemplary. You've grown to become one of my most effective agents. Your insight and instincts have proven correct during any number of missions. But I find myself in a difficult position. Never has there been public scrutiny as we're presently experiencing."

In a flash, she saw her entire SIS career... the training... the stakeouts... tense standoffs... surviving explosions... gun battles... a montage of growth and achievement, and now it was all about to go away.

"I'm going to have to separate you from the Service."

Tears formed in her eyes, but she was determined not to cry in front of C.

"I've ordered your mustering out to be streamlined. This needn't be the end, Hannah. In time, we may be able to bring you back. Quietly, of course."

Without another word, Hannah left the office.

Leaving SIS was like taking a perp walk of shame. Even Emily Fallon couldn't look her in the eye as she left the executive offices. The sting of C's dismissal was the last straw. She felt betrayed and abandoned. It seemed everyone in the building knew she'd been dismissed. People avoided her as she passed.

Back in her office, she found a large manila envelope on the desk. It contained separation papers, as well as instructions and reminders of British statutes and laws, and her confidentiality agreement. Alone now, she allowed herself to cry.

She didn't know how long she was in that state of grief, but finally, the crying stopped. With great difficulty, she got control of her emotions. With hands still shaking from the humiliation of her dismissal, she filled out the separation forms. Then, with a sigh, she placed the completed forms back in the envelope.

And then, in perhaps the most tangible expression of the separation, she placed her SIS credentials, the Beretta Nano, and her company mobile phone on the desk.

Taking one last look around, she wiped her face with her hands. She left with as much dignity as she could muster. *All I have to do is hold it together long enough to get to the elevator.*

She didn't remember the drive back to Islington, just suddenly found herself at her own front door. Entering her flat, she had a strange sense of disconnect. It was like she was walking around familiar things, but they were now strange or different. She had a hard time focusing her thoughts, and that scared her. Looking at her reflection in the hall mirror, she was alarmed.

"My God, I look a wreck." Wiping mascara from beneath her eyes made it better. Not good, just a little better.

She drew a bath. Soon, steam filled the bathroom.

Sliding into the hot, bubble-filled water, she sank down and let the warmth envelop her. She began to sob. She felt so powerless. She'd let so many people down, beginning with her deceased father. He believed in her, encouraged her through her childhood and university years, pushed her to do things she didn't think she could.

The memory made her weep all the more.

Her life flashed before her eyes, memories overlapping in crazy sequences... the people she'd known and lost... the hurts... the triumphs... and most of all, the loneliness of her life. She had no life partner, and now she had no career.

What's wrong with me?

It was a long time before she could collect herself and get out of the tub, or maybe it was the water beginning to cool. After toweling off, she crawled under her bed covers and put a pillow over her head. *I can't face the world right now.*

It was dark when she finally got up.

She wandered into the kitchen, searching for something to eat. Opening the refrigerator, she stared for a long moment at the silver canister and thought about the deadly narites inside. *Does it matter anymore?* With a shrug, she refocused on her present objective: Finding something to eat. She decided nothing interested her, and she certainly didn't feel like going out in public.

There was a bottle of white wine. "What the hell..."

She called out to her virtual assistant, "Alexa, play some gentle, soothing music."

Sitting in an overstuffed chair, she took a large swallow of wine and threw her head back on the cushion. The music and wine calmed her emotions, her mind beginning to fill with thoughts and questions she'd been suppressing. *What will I do now? Do I stay here, or go somewhere else—somewhere I'm not known?*

As she wrestled with these thoughts, her mobile rang. It was Joel.

"Sorry I didn't call you back," she said apologetically. "It was a rough day."

"I figured as much," Joel said. "What happened?"

"I got sacked."

"Just like that?"

"Just like that. Now I feel adrift. I'm not sure what to do or where to go."

"I don't want you to worry. You just need to get your feet back under you."

"How?"

"I've never seen you back down from anything or anyone. You're the smartest, toughest woman I've ever known. You can't let this knock you down. Sure, they've put you out of the Service, but that doesn't mean you can't continue."

"You mean freelance?"

"Yes, freelance. As a matter of fact, that could give you more freedom than you ever had with SIS."

"Freelance..." It was a new thought. She began to warm to the possibility. "Who would I work for? SIS is certainly out of the picture."

"SpartanZ will hire you. As it turns out, I have an in with the management."

"How would that work?"

"Leave it to me. There's more than one way to skin a cat. Meanwhile, I've gotten clearance from my division to pursue this line of inquiry. It turns out, they're as interested in nailing the Buchanans as we are."

"That's good news," Hannah said. "What's your next move?"

"I'm going to San Francisco. Can you meet me there?"

"Joel, I can't be seen anywhere near ASRI—and especially by the Buchanans."

"We're neck-deep in this nanotech thing, and we could really use your help."

"I—I don't know... Maybe."

"Just come to San Francisco."

CHAPTER 28

Applied Science Research Institute headquarters is located in San Francisco. Not actually in the city, but on the Peninsula—Silicon Valley. Close enough to the city to claim it as home.

Callum Robertson had no trouble setting up the proof-of-concept operation. A few phone calls revealed that a building adjacent to ASRI headquarters was vacant and available. It had been occupied by a tech company that, like so many others, gathered huge amounts of investment cash, prospered for a time, and then failed. Robertson believed the vacant building would work perfectly for Corbyn's plan.

A telephone call to London gained the director's approval to proceed. A one-year lease was entered into.

Corbyn dispatched her senior technicians, along with Dr. Hughes, to America. There, they would conduct the proof-of-concept testing, all under the watchful eye of Callum Robertson.

Before the group left for America, she gave them specific instructions.

"You will tell no one about the PoC. Since you'll be in a separate facility, I don't anticipate any interaction with ASRI's headquarters staff. However, should there be contact, you may allude to the biological nature of the project but give no specifics. You will direct any determined questioners to Mr. Robertson.

"Next, you will maintain regular contact with me and only me. I will be consulted on any actions taken, as well as resulting data from the PoC."

George Kraft looked at the director. "Where will the participants come from?"

"There's a large homeless population in San Francisco," she said. "Nobody knows who they are, and no one's interested in keeping track of them. Our 'participants' will come from this population."

Kraft pressed his questioning, "Are we going to inform those people about the nature of our study?"

Corbyn gave him a stony stare.

Kraft shifted uncomfortably and said, "Are you saying we won't be following informed consent protocols?"

Corbyn's silence continued, her response obvious.

"I see..." Kraft slunk down in his chair.

Oliver Buoy asked, "How will we produce nanites?"

"An incubator and full laboratory are being shipped as we speak. When you've set it up, I'll send you the seed canister."

Oliver continued his questioning, "Assuming the nanites follow their previous course, what do we do with the, ah, participant remains?"

"Mr. Robertson has made arrangements to access a crematorium." Corbyn looked at the three sitting before her. "If there is nothing else, you may go. Your flight is in the morning."

None of the three ASRI technicians had previously been to San Francisco. Dr. Hughes had visited years earlier on holiday.

Ground transportation had been arranged for the group. The

limo took a route south on US 101 from SFO that didn't go through the city, which was a disappointment for the three technicians. The short drive passed through uninteresting, heavily industrialized areas. Reaching an intersection with Highway 92, they turned toward the surprisingly green and rugged coastal mountains visible in the distance.

In San Mateo, they exited at Hillsdale Boulevard and turned left on Campus Drive, where they came to a modern, four-story red brick building. A prominent ASRI monument sign was situated on the manicured lawn in front of the building.

The driver didn't turn in but went past ASRI to an adjacent building. It was drab by comparison, light gray in color with tall, skinny windows. There was no identifying signage, although there was a lighter space above the front doors that presumably once displayed the previous tenant's business name. Robertson was out front to greet them.

"This is our building," Robertson said as they exited the limo.

Everyone looked at the building, wondering what the future might hold.

The group wasted no time settling into their new workplace. The good news was that an incubator and other lab equipment had already been delivered. The bad news was, it came in several crates. They would have to unpack, inventory, and install everything themselves. They couldn't risk getting help from headquarters staff. In addition, they had to manage computers, furniture, and other office equipment.

Dr. Hughes supervised the lab equipment and incubator installation. He selected a large central room. "There are no windows, and the ventilation system can be disabled," he said with an approving nod.

Most of the heavy work of lifting and placement fell to Oliver and George. Myra occupied her time getting the documentation materials arranged and ready for the test.

Meanwhile, Robertson paraded around like a feudal overlord. He rarely spoke with the others, and when he did, it was to prod them to work faster.

"Bugger thinks he's better than us all," Oliver groused in private. "Why not lend a hand once in a while?'

Robertson spent a good part of each day away from the facility. What he was doing was anyone's guess. When he was gone, Myra would go into his office and search. She finally gave that up. There was nothing worth transmitting to the Buchanans.

Callum Robertson had received private orders from Margaret Corbyn before leaving for San Francisco. He thought about the director's final instruction as he drove up the 101 Freeway into the city. Corbyn told him, "The others aren't fully aware of all aspects of this project. They know about the nanites, of course, but not their purpose. You are the only one who knows my intention for deploying what is, by any definition, a bioweapon."

His destination was the Tenderloin District. Using the Marriott Hotel as a landmark, he exited at Geary Street. The Tenderloin was an area bounded by Mason and Market Streets and ground zero for San Francisco's homeless population. Driving slowly, he confirmed that collecting subjects for the proof of concept would be no problem. Homeless were everywhere, literally lying on sidewalks, high on drugs, or passed out.

"I'm going to need help. Grabbing them won't be a problem, but I'll need a crew to gather and transport them back to the facility."

He thought through the people he knew. "The team that I

hired for the Paynim hit would be good, but I'm not sure they're right for this job. I need someone I know—someone I can trust to take orders—and ask no questions."

He knew just the man to call: Eric Reid.

Reid had been one of the *Shadow Hawks*. The Hawks were five men, including himself, trained to hunt down and kill the enemy.

His team had been one of the deadliest in the Middle East. Until he ran afoul of a know-nothing lieutenant who ordered the Shadow Hawks to support a mission that was sure to be a suicide assignment.

Robertson's memory of that night hadn't dimmed through the years. He could still see that idiot lieutenant waving his arms around like John Wayne, directing everyone to charge an insurgent stronghold.

He watched the lieutenant's men fall left and right. The lieutenant himself cowered behind a low wall, held down by vicious enemy fire. He couldn't help himself. He aimed at the lieutenant's feet and tapped off three rounds. The gunfire from behind startled the lieutenant. He jumped up.

The memory of that pompous idiot being instantly shredded by enemy fire was satisfying. The Shadow Hawks escaped. The others, including the lieutenant, were all killed.

The loss of an entire squad triggered an after-action inquiry. He stood before a court-martial and was ultimately discharged. The Shadow Hawks were disbanded.

Over the years, Reid had formed a protective services company using the name Shadow Hawks. Robertson knew that was shorthand for "Have gun—Will travel." A mercenary unit.

He pulled into the Union Square Plaza Hotel and went to the lounge. There, he could relax with a drink and reach out to his old teammate.

An hour later, he was back on the road, pleased that he'd been able to recruit Reid and his men to do the job. It would cost, but that was of no consequence. He'd simply request cash from Corbyn.

CHAPTER 29

Corbyn had been receiving regular reports from Robertson—they were getting close to beginning the proof of concept. It was time to send the seed colony. She went to the morgue room and opened the bottom refrigerated cabinet drawer.

It was empty.

Furrowing her brow, she moved to the middle drawer. Still nothing. Slamming the drawer shut, she moved to the top, yanked it open and let out a cry: "No-o-o!"

In a frenzy, she searched through a cabinet of medical equipment, the small desk, anywhere the container might be. Standing in the middle of the room, she spun around, frantically seeking the container. Finally, she had to admit the canister was gone.

The morgue was one of the few areas not covered by security cameras. Corbyn cursed. It was her decision to forgo camera installation. The log book on the desk was no help; it was a voluntary procedure. If someone wanted to enter anonymously, it was easy. There had to be some other way to discover who had been in the morgue.

As she returned to her office, she considered the question: *Who would have reason to go in there?* Slamming her office door, she felt alone without Callum Robertson. After all, this sort of investigation was his specialty. She lit her incense candle, sat back, and massaged her temples to soothe frayed nerves and calm her mind.

Regaining her composure, she considered her next steps. Both Robertson and Dr. Hughes were in San Francisco. There was no one else with even a remote reason to enter the morgue. *There was the SIS woman and her partner, but I shut down that interview as soon as it began to get into sensitive areas. Besides, they never returned with a court order.*

When she saw the SIS pilloried over its investigation into her company, she put the entire incident out of her mind. Until now. *What if that hadn't been the end of it?*

She called the HR department and asked for the director. After exchanging brief pleasantries, she got to the point of her call, "Have you had any recent visits from the government?"

"Yes, we get inquiries from various regulatory agencies on a regular basis. Let me see… there was one last week. It was the Department of Public Health. They come out quarterly to monitor groundwater and check our wastewater disposal systems."

"No other government visits?"

"Now that you mention it, there was one. It was some weeks ago. It wasn't really an official visit. I'd have to look up the exact date…"

"Who was this visit from?"

"I remember because it was odd to have someone from the Secret Intelligence Service call on us."

"Was it a woman?"

"Yes. Attractive, but serious."

Corbyn's mouth went dry. She was almost afraid to ask the next question.

"What did she want?"

"She was looking for an employee who disappeared. She asked to see where she worked, and I gave her directions."

Corbyn hung up without saying another word. Somehow, the SIS officer found her way to the morgue, discovered the canister, and pinched it.

"This is a disaster."

———

Corbyn didn't bother to check the time difference between London and San Francisco when she called Robertson. He answered, but he was clearly groggy. "Robertson here…"

"We have a problem. The seed canister is missing."

Robertson came fully awake. "What! How…?"

"This isn't the time to fix the blame. We have to find the thief and get our property back. Do you have resources here that can do that?"

"Yes, of course," Robertson replied. "Who are we looking for?"

"The SIS woman. You remember her?"

"She's been dealt with. You saw it play out on television."

"I'm not as confident as you. Contact your people here and have them find the woman."

"I'll get Walters and Smith, the team I used before."

"Fine. Just get our seed canister. That's the important thing."

———

Walters and Smith presented themselves to Director Corbyn the next day. She'd had time to consider how they should dispose of the SIS woman. The pair stood quietly before her desk.

Smith was distracted by the wisp of smoke drifting up from the credenza. He leaned to his partner and whispered, "Smells funny. Like a Turkish bathhouse or something." Walters gave Smith a stink-eye look.

"I have a new job for you two. Do you remember the flat where you retrieved the body?"

"Of course," Walters said.

"I want you to go back to that flat. The woman who lives there has taken something important."

Smith asked, "You want us to find whatever it is she stole?"

"No. You don't know what you're looking for. I'll go afterward and collect it. Your job is to subdue her and take her to the basement of this building..." She handed them a sheet of paper with an address. "It's abandoned and close to the Islington flat."

"What if we're seen?" Smith blurted out.

"Don't interrupt me! Once you've got her in the basement, you kill her." She could see the questioning looks on their faces. "It's isolated and abandoned. No witnesses about, and no one to hear her scream."

"How do you want us to do it?" Walters asked.

"I don't care how. A bullet to the head, strangulation, it doesn't matter so long as she dies. I don't want you to leave that basement until you've confirmed her death. In fact, here, take this Polaroid camera. Bring back proof that you've accomplished your assignment."

Smith took the camera. Walters said, "We'll do the job, don't worry."

CHAPTER 30

Walters and Smith set up surveillance in the same coffee shop Robertson had used. The end window was perfectly situated to observe the SIS woman's building. It was boring, and they were eating too many sweet rolls and drinking too much coffee.

"Is she ever gonna come out?" Smith asked. Walters didn't bother answering.

That afternoon, they noticed an Uber Eats bicycle delivery arrive at the building. The rider, carrying a large square insulated backpack, went inside.

When the Uber Eats delivery rider emerged, they could see his load was considerably lightened—the bag was slung casually over one shoulder. Walters and Smith looked at one another. "Who do you think he was delivering to?" Walters asked. Smith jumped up and ran out of the coffee shop.

Walters watched as his partner stopped and spoke with the Uber rider. After a minute, Smith let the rider go and returned to the coffee shop.

"He said he couldn't give out his customer's names. I gave him a twenty-pound note and he changed his tune."

Walters lifted a questioning eyebrow.

"It was her."

"I wonder how we could get one of those Uber backpacks," Walters said.

"What are you thinkin'?" Smith asked.

"I think we should make the next delivery. That's how we'll get her out."

Getting the Uber bag wasn't as complicated as they imagined. The coffee shop had WiFi, so Smith went to the Uber site and signed up to make local London deliveries. He gave a fake address and contact information and, within a minute, received a text message welcoming him to the Uber family. He was directed to a warehouse to get outfitted.

An hour later he returned, grinning as he held up the delivery bag.

"You look like the cat that caught the canary," Walters said.

"You should be proud of me," Smith said. "I got our bag." He held up an Uber ball cap. "And this, too."

"I guess when this is all over, you can turn that into a side hustle."

Smith sat down, shoving the Uber bag and hat under the table. "When do we move?"

"What time did the regular delivery guy come?"

"About five o'clock."

"We go at four tomorrow. Close enough in time not to arouse her suspicions. It'll also give us a comfortable window to grab her and get her to that abandoned building. And we'd better call Corbyn, tell her she can come after we're done and get whatever it is she's after."

CHAPTER 31

Myra Shipman received an unexpected call. Looking at the caller ID, she put down the glass vial she was holding. Her hands were shaking. She wasn't afraid exactly; it was just that she'd never received a personal call from Kurt Buchanan. All of her reports to him were through secure Tor messages on the Dark Web. This call made her nervous. She answered the phone.

"Good morning, Mr. Buchanan. This is a surprise."

"I don't mean to alarm you, Miss Shipman," Buchanan said. "I've got some questions, and I thought it better to speak directly."

"Yes, sir..."

"In fact, I think we should meet."

"Uh, okay. Where?"

"My father's compound in Hillsborough. It's not far from where you are."

"I don't have transportation."

"I'll send a car for you. One o'clock this afternoon."

Buchanan didn't wait for a reply; he simply hung up. She held her mobile out with a perplexed look. "I suppose it doesn't matter if it's convenient or not."

Myra was waiting in the lobby. At precisely one o'clock, a dark sedan pulled up to the front of the building. No one got out; it simply sat there. As she approached, the rear door opened, seemingly by itself. She got in, sitting on the soft leather seat. Looking to the front, she could see the back of the driver's head but he said nothing as they pulled away.

Buchanan was correct about the proximity of the satellite facility to Hillsborough. The drive to I-280 was less than three miles. Then, up the freeway for a couple of miles before exiting onto Highway 35, paralleling the freeway. They turned on Summit Drive and arrived at an impressive home. *This isn't just a home,* she thought. *It's huge. More like a compound.*

The car pulled under a porte cochère. The large double-door entry was intended to impress, and it did. As she got out of the car, one side of the massive wooden doors opened, and a well-dressed man stepped out. She imagined he was a butler of some sort.

The butler (or whatever he was) gestured for her to enter and showed her to a door on the right. The butler opened the door to reveal a cozy parlor. A rich Persian rug sat in the middle of the floor. Natural lighting streamed in through large curtained windows, and satin-finished damask silk chairs were positioned in groupings. There was the obligatory grandfather clock ticking out low, subdued tones.

The center of the room was occupied by two leather couches facing one another. A man was seated in one. It was Kurt Buchanan. With a wave of his arm, she was directed to sit opposite.

"Myra, it's good to meet you in person. Have we been treating you well?"

"Yes. Of course. No complaints."

"I'd like you to give me a summary of what you and the team are doing. You can leave out the jargon, just give me the high points."

Myra straightened up, placing her clasped hands on her knees. "As you know, we've taken an experimental biotechnology procedure and modified it. The nanites—"

"What's a nanite?"

"They're microscopic constructs, like robots, except these are biological—built on viruses. Like any robot, they're programmable. We've been able to change their basic programming to target... well, almost anything, like dissolving tumors or other inoperable conditions, and then self-destruct and flush out of the host's system." She cleared her dry throat. "They can also be programmed for other purposes."

"That's a little vague," Buchanan said.

"I'm sorry, it's just, Director Corbyn doesn't want anything to get out. I don't know how much I should say."

"Corbyn's wishes can go to hell. I'm a board member."

Myra lowered her eyes, trying to hide her embarrassment.

"What other 'purposes' are you working on?"

"Corbyn wants to use the nanites to target specific people."

"What people?"

"I'm not sure. All we need is a sample of the target's DNA."

"Why are you here in San Francisco?"

"There's a large homeless population. Corbyn wants to conduct an extensive proof of concept."

"That doesn't sound like you're targeting an individual. What kind of concept are you trying to prove?"

"The intention is to confirm this technology can be used to target not only individuals but groups of people as well. It could be based on race or ethnicity... even blood type, or eye color. It could be anything. At least, that's what the proof of concept hopes to show."

"Are you saying these little robots could be let loose in a boardroom, say, and no one would walk out?"

"I hadn't thought about that. I'm a research scientist, not involved in real-world applications..." Her nervousness ballooned into worry. "What have I become involved in?"

"You really have no idea?"

"No. I thought she moved our team out here because it's close to ASRI headquarters and the legal resources necessary for FDA approval."

Kurt changed the subject, "What's supposed to happen next?"

"We can't begin developing different strains until we have the seed colony."

"Where is this seed colony?"

"Director Corbyn has it. In England. She's going to bring it to us."

"I want you to go back and wait for my instructions. This could be very useful."

Kurt Buchanan was excited by what he'd learned. He considered the possibilities presented by this rogue project. *It could be used to eliminate competitors, critics, enemies...* He couldn't wait to tell his father. He took the next flight to Washington, DC.

Senator Buchanan had a local residence in Georgetown. The Northwest DC neighborhood was known for its Federalist-style architecture, cobblestone streets, upscale shopping, and dining. His father's home faced the Potomac River, overlooking Waterfront Park with its promenade and peaceful gardens.

He found his father in a small front room facing the river. It was his office. Consistent with the style of homes in this historic neighborhood, it was paneled in walnut. Tung oil, having been applied for generations, gave the paneling a rich patina. Heavy, embroidered curtains covered the windows, and antique furniture filled the room. A grandfather clock, once in the White House during the Harrison administration, sat against one wall, its deep ticking contributing to the air of dignified comfort.

The senator was seated at an antique rollup desk with numerous drawers. A small antique light with a green glass lampshade sat atop, casting a warm glow over the workspace. Greeting his father, he was met with a wide grin. "Kurt! You made it. I don't mind telling you, my curiosity was aroused by your call."

He took a seat in an area adjacent to the senator's desk. His father joined him. "Now, tell me what's on your mind."

"As you know, I've been keeping track of certain activities in ASRI."

"With an eye to enriching our family, I hope."

"That's why I came. I've discovered the operations manager in England has been working on a side project—not approved by the company's review board and certainly not registered with the National Health Service. We have a person embedded in this project, and I met with her yesterday. They're altering a biomedical experiment in nanotechnology." He could see the perplexed look on his father's face.

"They've figured a way to program nanites—tiny robots—to attack and kill a specific person or groups of people. The nanites can be programmed to attack a particular race or ethnicity, even a blood type."

"Hold on now," the senator said. "Remind me what these nanites are…"

"You know about robots in factories and on assembly lines?"

"Machines that are programmed to do repetitive, boring work."

"That's right. These nanites are microscopic *organic* robots. They were originally being developed to treat medical conditions that can't be reached with traditional surgery. ASRI has been funding a doctor who was working on an alternative to inoperable brain surgery. It seems the operations director decided the potential applications, not to mention the financial rewards for such a technology, would be astronomical.

"This was the genesis of the rogue project. The research doctor mysteriously disappeared, but the project continued. I don't understand the science of it, but the possibilities of this technology for us... well, you can imagine."

Senator Buchanan moved to a window. "Is this bio-robot thing operational?"

"It's not a single device. They're microscopic, and it takes a large number of them working together to complete a task."

"And when the task is complete, then what?"

"Part of the programming is a self-destruct sequence. The nanites become inert and simply flush out of the host's system."

"You mean, there's no trace of them?"

"Correct."

"Oh, my..." The senator stilled, deep in thought. After a time, he turned back. "Son, if what you say is true, these nanites could solve a great many of our problems."

"I was thinking the same thing."

"Where does the operation stand? Is it tested and ready to go?"

"Not exactly. The technicians working on this are preparing what they call a proof of concept. They only lack what our spy said is the 'seed colony' to get the PoC going."

"Where is this seed colony?"

"Supposedly, on its way to the test facility in San Francisco."

"I think it would be prudent to let that operations manager complete the testing, then we can swoop in and take it over."

"Do you have a plan, Dad?"

"By the time you 'acquire' this technology, I will."

CHAPTER 32

Myra returned to the satellite facility, her mind filled with questions and doubts. Walking through the lobby area, she had to weave her way around the new construction. She looked at the unfinished cubes and wondered anew about the purpose of such a large number of enclosures. Coming to the laboratory door, she punched code numbers into the keypad.

Why such security?

There were many things that had been right in front of her that went unquestioned or unnoticed. She found Oliver and George in the lab, both bent over rows of test tubes. Dr. Hughes, as usual, was sitting apart at a computer console examining a screen full of numbers.

Oliver saw her enter. "Hey, Myra. You're back. Where've you been? We were getting worried about you."

She deflected, even though she wanted very badly to air her doubts to her colleagues. "Sorry... I had something that needed attending to upstairs." She put on a lab smock and joined Oliver and George. Taking up a clipboard, she began filling in test results.

Death Mist

After a time, George looked over. "Are you okay? You seem distracted."

She leaned over and answered with a hushed voice, "I've been wondering, why are we preparing for such a large sample? Do you know?"

"I... I'm not really sure. I hadn't thought about it. The number came from Dr. Hughes—and Corbyn."

"Why is the door to this lab reinforced, and why does it have a security lock?"

George gave a questioning look. "I'm not really sure. I guess maybe because there are going to be a lot of test subjects in the building, they didn't want any of them to get access to the lab."

"Sounds reasonable," she said. "It just seems, well, like overkill."

"You're simply getting the jitters because we're closing in on the testing phase. Besides, it's not for us to know everything. We just need to do our jobs."

She looked over to Dr. Hughes, who was focused on the data he was inspecting, oblivious to the others in the room. "What do you suppose he's doing?" George shrugged in response; Myra pressed, "And those containers," she pointed her chin to the large, stainless-steel cylinders stacked against one wall, "why so many?"

George could offer no explanation. She went back to work, but she was feeling trapped. *They never let us out of his building. We even have to sleep upstairs.*

Her misgivings were beginning to cause deep concern. *When this is all over, what happens to us?*

Later that night, after everyone had retired to their rooms, Myra snuck down to the lab. Since she had the access code, getting in raised no alarms. She stood in the middle of the lab and looked around. *Where to begin?*

She knew all the equipment intimately; after all, she'd helped assemble and install almost everything. It was her understanding that they were developing a radically new biomechanical remedy for many inoperable situations. She didn't question when Dr. Perry stole samples from the morgue, and at the time, she thought it served her right that she'd become infected and died. In retrospect, the sequence of events since then were oddly rushed. What was the hurry? These things take years to bring to market. For some reason, Corbyn was pushing and not necessarily following standard protocols.

Maybe the answers are in Dr. Hughes' computer.

She stepped over to the solitary computer station used exclusively by Dr. Hughes. Hitting the space bar on the keyboard, the screen came to life.

Damn, there's a login. I can't even imagine what that might be.

She was stumped, and her curiosity was significantly aroused. She'd have to be more observant as they moved forward, see if she could glean any information about the true purpose of this experiment.

CHAPTER 33

Michael Roark was impressed by Senator Buchanan's masterful takedown of SIS. *I couldn't have done better myself.* He was confident the senator had it together; he wasn't so sure about the son, Kurt.

Kurt Buchanan had always played it fast and loose. His womanizing, drinking, and drugs required constant intervention by the senator to make charges and lawsuits go away. The senator's handling of his son's misadventures over the years did nothing to discourage the scion's dissolute lifestyle. But Kurt was a Buchanan, and the senior senator from California guarded his family like a she-bear.

Kurt Buchanan was a good-looking and outgoing young man who made friends easily. Besides his appealing looks, Roark had to admit the young Buchanan actually had a brain. Kurt turned out to be helpful in growing the senator's "outside" interests, becoming the front man for much of the family business.

He heard Kurt was in Washington. He wanted to take advantage of this visit, and called to arrange a meeting.

"Hello, Kurt? This is Roark."

"Michael... good to hear from you. You know, I was gonna call you while I was in town. You must have read my mind."

"How lucky for us both. I was hoping you'd be free for dinner."

"As it happens, I am. What do you have in mind?"

"How about The Dabney. Do you know it?"

"It's the place in Blagden Alley, right?"

"That's the one. Let's set it for, say, seven o'clock. Does that work for you?"

"You're on."

The Dabney was a small, Michelin-starred restaurant located in a historic row house. The open kitchen and its wood-burning hearth formed the focal point of the restaurant. The chef prepares mid-Atlantic specialties like Rohan Duck, Roasted Palmetto Farm Squab, and Chesapeake Rock Fish. With limited seating and an extremely talented chef, last-minute reservations were almost impossible to get. Not for Roark. He was a power figure in Washington and well-known. His reservation request was accommodated.

A little after seven o'clock, Kurt Buchanan entered. His bearing was self-assured, even pompous. Roark smirked. He knew better. Any importance the young man enjoyed came through his father.

Spotting his host, Kurt Buchanan took a seat. "Wonderful place. Last time I was here, I was entertaining some oil people. Dad came by, shook hands with everyone, and left."

"What was the result of that dinner?"

"They gave us everything we asked for."

After ordering cocktails, Roark opened the subject that was on his mind, "I've been wondering about your directorship at ASRI, how it's going..."

Kurt set down his martini. "Why are you asking?"

"No reason," he said evasively. "It's just, there's been some talk."

"About what?"

Roark squirmed, trying to phrase his response in a way that wouldn't set the volatile young man off.

"A woman from the British government came by my office, asking questions about ASRI. I thought the woman was doing background research. It began that way but then turned to your father's involvement with the company. She asked why you had been appointed to the Board of Directors. She wondered why Kurt Buchanan, who doesn't have any scientific credentials, not by schooling or employment, should hold such a position. The unasked question was, what qualified Kurt Buchanan to be appointed to ASRI's board? She was obviously trying to figure out what ASRI expected to get from the relationship."

Kurt's former bravado turned to discomfort. "What did you tell her?"

"Nothing. I ended the interview and sent her on her way."

"Good," Kurt said.

Roark leaned in close. "Look, I know about your various deals and shell companies. I'm good with that. Hell using influence to get something you want is the American way. I just get a little nervous when the press starts sniffing around in England. America can't be too far behind."

Kurt began to reestablish his self-control. "What's the woman's name? We may have a way to handle this."

The next day, Kurt Buchanan booked a flight to London. He'd decided the best course of action was to go to the source: Margaret Corbyn. He intended to find out more about the so-called *seed colony*.

Arriving at Heathrow, the town car and driver he'd arranged drove him out of the city to West Northamptonshire, the location of ASRI-GB. The countryside was picturesque with rolling hills, open fields of green, stands of trees scattered about... He thought it very relaxing, but this was certainly out in the boonies. From previous visits, he knew there was only one decent hotel: Fawsley Hall, and that was where they were headed.

As the town car approached the historic country estate, they passed through meticulously groomed parkland, originally designed in the 1760s by architect Capability Brown. Entering the stately building, he was greeted by a pretty attendant. He remembered her. *That was a wild night. Who knew these country girls could be so inventive in bed?* Unfortunately, he couldn't remember her name. Stepping to the baroque desk, he was relieved to find she was wearing a name badge.

"Stephanie... it's good to see you again."

The attendant blushed slightly and returned the greeting. "How long will you be staying with us?"

"A couple of days, I think."

"If you'd like to wait in the Tudor Great Hall, we'll get the Master Suite prepared."

The Tudor Great Hall's twenty-four-foot-high ceiling was impressive. There were windows across the top on both sides of the long rectangular room. The windows let in plenty of natural light, giving what would otherwise have been an oppressive and dark room a light, airy feel.

Stylish furniture, evocative of bygone aristocratic luxury, created a sense of grandeur. Every time he came to Fawsley Hall, it felt like stepping into the nineteenth century, like entering the world of Downton Abbey.

A liveried attendant came to his side, offering a beverage. "A sparkling water, please," he said.

In short order, Stephanie found him. "Your suite is ready, Mr. Buchanan." She lowered her eyes in a coquettish way.

Entering the suite, he found his luggage had been delivered. The rich wooden four-poster bed with a carved canopy was set behind a comfortable living room. A fireplace was on the outside wall, flanked by tall windows.

"As always, this is perfect."

As she was leaving, Stephanie turned and asked, "Will you need anything else?"

He knew she was talking about more than an extra blanket.

"Not tonight. It's been a long day, and I want to be ready for tomorrow."

The next morning, his hired car was waiting in front of the estate house. Before leaving, Kurt called Corbyn's office, alerting them he was coming to meet with the director.

The sleek, contemporary ASRI building sat in stark contrast to the old-world elegance of Fawsley Hall and, indeed, the entire Northamptonshire vibe.

Kurt knew the way to the operations manager's office and only stopped at the front desk long enough to collect a VIP badge. He found Margaret Corbyn waiting for him in her office.

"Mr. Buchanan, this is a surprise." Despite the welcoming greeting, there was suspicion in her eyes.

Corbyn escorted him to a small seating area in her office. The pungent smell of incense infused the atmosphere, and he wondered why Corbyn always had that thing burning. It was noticeable, and frankly, he found it distracting.

"I was going over the various projects you're managing. It's an impressive workload."

Corbyn wasn't sure how to respond, so she said nothing.

"One in particular caught my attention. It has to do with using nanotechnology to develop new brain surgery therapies."

"You're referring to the Perry study."

"Yes, that's the one. Can you update me on that study?"

"I'm afraid there's nothing to tell. You see, Dr. Perry disappeared a while back. We never knew why, but I suspect it was to avoid the shame of failure."

"Failure? From what I understand, the experiments were yielding results."

"Sadly, those reports were premature. Testing on rats and rabbits at first looked promising, but in the end, they were unsuccessful. More than that, Dr. Perry's experiments were dramatic failures. As a matter of fact, I was going to pull the plug on her research when she disappeared."

Corbyn was clearly gaslighting him. He was about to confront her with the fact that she'd set up an unauthorized operation in San Francisco but stopped. *Playing dumb may actually be more advantageous.*

"I'm sorry to hear that," he said. "What happened to her research—notes, experimental data, et cetera?"

"Dr. Perry's entire premise proved to be flawed. The time and money it took to discover that... Let's just say it was an intellectual and fiscal drain. From the beginning, hers was a highly speculative venture—a shiny object, if you will. These sorts of projects are often taken in the early years of a company's growth when venture capital is flowing, and investors are looking for quick results. In the end, if the project doesn't pan out, we eliminate it."

"You don't keep records?"

"I'm not saying that. There is a record of Dr. Perry's time with ASRI, but the specific materials you're asking about have no value to the company. They've been destroyed."

"Wouldn't the researcher keep a copy of the work?"

"Virtually all work is considered 'work for hire,' and as such, it's owned by the company. The researcher may petition to return materials to private ownership, but I've never seen it done." Corbyn sat back, satisfied she'd deflected any real inquiry.

Kurt said, "I heard something about a seed colony. What does that mean to you?" Her complexion turned pallid. He imagined images of a carefully planned scheme being exposed were flashing through Corbyn's mind.

"There were several colonies in development. When Dr. Perry disappeared and I shut down the project, the colonies were destroyed." Corbyn made a quick glance toward the small refrigerator next to the credenza.

"I see…" He was starting to get the picture of what was happening. *She didn't destroy anything. She kept it for herself.*

CHAPTER 34

Margaret Corbyn wasn't exactly anxious, nevertheless, she fidgeted and rubbed her hands together. Buchanan's unscheduled visit unsettled her.

What does he know? It can't be the satellite office. I covered my tracks with that deal. Could he have found out? God, I hope not. That would be a disaster... Well, maybe not. I've known from the beginning the company traded a board seat for the political influence that Senator Buchanan brought. I even heard rumors about a large sum of money being paid off-the-books to the Buchanans. Yes, maybe there's a deal to be struck.

Breaking out of her reverie, she asked, "Why hasn't Robertson called?" There was no one to respond to her rhetorical question. She opened the small refrigerator in her office for the hundredth time. The canister she'd collected from the SIS woman's flat was still there. "Good." It was an irrational act, checking and re-checking to assure herself about the canister.

Looking at her desk clock yet again, she calculated the eight-hour time difference. She couldn't understand what the problem might be. "Why hasn't he called? It's almost six o'clock. He should have called me hours ago."

She was just about to give in and call Robertson when her mobile rang.

"It's about time," she muttered as she answered. Before Robertson could get out a single word, she plunged right in. "Where have you been? You can't leave me hanging like that. Tell me the woman's been dealt with."

"Good day to you, too," Robertson said, and took a deep breath. "I have to report that things didn't go quite as planned."

She covered her eyes with one hand, rubbing her temples with her thumb and ring finger. "Tell me."

"There's no easy way to put this... My team failed." Robertson gave a digest version of the operation.

"Have those men report to me here at ASRL."

"They'll be there in the morning."

She looked at the refrigerator. "Are you ready to receive the colony?"

"Almost," Robertson said. "The lab equipment's been installed and the support systems are ready to go. We just have to conduct some final tests."

"I was going to ship the seed colony to you..." she began.

Robertson interrupted, "Once we get the seed colony, we'll begin the duplication process. When we have a sufficient population, we'll be ready to begin the proof of concept."

"You're not hearing me," Corbyn said, almost shouting. "I *was* going to ship the colony to you. Not now.' She let that declaration hang. "Once I get things settled, I'll *personally* come out—with the colony."

Kurt Buchanan returned to Fawsley Hall, his mind churning with possibilities. First, he'd established that Margaret Corbyn was as ruthless and self-serving as any mercenary. Never mind the oaths and agreements she'd made with ASRI, she found something of great value and was taking it for herself.

He had to find out where she was hiding the seed colony. "There's no question it's in her possession. It was written all over her face." He'd begin with simple surveillance. Watch where she goes, see who she meets with.

He scanned through the contacts on his smartphone, stopping on one that had worked for the family in the early days of ASRI's IPO launch. Even then, his father had a sense that this was a company to watch. When ASRI announced plans to open a laboratory in England, the elder Buchanan sent his son to act as an emissary. That was when he found Joe Dixon. He hoped Dixon was still in business.

"Dixon Investigations," announced a perky female voice. "How may I help you?"

I guess he's done well. He used to answer the phone himself.

"Is Joe in?" Kurt asked.

"May I ask who's calling?"

"An old client. Kurt Buchanan."

"Yes, sir. I'll put you through."

He heard a couple of clicks, then a hoarse voice. He knew it was from Dixon smoking of two packs of cigarettes a day. "Mr. Buchanan! Great to hear from you. It's been, what... a decade?"

"Not quite that long, Joe, but it's been a while."

"I'm guessing this isn't a social call," Dixon said. "What's on your mind?"

"I've got a little job I'd like you to handle."

"Is this about that ASRI company?"

"Sort of. There's a person I'd like you to follow..."

"Any abductions or wire-tapping or anything?"

"No, nothing like that. Just straight surveillance. Can you do the job?"

"Sure. I'm a little busy with other jobs at the moment, but

since it's a straightforward observation job, I can put one of my operatives on it right away."

Kurt thought about the offer, then decided Dixon was right. It was a simple follow-and-report assignment.

"That'll be fine. Have him contact me as soon as possible."

"Are you here in England?"

"Yes, at Fawsley Hall."

"Oh, yeah, I remember. The country estate house that's been converted to a hotel."

"Have your man contact me. I'll fill him in on the details."

CHAPTER 35

Joe Dixon's operative, an unassuming middle-aged man, watched with interest as two men, who looked to be anything but scientists, parked in the visitor's area and entered ASRI, almost like they owned the place.

He got out and went to the reception desk, attended by a pretty young woman. He asked for the operations manager, Margaret Corbyn. He was told to wait, and took a seat. In a few minutes, the receptionist motioned him over.

"Ms. Corbyn is in a meeting at present."

"Is it with the two men who came in before me?"

"Yes," the receptionist said, not certain if revealing that information was allowed. "May I take your name? I'll see if we can get you in another day."

"That won't be necessary." He left the lobby and returned to his car.

He waited only ten minutes before the two men reemerged from the building. *They look suspicious. I hate to let them go, but the job is to watch Corbyn.*

The men took off. The operative wondered if they were heading back to London. He waited all day before his mark pulled out in her late model Land Rover. He recognized it from the briefing document Dixon had given him. As the Rover passed, he saw the driver. A woman. Medium-length hair, streaked with gray. "That's her."

He followed the mark to what must be her home in a townhouse community. It wasn't far from ASRI. As she got out, he watched her lean in and grab something from the passenger seat. It was small, cylindrical, and looked metallic.

The mark went inside. He watched for a while, but decided she was in for the night.

Margaret Corbyn sat in her office, glad that Robertson had done some surveillance of the Islington neighborhood. It was Robertson who'd found the empty building. He said at the time, should they need to abduct the woman and take her somewhere, that building would be more suitable than bringing her back to ASRI. She agreed.

Events developed differently than expected, and the need for the abandoned building lessened. Until now. Today, she was happy to have it in her back pocket. Unfortunately, she was committed. She could only hope those two fools, Walters and Smith, could actually come through. They knew too much. She wondered if this fact bothered Robertson... regardless, she had to see it through.

CHAPTER 36

Hannah was grateful for Joel's lifeline—but it was more than that. It was something she hadn't considered before: SpartanZ. "Who'd have thought...?"

Beyond the freelance offer, Joel made a good point: It wasn't in her nature to back down from challenges or difficult situations. She had only to look at her recent missions for confirmation. She made up her mind. "I'll go to San Francisco like Joel asked. I may have to keep a low profile, but there's no way I'm going to be put out to pasture like this."

She booked a United Airlines flight the next day from Heathrow to San Francisco. With the decision made and ticket purchased, Hannah settled down. "I don't know how long I'll be there. I'd better pack extra clothes, just in case."

Then she remembered the canister in her refrigerator. "Can't forget that!" She went to the hall closet and found a collapsible cooler bag and decided it was perfect for transporting the canister. She wondered how she'd keep the nanites cooled for the nine-hour flight. Then it struck her—dry ice. This wasn't something she normally purchased, but since her flight wasn't until the next day, it gave her time to find a source.

After returning from her hunt for dry ice (It wasn't that difficult. The local grocery store had a cooler of dry ice), Hannah was still feeling restless. A great deal was happening around her case. She paused mid-thought. *I guess it's not really my case anymore.* Nevertheless, she was anxious to get back into the action.

It was late afternoon. She'd already placed her Uber Eats order, and it was too early for Joel's call. She switched on the telly and flipped through channels. Nothing caught her attention, so she left it on Channel 4. There was some cooking show playing. As she rummaged through her kitchen, the doorbell rang.

"Is that Uber already?" She went to the door and looked through the peephole. She saw the Uber delivery man, his hat and bag. As she opened the door, there was a hard push. The shove left her off-balance. Suddenly, she was grabbed by two men.

"You!" She remembered the pair. They were the ersatz detectives, Smith and Walters. Smith was dressed up like an Uber Eats deliveryman, Walters wore a suit.

She struggled to get her wrists free from Walter's grasp while Smith poured something onto a handkerchief and pressed it over her mouth and nose. She recognized the scent on the cloth—ether. She'd been dosed with ether before.

It wasn't long before her attempts to free herself weakened and finally stopped. Smith nodded to his partner, and they laid her down.

"What's the time?" Walters demanded. Smith looked at the microwave clock. "Four fifteen. We got plenty of time." Walters spotted a rug under a small table and chairs in the kitchen.

"Grab that, will you?"

Smith moved the furniture off the rug and dragged it to Walters.

"Help me put her on there."

Once Hannah was in position on the rug, they rolled her up. "There you go—a rug ready to go to the cleaners," Walters said.

Hoisting the rug over their shoulders, they left the flat and headed for the parking area behind the building. They opened the rear door of their sedan, and the rug—with Hannah in it—was placed on the back seat.

Corbyn was confident that the plan Walters and Smith laid out would allow them to complete this assignment. She left her office, and during the two-hour drive to London, she couldn't help but brood about the seed colony. She couldn't imagine how that SIS woman managed to find the morgue room—much less the canister—and escape undetected.

That damn HR director! He should have notified me or Callum. Damn him!

Arriving in Islington, she parked and went directly to the flat Walters and Smith had visited. She found the door open. *At least those two did that right.* There was only one place someone would store the canister, the refrigerator.

Relief washed over her when she opened the refrigerator in the SIS woman's flat and found the canister. In the freezer, she discovered a bag of dry ice. *All is forgiven!*

Tucking the canister under one arm and the dry ice in the other hand, she left the flat, careful to close the door behind her.

CHAPTER 37

Joel watched every deplaning passenger. It was the only United Airlines London flight scheduled that day. He searched, but Hannah wasn't among the passengers. He checked his watch, looked up to the flight board to see if there was another flight from London. That confirmed this was the only United flight. He tried calling Hannah. It went to voicemail. "Where the hell is she?"

He went to the United Airlines service counter asking about Hannah. "I'm sorry, sir," the counter attendant said smoothly, "we show a ticket sold in that name but it hasn't been used. Perhaps your lady friend is taking another flight."

The counter attendant's speculation did nothing to quell his growing concern. He called Davies, "Hannah wasn't on the flight. She had a ticket, but United says it wasn't used. Can you do your computer thing and see if she's on another flight or airline?"

"No problem, Mr. B. We're on it. Are you staying at the airport?"

"I'll come back, but I have a bad feeling about this."

Joel returned to his hotel in San Mateo where he'd booked adjoining suites, accommodating himself and the SpartanZ. A large central living room connecting the two suites and had been transformed by Davies and Shadow into something resembling a NASA control room: computers, monitors, folding tables, routers, and other equipment that Joel couldn't identify. He had to admit, the blinking red, yellow, and green lights in open racks were impressive.

Davies greeted him and said, "We gotta thank you for all this equipment."

"No problem," Joel said. "My department was happy to fill your shopping list. By the way, have you found anything?"

"This is a little strange," Davies said. "We've gone through all the normal channels, but nothing shows up. It's like she dropped off the face of the earth."

"What about the not-normal channels... you know, your Dark Web buddies?"

Shadow spun around in his task chair. "We were just beginning to go down that path."

Davies rolled his chair over to his partner and both went to work.

Neither acknowledged what he didn't say. The knot in his stomach said it all.

CHAPTER 38

Joel tried again to check on Hannah. Still no answer. He couldn't shake the sense of dread that he felt. Meanwhile, he'd set up a surveillance duty schedule to watch the ASRI satellite building. At this point, there wasn't much to do except watch the building.

Joel had determined there were only five people inside. Which was a lot of space for only five people. One of the five went out virtually every day; the others had no transportation and were confined to the building.

This day, something unusual happened. It was about one o'clock. A dark sedan pulled up to the front of the building. A woman came out and got into the rear seat. After a moment, the sedan drove off.

I wonder where they're going?

He followed the sedan to a home in Hillsborough, an exclusive community catering to its rich and famous residents. Tree-lined streets were set off by colorful flowers and bushes. Hand lettered street signs were placed at each corner. The entire community looked manicured.

The few cars he passed were all expensive or exotic, the kind one would expect in this obviously genteel neighborhood. He felt out of place driving a Ford sedan. *Maybe they'll think I'm a workman.* His rationale did little to ease his discomfort.

Following the limo, he watched it turn onto a private drive. It was gated, of course. He went a little farther up the street and pulled over to watch in his rearview mirror. He saw no movement from within the compound. Picking up his mobile, he called Davies.

"Would you mind running an address for me?"

"No problem. Where are you? Are you calling off the surveillance?"

"Don't get your hopes up. Our reconnaissance operation is still in place. It's just, this afternoon, a car pulled up to the front of the building and a woman got in. I followed them to an address in Hillsborough." He gave Davies the house number. "Find out who lives there."

Davies called back ten minutes later, "You're not gonna believe this, boss."

"Give it to me," Joel said.

"Senator Jack Buchanan lives there."

Joel was quiet, his mind sorting through the possible scenarios. "He's the one who railroaded the SIS and got Hannah fired. Now he brings in one of the ASRI technicians... Why?"

"Beg your pardon," Davies said, "but there's more than the senator living at that address. His son, Kurt, also lists that as his home."

"Maybe the woman was being brought to meet with Kurt Buchanan."

"Given he's on the ASRI board, it would make sense," Davies agreed.

"Even so, why bring a technician to his home? Especially one from this renegade group occupying that other building."

"Do you think he's onto their off-the-books project?" Davies asked.

"I'm wondering the same thing. I'll try to get a picture of her and send it to you. Let's find out who she is."

Joel pulled onto the street and drove back around, passing the property gate. The limousine was no longer parked in front. He pulled off to the side of the street and walked up the entry drive to the gate. It gave him a good view of the home and its massive front doors.

Thirty minutes later, one of the double doors opened. The woman stepped out. She looked a little confused as she swept her gaze left and right. *She's looking for the car. I've only got moments.* He opened the camera app on his phone, zoomed in on the woman, snapped off a shot, and scurried back to his car.

In the rearview mirror, he watched the limo pull out and head back toward the freeway. *Taking her back, I'd say.*

He texted the picture to Davies, then returned to continue his surveillance.

Shadow was Joel's surveillance relief. He drove up and parked next to him, passing on a message, "Davies says he's got some preliminary information for you."

"Thanks, Shadow."

Back at the hotel suite, he sat down with Davies. "I understand you've got something for me."

"I do. The woman's name is Myra Shipman. I found her listed on the ASRI website. She's a microbiologist. Graduated with a Master's from Newcastle University, began with ASRI three years ago."

"That was about the time ASRI opened the UK facility, wasn't it?"

"Not long after."

"Why is she involved with Corbyn's scheme?"

"After getting the corporate fluff, I dug in a little deeper. In fact, I accessed Interpol's servers."

"Davies! I hope—"

"Naw, they never knew I was there. But it proved fruitful: I found a police report on her. In college, she was busted in Germany for carrying a dime-bag of cocaine."

"She's a user?" Joel asked.

"It seemed so, but for some reason, charges were dropped."

"This is beginning to fall into place. Do you suppose Kurt Buchanan, in his new position, found out about Myra, used his family's influence to dismiss the charges, and put her in his debt?"

"Revealing something like a drug charge would have killed her career," Davies said. "With all this research into the Buchanans, I can see Kurt doing just that—to buy himself a spy."

Joel thought for a moment. "And when Hannah's friend died, Myra was conveniently attached to Corbyn's project. The meeting I observed, presumably with Kurt, was a matter of convenience. Hillsborough isn't far from the satellite operation. I think Kurt wanted an in-person briefing about… what?"

"That's the question of the day," Davies said.

"Maybe it's one I should put to Hannah…" He checked the time. "It's about time to call her anyway." He selected Hannah from his favorites list and placed the call. After several rings, he was re-directed to voicemail. He frowned, tilting his head to one side. "Damned odd…"

"What's odd?" Davies asked.

"She's still not answering."

He couldn't shed the feeling of dread. He waited another fifteen minutes before redialing. The result was the same.

"Where the hell could she be? She missed her flight, and now she doesn't answer her phone."

CHAPTER 39

It was only a short drive to the address Corbyn had given Walters and Smith. They'd checked it out ahead of time, so they knew where they were going. They carried the rug with the woman's inert body inside into the empty building and down to the basement.

As they reached the basement floor, she was beginning to move inside the rug.

"Let's get her out of there and finish the job," Walters said.

They dropped the rug onto the floor and unrolled it. The woman's eyes were fluttering, and she gasped for a breath of fresh air.

Walters asked, "You got the Polaroid?"

Smith's mouth fell open. "Uh…"

"You forgot it?"

"No, it's in the car. I'll go back and get it."

———

Hannah was shaken into consciousness as she was unceremoniously dropped and then unrolled from a carpet. She lay in a confused bundle on the floor, half awake. The effects of the ether would wear off, but until then, she was seriously handicapped, both mentally and physically.

She watched Walters engage in a discussion with Smith but had trouble hearing clearly. From Smith's body language, it looked like Walters was rebuking him. Smith left, and Walters stepped to one of the small windows mounted high on the wall.

This must be a basement.

It was stark and unfinished. The walls were cement. Iron support pillars marched down the middle of the room, a strictly functional structural feature. A stack of boxes occupied a far wall, and next to the boxes, a broken bookcase. Lighting came from a pair of bare bulbs hanging from the ceiling. There was a stuffy smell to the air. Not dank, more like musty or neglected.

She lay very still, allowing the ether to work its way out of her system. She took note of the open basement door, then glanced back to Walters, who was still gazing out the window, his back to her.

He's not paying attention to me. It's an opportunity I have to take.

She rolled onto her side, pressed her hands under her body, and pushed. She was up! Without looking back, she ran—more like a stumbling shuffle—through the door and up a flight of stairs.

Walters shouted the alarm, calling for Smith.

Her first order of business was to get out of the building. As she reached a landing, she saw a door with a small window. A man was approaching from outside.

There was no hiding place on the landing, just more stairs going up to the next level. Out of options—and time—she went to the door, flattening herself against the wall. Her only hope was that Smith, for that had to be who was coming through the door, would be responding to Walters' alarm and be in a hurry, not looking around the landing.

The door swung open, covering her. She peeked around the door and watched Smith enter, still in his Uber uniform. He was carrying a weapon in his right hand and a Polaroid camera in his left. He moved quickly to the stairs and ran down to the basement.

She stepped around the open door and ran outside.

I'm moving better. That's a good sign.

Walters, running up the stairs, and Smith, running down, crashed into one another. After untangling, Walters began accusing his partner, "She went up! Didn't you see her? Did you let her get away?"

"I didn't let her get away—you did!"

"No time to waste. Let's get going," Walters said.

The pair moved up the stairs, looking for any sort of hiding place. There were only solid walls all the way up to the landing. When they reached the landing, no one was there.

"Goddammit, somehow she's gotten away," Walters said, throwing open the entry door. He looked up and down the empty street. "Get the car. We'll run her down."

Smith jumped into action, and they were quickly under way.

"Which direction?" Smith asked.

Walters pointed to the left. "That way."

They cruised along the street, carefully checking doorways and narrow alleys separating buildings, but without success.

"Should we turn around?" Smith asked.

"She couldn't have gotten this far... Yeah, turn around."

They reversed course and continued their search. At one point, Walters shouted, "Stop!" Smith braked sharply, causing Walters to lurch forward and bump the dashboard.

"What is it?" Smith asked.

"Look, down that alley…"

A figure was moving away from them toward the main road beyond the buildings.

"That's her!"

"We can't fit down that," Smith said, "it's way too narrow."

"Go down to the end of this row," Walters ordered. "There's a turn."

Hannah moved as rapidly as possible, but in her half-drugged state, that wasn't too quick. She was out but unsure of her location. *Left or right*, she wondered. She chose to go right. *More buildings to hide in.*

She heard the sound of a car. There was a small doorway, and she pressed herself into it. Peeking around the door frame, she saw a dark sedan. *The same as before.* It pulled up to the access road that ran between rows of buildings and stopped. After a moment, it turned left. She let out a sigh of relief.

As the sedan drove out of sight, she felt it was safe to move.

She searched for an escape route. The buildings were all attached to one another. On the left, she spotted what she hoped was an answer. "An alley!" Stepping into the narrow divide between two buildings, she decided *alley* was too generous a word. It was more a breezeway, just wide enough to walk through.

Down the breezeway, traffic streaked past. *A main road*, she told herself. *There'll be people—and freedom.* She went as quickly as possible down the narrow passage.

Reaching the road, she turned right. The traffic was heavy; cars, trucks, and buses, all whizzing frantically in both directions. In her still murky mind, it was a kaleidoscope of color and noise.

She didn't know if that sedan was tracking her, but had to assume it was. Running would only draw attention to herself, so she purposely walked at a slow pace. Ahead was a turn. She approached the intersection with care, looking to be certain the sedan wasn't there.

Taking a step into the crossing, the dark sedan unexpectedly appeared. She halted and watched as the vehicle accelerated. She knew they it intended to run her down.

———

Walters shouted as soon as they turned down the street. "There she is!"

"What do you want me to do?" Smith asked.

"Run her down, you idiot!"

Smith gunned the engine and set off at a high speed, tires squealing, aiming directly for the woman crossing the street. He paid no attention to the busy traffic on the main road—he was focused on the woman. He gripped the steering wheel and gave a vicious grin.

"We've got you, bitch!"

———

Hannah dove to the far sidewalk as the sedan flew by. She felt the draft of its passing. And then, a terrible crashing sound. The sedan was a mangled mess of metal under the massive front grill of a transport with a load of gravel.

Standing and straightening herself, she, like a dozen other onlookers, walked over to the scene of the accident. She heard several overlapping questions.

"What happened?"

"Did you see that?"

"How horrible."

She had to agree, it was horrible It was clear both men in the sedan were dead. The driver of the transport was circling around the crushed car, obviously upset.

"It came out of nowhere... just appeared in front of me... there was nothing I could do."

Police sirens could be heard in the distance. Hannah's only thought was to go back to her flat.

CHAPTER 40

Corbyn returned to ASRI and resumed her normal duties while waiting for a report. *Why haven't they checked in?* By four o'clock, she still hadn't heard from Walters and Smith. *Odd... surely, I would have heard by now.* She picked up her mobile to call Robertson. The desk clock reminded her that, in San Francisco, it was eight o'clock in the morning. "Well, he'll have to deal with it."

It took four rings before Robertson answered, "Hullo."

"Callum, I need you to check on your boys."

"My boys...? Oh, you mean Walters and Smith. What's wrong?"

"I met with them, laid out the new assignment, and sent them off. I haven't heard from them yet."

"What were your orders?"

"Wait until the woman came out, then take her. I gave them the address of that empty building you recommended. I told them to eliminate her there."

"Maybe she hasn't come out."

"I went myself to retrieve our seed colony. The flat was empty."

"Sounds like they grabbed the woman," Robertson said.

"Just contact them, if only for my peace of mind. Also, I told them to take a Polaroid picture to verify the task was complete. Find out what they're doing."

It was the next day before Corbyn heard back from Robertson. As soon as she picked up her mobile, she knew it was bad news.

"I'm sorry it's taken so long to get back to you," Robertson said. "I couldn't reach either Walters or Smith, so I began checking with others who know them. No one knew where the two were. I had the uncomfortable thought that maybe they got cold feet and took off."

"What about the woman?"

"I called her mobile. She answered. I didn't say anything, just hung up."

"She answered? How can that be?"

"When I heard the woman's voice, I put two and two together. I think they managed to grab her, but somehow, she got away. That's when I thought to look at the news services."

"Oh, God," Corbyn said. "Don't tell me…"

"There was a terrible traffic accident in Islington. A sedan reportedly shot out of a side street, right in front of a M.A.N. truck. The car was mangled beyond recognition, and the two men inside were dead. At present, the police haven't been able to identify the bodies."

"You think it was Walters and Smith," she said, almost in a whisper.

"I know it was them," Robertson said. "I also know from that other call that the SIS woman is out there, free. How do you want to proceed?"

"We can't just let her run loose. She's seen the nanites... seen what they do."

"We'll have to find a way to lure her out, get her somewhere where we can end this once and for all."

"How do we do that?" Corbyn asked.

"We bait a trap."

"With what?"

"How did she come to us in the first place?" Robertson asked.

"She was looking into the death of her friend, a researcher who worked for me."

"The one who ran off?"

"Yes. The one you originally sent Walters and Smith to investigate."

"Of course," Robertson said. "They brought the body back to ASRI, and Dr. Hughes performed an autopsy. I assume she wasn't able to find out what happened to her friend."

"No, and that's why she was back snooping around the morgue room."

"Was there anything there to find?"

"Only the canister—the nanites."

"But there was no body, right?"

"The remains were already destroyed."

"That's good... that's very good. Discovering her friend's body will be the bait."

"How do we do that?"

"We have to let her think she can find the body."

CHAPTER 41

Hannah had recovered enough to travel. She found her bags where she'd left them. The memory of the assault caused a slight shiver. She decided a drink was in order, and after all, it was past five in the afternoon. Opening the refrigerator to get a chilled bottle of Sauvignon Blanc, she stopped with a start. The space occupied by the canister she'd pinched from ASRI was empty.

"Oh, my God! Did they take the canister?" The image of the mangled car beneath the M.A.N. truck came to mind. "If they had it with them..." Beyond the thought of a massive slaughter in the streets of London, the loss of the canister meant she had no proof that ASRI was behind Amy's death.

As she worked through the options, she came to a conclusion. *If it was with them, dozens of people would have been exposed. So far, there are no reports of strange illnesses or death.*

She turned on the local news to verify her reasoning. There was still some reporting about the accident, but nothing about mysterious illness or death. *Someone else must have taken the canister.*

There was no use pining over the loss. She'd just have to find some other way to bring Amy some justice. Looking at the unused ticket to San Francisco, she thought that might be where she'd find answers. As she called to re-book her flight, her laptop dinged. She gave the computer a questioning look. *Who would be messaging me?* The reservations agent came back on the line and she completed the alteration of her travel plans. Then she went to the laptop to read the message. She read it twice to be certain she understood.

You'll find your friend in the Brookwood Cemetery, Surry.

The Zoroastrian section—North area.

There was no signature. The message had been sent anonymously.

"This could well be a trap. It's not like they haven't tried to kidnap and kill me already."

Despite her misgivings, the possibility of finding Amy and getting a measure of closure was too compelling to pass up. She stopped to think. *Where do you hide a body? In a cemetery, of course.*

The drive to Surry took almost two hours. She wondered who sent the message—and why. As she drove, her thoughts churned over all that had happened since Amy's death... *The root cellar... Agent Simmons' suggestion to meet with the K Street lobbyist... finding Amy's canister at ASRI... the public pillorying of SIS... finding the Buchanan connection... dismissal from the Service... and then, my abduction...*

She was having a hard time assembling all these pieces into a meaningful picture. The only connective element was ASRI. Everything was coming back to that company.

The GPS on her smartphone took her straight to Brookwood Cemetery. Entering the gates, she paused. "This place is huge. How in the world do I find anything?" She pulled up to a large sign showing a layout of the cemetery. It took a moment to get oriented, but she found the north area. She located the Zoroastrian section and said with satisfaction, "All the way to the end of the road, then left. What could be easier?"

There was a surprising volume of traffic within the cemetery, but it lessened as she reached the outside perimeter road. Turning left, she came to the end and parked in a small gravel lot. *I guess it's an Easter egg hunt from here.*

Most of the tombs in this particular section of the cemetery were mausoleums scattered throughout the heavily forested grounds. Wandering a manicured trail through the trees, she noticed the crypts varied in size and splendor. She wasn't sure what she was looking for. *Should I be looking for a sign saying, 'Amy is buried here?' I don't think so. How will I find her?*

Passing through the various tombs, she noticed reliefs cut above each mausoleum entry. The reliefs were slightly different, but they all had a Mesopotamian theme. Every mausoleum had a carved figure of a berobed Ahura Mazda wearing majestic Paghdi headgear. The figure's right hand was lifted in a gesture of welcome while the other held what looked like a handbag. The Ahura Mazda figures had huge wings extending left and right as if ready to fly.

As she wandered, she noticed a distinct aging of the tombs. The newest were bright white; the older ones had patinas in varying shades of gray. She also noticed she was quite alone. Coming around one especially large mausoleum, she noted the immediate area around it was cleared and had meditation benches placed at wide intervals.

Rounding the corner, she saw the tomb door was open. Her curiosity was aroused, but suspicions also went on high alert. *Too obvious.*

She moved with caution, circling around the crypt. There was no one in sight, but her internal alert system was pinging like crazy.

A stand of trees separated the crypt from the others in the area, providing seclusion and a sense of privacy. *It also gives a lot of cover.* She sensed no movement or other signs that someone was about.

After going fully around the open mausoleum, she believed she was alone. *Time to check inside.*

Placing her hand on the open door, she found it was made of iron. Thick iron. *Why does an interred body need such strong doors?* She wasn't going to wait around to find out. Making a quick survey of the open area, she felt eyes watching her. *Time to go.*

She made a hasty return to the path, silenced pistol in hand. Reaching the trees, she looked back.

Movement! The figure of a man was moving through the trees on the opposite side of the mausoleum. *He must think I'm inside.*

Quiet as a cat, she returned to her car, thankful to have avoided an ambush.

CHAPTER 42

Margaret Corbyn was uneasy. "There's so much riding on this…" Sitting in her living room, she knew it was time to get her project moving. She went to the kitchen, opened the refrigerator, and took out the canister.

She considered what she held. "These nanites will change the balance of power worldwide… and they'll make me rich." She placed the canister in a collapsible cooler bag, the type one would use to keep cans of soda cold on a picnic. She placed the dry ice into the cooler bag, zipping it closed. Placing her hand on top, like she was blessing it, she prayed that her dreams would finally be realized.

While packing and preparing for a long trip, she made a call to the corporate transportation office, "This is Director Corbyn. I wish to be placed on the list for the next flight to headquarters in San Francisco."

"The jet is at your disposal, ma'am," said the coordinator.

"Are there others scheduled to fly?"

"No, ma'am, but there is an order for a pick-up in San Francisco."

"Very well. I should be there in..." she checked her watch, "an hour."

"We'll have the plane fueled and ready to depart. Will you have anything to declare?"

"Only a small canister of biological materials that need testing at HQ."

She ended the call, knowing full well the only way to get the canister into the United States was to bypass customs. The company had an open approval to transport small samples back and forth without a customs check—another favor from Senator Buchanan.

Once her packing was complete, she called for a company driver, who picked her up and took her to London Oxford Airport, a private aviation field twenty-five kilometers away. She passed through the airport lobby, made a quick stop at the customer service counter, and then onto the company jet. As she expected, there were no questions about her luggage.

A crystal bud vase with a single rose and a glass of champagne were waiting as she boarded the aircraft. Sitting in one of the jet's comfortable seats, she thought, *This is the way to travel.*

A male flight attendant greeted her, asking if she was familiar with the safety features of the Gulfstream G650ER. She replied that she was, clipped her seatbelt, and took a sip of champagne.

She was in the air within twenty minutes, on her way to her destiny.

Joe Dixon's operative watched a dark sedan pull up to Corbyn's condo. A minute later, Corbyn herself came out. The driver took her bags. The operative was focused on one particular item: a small cooler bag, the type that holds a six-pack of soda. He noted she wouldn't let the driver take the cooler bag as she got into the rear seat.

The sedan drove off, and the operative followed at a discreet distance. When they didn't take the turn to London, he wondered where Corbyn was going. They went on M40 until reaching the intersection with A34, which they followed until reaching A44 where they turned right. By this time, the operative had a good idea of the destination.

When the sedan pulled into the London Oxford Airport, it confirmed his suspicions. *She's getting out of town—most likely, out of the country—and she's still holding onto the small cooler.*

He sent a text message to Dixon. The reply was immediate.

Get in there and see what airplane she gets on.

The operative made quick work of obeying Dixon. Questioning the attendant at the customer service desk, he learned that Corbyn had already passed through and boarded her flight.

Dixon's operative asked, "Where does that flight go?"

The attendant tapped on her computer. "San Jose, California is the logged destination."

Thanking the woman, the operative stepped to a private area of the small terminal to report back to Dixon. This time, the response took several minutes.

Let her go. We'll arrange someone on the other end to continue the surveillance.

Joe Dixon wasted no time messaging Kurt Buchanan. It was probably the wisest way to deliver the news, because he knew Buchanan would explode in anger when he read the text.

"What the hell!" The expletives continued for a full minute as he reacted to Dixon's text message. Once settled down, he realized what he had to do. "I need to let Dad know."

Kurt called the senator.

Senator Jack Buchanan knew immediately something was amiss and didn't waste time on pleasantries. He asked his son what was wrong.

"The ASRI woman, Margaret Corbyn, the one we've been keeping an eye on, just boarded a private jet. It's going to San Francisco. More specifically, San Jose."

The senator asked, "Why are you so worked up?"

"Dad, our man here saw Corbyn with a small cooler bag. She wouldn't let the driver take it, holding on like it was filled with priceless jewels."

"I see... Were you able to confirm the cooler went on the plane with her?"

"The check-in counter attendant said she boarded the private jet with all her baggage. I believe she's headed to the satellite operation. I think she's going to do something with the nanites."

"Arrange someone to watch that satellite building," his father said. "Can you do that?"

CHAPTER 43

Margaret Corbyn arrived carrying the seed colony as if it were a newborn infant. She'd taken the precaution to mark the canister with red tape to indicate this was the original from which other variants would be developed. Her technicians, Buoy, Shipman, and Kraft, waited for her at the entry to the laboratory area. She carefully handed the canister to Myra Shipman.

"It's in your hands now," she said, giving Myra and her two companions a stern look. "I expect only your best work. Understood?"

All three nodded. Myra spoke for the group, "We won't disappoint you, Director."

The technicians moved as a group into the laboratory. There was a slight *hiss* as the hermetically sealed door closed behind them. Corbyn turned and saw Robertson coming toward her.

"I take it the seed colony is safely delivered," Robertson said.

"It is, but there are other matters we need to discuss. Where can we have some privacy?"

"Follow me. There's a small meeting room over here." They crossed the open floor to a door on the opposite wall. "I think it may have been a cry room for the sensitive programmer types."

She gave a guttural laugh. It wasn't an expression of amusement, more of an appraisal of people she considered inferior. Entering the room, she wasn't surprised to see soft pastel walls and thick carpet. Robertson carried two chairs into the otherwise empty room.

"This room, and the others like it, we intend to use as testing cells. We've already removed any furniture and created air-tight closures for the doors."

She looked around with a new eye, seeing how nicely this room would fulfill this new purpose. "No windows, no furniture or bookcases, and only one way in or out. I approve."

"Thank you."

She took a seat and began, "Can you verify the SIS woman has been taken care of?"

"I've yet to hear from the guys I've brought on to replace Walters and Smith, but I assume they'll call once they leave the country."

"Assuming is a dangerous thing, Callum. Alert me the moment they contact you."

"Of course."

"Very well. Let's review the process..." They fell into a discussion about final preparations for the physical plant as well as the laboratory. Robertson assured her that everything was on schedule.

"In fact, we may be finished with the overall building sooner than expected. As I mentioned, existing rooms have all been stripped and equipped with hermetically sealed doors. Let me show you."

Robertson went to the room door, which was still ajar, and pushed it closed. She felt a pressure wave in her ears, causing her to yawn.

"How many subjects can be handled in these rooms?"

"As many as fifty to a room. The rest will be placed in isolation tents on the main floor. I'm sure you saw the framing going up."

"And the test subjects? How are we doing on that front?"

Robertson launched into a description of his arrangement with Reid, a former special forces colleague, and his rationale for selecting him. He then went on to tell her about the collection system Reid would be using, and how they planned to process the subjects once they were delivered. Finally, he sketched out how the remains would be handled.

"In short, everything is in place," Robertson said.

CHAPTER 44

Hannah returned to her Islington flat and thought it might be a good time to call Joel. The call was answered on the first ring. She gave him a quick recap of recent events and could hear the anxiety in Joel's voice. "Do you know *why* these people are trying to kill you? First, they managed to discredit you, then they got you fired from SIS, and now kidnapping..."

"There's something else." She recounted her trip to the cemetery.

"You didn't see anyone?" Joel asked.

"Not clearly, only a figure heading to the mausoleum I'd just left. In any event, it was clear they'd set a trap for me. I got out of there."

"We're back to the initial question: Why are they trying to kill you?"

"The only reason I can think of is that I discovered Amy's seed colony. I held it in my hands. I took it home."

"You have the seed colony with you?"

"No. It's gone. That must have been the reason I was abducted."

Death Mist

"They don't want anyone to know about the seed colony," Joel said.

"How do we stop these people?"

"You may no longer be with SIS, but we're still a team, remember? Let's get you out here so we can make a plan."

―――――

Landing at San Francisco International Airport, Hannah took a taxi to Joel's hotel in San Mateo. There was a room reserved for her, and she was grateful for Joel's thoughtfulness. There was a note on the coffee table in her room.

Rest well. Come to Suite 410 when you can. JB

The next morning, much refreshed, she went up to Suite 410. Joel answered the door. The room wasn't at all what she expected. There were racks of equipment, flashing lights, and computer workstations. Davies sat with his back to her, hunched over a keyboard. Joel invited her inside.

"Did you have breakfast?"

"Just a cup of coffee in the room."

"That won't do. Let me order you something." He picked up the house phone and ordered a fruit plate, yogurt, and wheat toast. "They'll be up shortly. Meanwhile, it's good we're finally all together."

Davies heard the discussion and turned around. He looked very happy to see her.

She glanced around the suite. "Where's Shadow?"

"He's on surveillance duty," Joel said.

"I relieve him in an hour," Davies added.

She took a seat in a comfortable chair. "I'm so happy that

we're together. You don't know how much it means to me. What's this about surveillance?"

"We've conclusively established that the Buchanans are involved in all this," Joel said.

"What's their angle?" Hannah asked.

"We think they know about the nanites and their potential. They don't want to miss this boat."

"They're gonna make a move on Corbyn's project," Davies added. "I just know it."

"We *think* they're going to insinuate themselves, somehow," Joel clarified.

Hannah asked, "What about Corbyn?"

"She's the linchpin," Joel said, "the one calling all the shots. She's got some kind of game plan; we just don't know what it is."

"Does she know about the Buchanans' plan?" Hannah asked.

"I don't believe she's aware how much Kurt Buchanan knows. He's got a spy in her team."

"I see… but isn't Corbyn in England?"

"She arrived here thirty-six hours ago."

CHAPTER 45

Kurt Buchanan arose early. There was much to do this day. Dixon had given him the local operative's name: Ed Pearson. Using Pearson's cell number, he sent a text introducing himself and asking for a situation report.

It took only a couple of minutes for Pearson to respond.

In place before the subject's flight landed.
Observed her deplaning, gathering luggage, and getting into a town car.
Followed the car to ASRI in San Mateo.
The car didn't stop at the ASRI building. Instead, it dropped the subject at a building next door.
No identifying signage on that building.
Presently watching the building. What are your orders?
—Pearson

Kurt thought for a moment before replying.

Get a count of the people inside. Also, any deliveries or outside services coming to the building. KB

A return message came almost immediately.

Need to bring on at least two more men to set up full 24-hour shifts. Will you approve budget increase?
—Pearson

Kurt replied,

Budget increase approved. KB

He relaxed, not realizing how tight he'd been holding himself. *I've got control again.*

After getting settled in her private quarters in the satellite building, Corbyn's first order of business was to assemble her people. She asked for, and received, a comprehensive debrief on the group's progress. Dr. Hughes led the review.

"Most of our time has been spent assembling and testing laboratory equipment. As you know, there's a great deal of sophisticated—and delicate—hardware, not to mention the software. In order to manage the software side, we had to contract an outside computer technician. We got Mr. Robertson's approval."

Dr. Hughes glanced over at Robertson who was leaning against the wall, listening.

"The tech area, including servers and other computer paraphernalia, is upstairs, totally separated from our main activities. Don't worry, the contractor's been kept out of the loop. There's also a cleaning staff that comes twice a week. They're equally uninformed.

"With Myra's assistance, the lab equipment's been set up and is now in place. We're ready to begin a series of diagnostic tests to be certain everything is running as designed." Dr. Hughes looked at Corbyn. Seeing no particular emotion on her face, he continued.

"While completing the lab setup, we also began preparing this facility to accommodate the scope of test subjects you've asked for. The facility's modifications are being done primarily by George and Oliver," he nodded to his two associates. "They can speak more directly to the progress there."

George Kraft picked up the narrative, "As Dr. Hughes mentioned, preparing for a large number of subjects requires some unconventional thinking. This building was originally designed for software developers. Lots of open space, conversation pits, cubicles, game areas... Not at all like our ASRI facility in England.

"At first, we were stumped about handling a large number of test subjects—how to isolate them and prevent the research team from contamination. I think we've overcome that obstacle. Oliver will give you more details on that.

"Next, we had to build out a space where we could increase the volume of nanites. Now that you've delivered the seed colony, we can begin growing and differentiating the new population."

Corbyn interrupted, "What's the timeline for production?"

"We estimate about thirty days," Kraft said. "We'll need first to confirm that the new colonies are as effective as the original. I'd suggest we identify two, maybe three, subgroups. After that, we can expand."

"Thirty days..." Corbyn complained. "We can move faster than that."

Dr. Hughes stepped in, much to Kraft's relief, "Let me take

this, George. We learned a great deal from the previous, ah, subjects. As you know, our new generation of nanites was programmed to work within the entire human circulatory system. When the nanites are in stasis, that is, refrigerated to a temperature below fifty degrees, they develop an insulating mist. I'm not sure why this is. There was no mention of such a mist in the late Dr. Perry's notes, and I'm still studying the phenomenon.

"In any event, during the mist stage, the nanites are dormant. It's only when the temperature is elevated, like being introduced into a living body, that they warm up, activate, and carry out their programming. The seed colony you've brought is the undifferentiated strain. George is technically correct; it should take about thirty days to incubate differentiated nanites. However, based on what I've learned, the process could be shortened by seven, perhaps ten days."

Myra raised her hand and asked meekly, "Director, I was wondering... why such a large sample size? Is it necessary for certifications and approvals?"

Corbyn gave a look that would have melted lead. Myra quickly withdrew and became silent. Corbyn turned her attention back to Dr. Hughes.

"Make it happen. You have two weeks to increase and differentiate the population to our target size."

"Two weeks...!" George Kraft couldn't contain his outburst. Dr. Hughes intervened.

"That's very... aggressive, but we'll try to make that deadline."

Corbyn sat back. She was happy to have re-established control over these people.

"Now," she said. "What about the handling of the test subjects? What's our plan there?"

Oliver Buoy stood. "Let me walk you through that." He stepped to a small table and plugged a laptop into a video projector, then pulled up a rollup screen. "I thought visuals would be helpful." The projector came to life and a company logo appeared on the screen. "As George said, this building is very different from our UK facility, or even the headquarters complex next door."

A plan view of the first floor appeared on the screen. Using a small laser pointer, he began.

"This area is the loading dock." The red dot flew around in a circle. "The dock's not big, only two overhead doors, but we don't think that will hinder our work. Now, moving inside," the red dot circled around an open area adjacent to the loading dock, "you'll see open space. This will be our initial staging area, where we number the subjects and separate them into individual test groups. And this is where you'll see the biggest change in the layout." He pointed to a different area of the floor plan, the open main floor. Here, there were modifications to several rooms and other areas.

"We had to keep this from becoming a major construction project. That would have triggered headquarters involvement, not to mention the need for various permits and certifications. Instead, we're creating a series of clean rooms using framing and heavy plastic. Since we haven't yet tested the nanites on a large group of subjects, Dr. Hughes thought, as a precaution, we should begin small. Perhaps a group of no more than a dozen."

Corbyn didn't react, so Oliver continued. "You'll see here, we've taken the half dozen break rooms around the perimeter and converted them. They're the easiest. We're presently working on the stand-alone enclosures, or 'clean rooms' as we call them. On Dr. Hughes' recommendation, we're keeping them separated by a minimum of five feet."

"And how long until they're complete?"

Oliver hesitated. "Well, it would go much faster if we had additional help."

Corbyn looked at Robertson who had been standing aside. "Mr. Robertson, perhaps you could give Bouy and Kraft a hand with the enclosures…"

Robertson opened his mouth to reply, and then thought better of crossing her in public. He nodded and said, "Of course."

"Done then," Corbyn said. "Build your enclosures as quickly as possible."

When Corbyn and Robertson left the lab area, taking Dr. Hughes with them, Myra felt the world was closing in around her. Her colleagues could see it on her face and asked what the matter might be.

"Why this rush to get everything complete? Why is Corbyn in such a hurry?" Myra asked.

"She must be getting pressure from corporate," Oliver said. "I've heard they hit a rough patch and need something big to take up the financial slack."

It was a reasonable answer, but it didn't diminish the anxious feeling in the pit of Myra's stomach. "You're probably right. Being cooped up here all this time has given me the jitters."

George overheard their conversation. "Don't you think if Corbyn was getting pressure from corporate, there'd be more people around? Have you ever seen even one corporate type in this building?"

Myra and Oliver shook their heads.

"So, what do we do?" Oliver asked.

"What can we do?" Myra responded. "We're essentially prisoners."

Oliver and George looked at one another, then back to Myra. They had no idea what to do.

CHAPTER 46

Joel called Shadow, asking him to return to the hotel. While waiting, Joel filled Hannah in on his activities to that point, "My first task was finding out about Margaret Corbyn. Thankfully, I was able to tap FBI resources for the investigation. Do you remember Special Agent Simmons?"

"As a matter of fact, I recently consulted with him—before the SIS blow-up," Hannah said.

"So that's why he was so cooperative... I was just happy to have the FBI's help. Here's what I've found: Corbyn has a distant, aloof personality. She apparently has, or had, psychological issues, probably stemming from being moved around as a child. She was seeing a psychologist for body dysmorphia during high school, but that stopped.

"Corbyn was a gifted student, which alienated her all the more from her peers. She remained solitary all through high school, almost a recluse. Her intellect got her into college, and then on to a master's degree in biochemistry. She managed to land a job with a Silicon Valley start-up—ASRI. She did well, and given the dynamics of the start-up culture, she advanced quickly.

"The company grew and expanded to Europe—specifically,

the UK. The new facility's focus was on emerging technologies in bioengineering. Corbyn was put in charge of operations but continued reporting to headquarters in San Francisco, making her virtually autonomous.

"In her new role, Corbyn recruited and nurtured your friend, Dr. Perry. She gave Perry her own lab and allowed her to operate, for the most part, independently. I couldn't find many details about your friend's research, only that it had something to do with the intersection of nanotechnology and medicine."

Shadow entered the suite, and everyone greeted him.

"It's good to see you again, Shadow," Hannah said, giving him a big hug. "We were just talking about Margaret Corbyn."

Once everyone was seated, Davies picked up the story, "Shadow and I were digging into the Dark Web side of this whole affair. There's always some rancor in the Dark Web community but there's rarely direct, physical violence."

Shadow interrupted, "That's what caught my attention. First, it was the aggressive way Paynim responded to my original post. Maybe they wanted to scare off any other interested parties, I don't know. Somehow, Corbyn got wind of my posting. I think she must have tracked down the Paynim Clan. She couldn't know if they did or did not know about the death of Amy Perry, but she wasn't going to take any chances. She discovered the cottage where they met..."

Davies jumped in, "And hired the mercenaries to eliminate the Paynim Clan."

"How would a research scientist find, much less contract, a mercenary group?" Joel asked.

"ASRI is a big organization with lots of resources," Davies said, "security resources. I bet if we look into that security man you encountered when you first tried to meet with Corbyn, we'd find someone more than capable of doing that job."

Hannah agreed. "He had the distinct feel of a military man,

and he didn't wear a suit like everyone else." She looked at Davies. "I think it would be time well spent looking into that man... what was his name?"

Joel murmured, "Robertson. Callum Robertson."

Hannah moved on and recounted her investigation, "I was focusing on the Buchanans. They're the real power behind the throne, and somehow, I think they're involved in my recent troubles.

"I think the Buchanans took an interest in Amy's research, not because it would benefit mankind, but because it had the potential to make a whole lot of money and, possibly, a weapon. Somehow, Amy became infected and died.

"Then, someone in ASRI—my money's on Corbyn—had Amy's body hijacked. After some unproductive inquiries as to her body's whereabouts, the Buchanans' name came up. That sent me down a new trail. I met with our FBI friend, Rick Simmons."

"I remember him," Davies and Shadow spoke out in unison.

"One thing led to another. I must have made the Buchanans uncomfortable, because that's when the smear campaign began. The rest, you know."

Joel leaned forward. "That's why I've brought you all here. My investigation into ASRI was a little different than Hannah's, but it was enough to make me suspect there's a wider conspiracy in play. The UN Terrorism Bureau sent me out here to conduct a little surveillance on the company headquarters. Interestingly, I found that the security man, Callum Robertson, had arranged a lease on the building right next door to headquarters. What do you suppose that's for?"

"I think things were getting a little too hot in England," Hannah said, "and Corbyn needed to move her secret operation out of the UK."

The group wandered around the hotel space. Davies and Shadow went to the kitchen in search of something to eat. Hannah sat down to the breakfast that had been delivered, and Joel went to the coffee bar to get a fresh cup.

Hannah looked up from her yogurt. "We've been playing defense this whole time. I think we should turn the tables on them."

Joel looked up from his coffee and gave a big grin. "It's good to hear you say that because I've been thinking the same thing." This led to re-convening for a brainstorming session.

After an hour of suggestions, some of them crazy, others not, Joel called an end to the session.

"I've been taking notes of each idea tossed into the ring, and I think there's something here that has a good shot at working. Let's begin with the infiltration idea that both Hannah and Davies suggested."

Shadow interrupted, "You said there were only five of them in there. How can you infiltrate what must be a tight group?"

"I misspoke. There are only four of Corbyn's team; you've seen them."

"You're right. There's a cleaning crew that comes in for half a day, twice a week, Tuesdays and Fridays," Shadow said, "and another guy who drives in daily."

"I'd say he's a local," Joel said. "I've seen him as well. He doesn't look like a bioengineering type. He looks more like you." Joel nodded to Shadow.

Shadow, taking offense at Joel's comment, sat back, squaring his shoulders, and straightened his shirt. "What's that supposed to mean?"

Hannah stepped in. "Easy, Shadow. What he's saying is the others look, well, doctor-y, if you take my meaning. You look like a computer guy—which you are."

Shadow was appeased by her interpretation.

"I've got a multi-part plan," Joel said, "if you'd like to hear it." There was acceptance from all.

"Great. Here goes… Davies, I want you to create a distraction that will require outside computer expertise."

"What are you thinking?" Davies asked.

"Something big enough to get everyone's attention but not so destructive it stops what they're doing. Maybe a power outage or something."

"Let me work on it," Davies said.

He turned to Shadow. "I need you to befriend the computer guy, see if you can get inside that way. He's American, you're American, and you're both computer geeks."

"What about me?" Hannah asked.

"You have the toughest assignment of all: infiltration. Of course, that's also right in your wheelhouse."

"And you?" Hannah asked.

"I'm going to contact Agent Simmons, see if we can enlist the FBI's cooperation. Once this goes down, there are going to be people who need to be jailed."

Hannah gave a pouty look.

"You have to do this, Hannah. You're no longer with SIS, and Simmons knows it."

Shadow had been busy texting with Greg Turner, the computer contractor. He told Turner he was looking for freelance work. After a back-and-forth with his experience and qualifications, Turner agreed to meet with him. He reported his success to Davies and Joel.

"I'm going to meet Turner at lunch tomorrow. He said it's the only time he can get away."

"Great work," Joel said. "Now we've got to get Hannah

working on the inside as well. Any progress on your end, Davies?"

"Yeah. It turns out, the company that originally occupied that building was trying to break into digital motion pictures. They had lots of graphics and needed full-motion capabilities throughout the building. To accomplish that, they had a T3 line installed."

"What's that?" Joel asked.

"It's really just a bundle of twenty-eight high-speed T1 lines, but all working in unison. The speed is really fantastic. Our SpartanZ office has a T1, but we don't come close to having the same needs as this company did. They managed to get a partnership with HP and got a movie into production. But the funding dried up, and the company had to close down. Sort of a 'here today, gone tomorrow' thing. But I'm getting off track. The point is, they still have that T3 line connected. That's going to be my point of attack. I'm betting Shadow's new buddy... what's his name?"

"Turner. Greg Turner," Shadow said.

"I'm betting Turner's a decent programmer but not an experienced repair technician. My plan is to access the line and disable some channels. That should be enough to ring alarm bells and generate a call for help. That would be me."

"Outstanding, Davies. But how do you get them to call you?" Shadow asked.

"Easy. I'll drop in a little worm that will intercept their internet search for a T3 repair technician."

CHAPTER 47

The surveillance phase was over, much to the relief of Davies and Shadow. Joel knew he was asking them to operate outside their comfort zone, but he couldn't mount a UN operation in the United States—not without authorization and cooperation from the US government. His next move would be contacting Special Agent Simmons at the FBI. Until then, SpartanZ was his best option.

At first, the boys were excited to be on an actual mission with him. After a few days of boring duty watching a mostly empty building where almost no one came or went, the bloom was off the rose. They didn't complain, but Joel could tell they were getting restless.

New assignments should cure that.

He'd been deliberately obscure when giving Hannah her part in the mission. He hadn't been patronizing when he said her role was going to be the most difficult. He meant it. She was accustomed to being the lead in an operation, but the circumstances had changed. *I hope she can yield control.*

Davies dove into his task. He looked up the electrical grid for the area and began figuring how to create a site-specific blackout.

Joel heard Shadow's exclamation of success when he found

out who the computer contractor was. "Here he is... A one-man operation based in Mountain View. His website says he's done contract work with HP, Oracle, and a bunch of startups. Interesting, ASRI isn't listed. I wonder why?"

"Maybe a non-disclosure, something like that," offered Joel.

"It doesn't matter. I'll bet he could use some help," Shadow said.

Joel took Hannah aside to discuss her infiltration mission. He could tell she was still uneasy. "Are you okay? I know this must all be a little weird."

"I'm sorry, does it show? I guess I've been a solo act for so long, it's a little strange to be part of a team and waiting for orders."

"I can understand that. But right now, you've got a part to play if we're to succeed. And that's what I want to talk about—playing a part." She looked at him with interest. "Can you do that?"

"Absolutely. And I apologize for my little pity-party. Go on..."

"I would like you to get hired by the cleaning company. They're big, and I'm sure they have a high turnover rate."

"How often do they service the building?"

"Twice each week, on Tuesdays and Fridays."

"That means they'll be there tomorrow," Hannah said.

"You'll need to do something to change your appearance," Joel said. "I think only Corbyn knows what you look like."

Hannah was getting into the spirit of the operation. "A wig, some frumpy clothes, and no makeup—I'll be a different woman."

"That's what I like to hear! Now, let's see if we can get you on the crew for tomorrow."

The cleaning company was based in San Jose, about a thirty-minute drive from their hotel. Hannah spoke on the phone with a very nice lady who told her they were always looking for qualified people and that she could come in for an interview.

"May I come today? I'm not far away." After they agreed to meet at two o'clock, she went to Davies. "I need you to cook up some professional cleaning references for me." Davies gave her a strange look. "I'm getting a job with the cleaning company."

He mouthed an *O-o-oh* in response.

"Today. Are you able to do it?"

"Are you kidding? I'll have it done in thirty minutes. What's your specialty—dusting, toilets, mopping floors?"

"Just show that I've worked with other companies, like Molly Maids."

"Good thought. They're all independent contractors, harder to verify."

"Meanwhile, can you find me a good second-hand store around here?"

A quick search on his laptop gave her several options, but the best was Goodwill, and they had a store in San Mateo.

"I'm off shopping. Thanks for your help!"

Hannah had to get up early Tuesday morning; "Kimberly Ryan" had to go to work. She, of course, was Kimberly. Her cover persona included used clothing, a wig, no makeup, a slumpy gait, and of course, an American accent. Her interview with the cleaning service had gone well and she was hired provisionally, pending a background check. Davies, of course, had taken care of her experience with a totally fabricated resume. A search for Kimberly Ryan would show a ten-year record of steady employment and no complaints.

Having learned earlier that this company was servicing the ASRI satellite building, she asked to be assigned to that crew. "You're in luck," the manager said. "There's an opening on that team."

When the manager saw her address was in San Mateo, it was a done deal. Now it was off to join her new crew for her first day of work.

The cleaning crew, three women and two men, were assembled at the loading dock in the rear of the building. They were happy to receive her. "Means less work and a quicker day for us all," said Patty, the team leader.

After getting her assigned areas, the team leader rang a call button at the loading doors. They had to wait several minutes. The others talked quietly among themselves while she stood silently off to one side. Finally, one door rolled up, and the team entered.

The men pushed wheeled buckets and carried mops. The women brought clear plastic bags and hand buckets with various cleaning supplies. They also pulled two vacuum cleaners behind them. Hannah/Kimberly was assigned the sleeping rooms on the second floor.

"They're used as staff quarters," Patty said.

Odd that they'd be housed here, in an office building.

She went about her duties, glad this assignment gave her a chance to snoop in each room.

Three rooms were rather small. *Must have been junior executive offices. Now they're bedrooms.*

After searching around, she found no real information. The last room was different. It was larger. *For a senior executive, no doubt.* This one had a front room with a desk and two chairs. The others were set up only as bedrooms. *This must be the security man's room.*

She went to the desk. It was typical: five feet wide by three feet deep. There were three drawers down each side and a wide drawer in the middle. A stack of three file folder trays sat on one side with a notepad and pen opposite. She noted there was no desk blotter, but a slender laptop charging cable lay across the desktop.

Placing her feather duster on the desk, she went back to the door and checked the hall. *All clear.*

She returned to the desk and pulled open the middle drawer. *Not much here. Pens, a letter opener, note pads, and a pad of sticky notes.* She pulled the drawer farther out, running her hand across the back. *What's this?* Grabbing the small object, she pulled her hand from the drawer. *A thumb drive... Now, that's interesting.*

She berated herself for not having a means to inspect the contents of the drive. Rolling the drive in her hand, she wondered what the best course of action might be. *I could take it and then return it on Tuesday. Would it be missed?*

She placed the drive back in the drawer. Moving to the other drawers, she was surprised to find them mostly empty. There were some papers in one. They didn't look revealing or important in any way. *Important stuff must be kept on the laptop.*

The bottom right drawer did have something of interest. A three-ring binder. No identifying title on the outside. Placing the binder on the desk, she began inspecting. There weren't many pages inside and only one divider. The first group of pages were printouts of a contact list. The title above the list read, *SFO Resources*. Below the heading were names and telephone numbers.

This could be useful.

She opened the camera on her smartphone and began clicking away. Turning the divider page, she found official-looking correspondence from ASRI. One document of interest was headed "Roles and Responsibilities." She took a picture of this page as well.

After returning the binder to the drawer, she went back to the center drawer and the USB drive. She was startled when the room door opened. She stood, pushing the center drawer closed with her thigh. Hastily, she grabbed the feather duster and made a fist with the hand holding the USB drive.

"Everything going all right, Kim?" It was the crew supervisor, Patty.

"Yes, just finishing up in here. One more to go." She made a show of passing the duster over the desktop.

"Oh, don't bother cleaning that one," Patty said.

"Whose is it?"

"I don't know. A woman. Apparently, a company big shot. She's arriving tonight and left orders to stay clear of her room."

Patty turned, closing the door behind her.

That was close! She pocketed the drive. Her decision was made.

The order to avoid the last room intrigued her. *It has to be Margaret Corbyn's.* She stepped into the hallway. It was empty. Patty had already gone to check on the others.

She went to the door of the last room. By the positioning of the door and its separation from the others, it was clear the room was bigger than the rest. *Top executive. Probably has a panoramic view.*

She made one last visual check of the hallway and tried the door. It was locked. *Nuts! Well, I can try on Tuesday—and I'll bring a lockpick set.*

CHAPTER 48

Corbyn had neglected to include Kurt Buchanan in her calculations. Ed Pearson, Dixon's local operative, had been keeping watch since Corbyn's arrival. So far, Pearson had little to report to Kurt Buchanan. "Five people, plus the woman who came in from England. There's another one who must be local because he drives in each morning and leaves about five or six in the evening. There's also a cleaning crew that comes twice a week."

Buchanan asked about the canister Dixon had seen in London.

"She carried a small collapsible cooler, the kind that holds a six-pack. That has to be it. Also, she rode with it on her lap. What are your orders?"

"Keep the surveillance going. Let me know the moment anyone leaves that building."

Two days went by before Pearson delivered a new report, "I don't know if this means anything, but the one guy, the local, went out for lunch. No one else was leaving, so I followed him. He met with another nerdy-looking guy. Thankfully, they were sitting at an outdoor table so it was easy to watch them."

Kurt's interest was aroused. "Did you hear what they were talking about?"

"I was too far away, but it looked like our local guy was interviewing the other one. They finished their business, and the one returned to work. Soon after, the one being interviewed followed him.

"Back at the building, the new guy went inside. I think he's an extra hand."

"Keep an eye on things," Kurt said. "Let me know when something happens."

While Hannah was playing the role of Kimberly Ryan, Shadow was meeting with Greg Turner. He found Turner at an outdoor table in front of Starbucks. Turner was munching on a turkey, provolone, and pesto on a ciabatta bun. He put the sandwich down as Shadow came to the table.

"Are you Greg?" Shadow asked.

"I am," Turner replied. "Sit down, please."

As he took a chair, Turner picked up his sandwich. "You want something?"

"I don't think so. This is sort of an interview, and I want to stay focused."

"Great. Let's get started," Turner said. "What's your real name?"

"It's Farrell—Dylan Farrell. My handle is 742369—*Shadow*. What's yours?"

"78734734—*StreGreg*."

"Cool. Nice to meet you," Shadow said, shaking Turner's hand. The fact this guy had a handle meant he was a serious Explorer. That was good and bad. On the good side, it meant he probably had a number of offers for work. On the bad side, Davies's plan to disable one of the T1 lines might be something Turner could figure out. He'd just have to go with it.

Turner began by asking about the sorts of problems he'd overcome in the past. He had plenty to draw on but made a conscious decision not to talk about the King Tut heist—or his association with Milton Davies and SpartanZ.

Finally, Turner looked satisfied. It was time to close the sale.

"I looked on your website, Greg. You have an impressive client list. I thought you might want a couple of days each week to take care of other opportunities."

"I've had inquiries for new projects, but with this commitment," Turner waved his arm in the general direction of ASRI, "I can't follow up. Though, you're right. They've hired my company and it's my responsibility to provide the talent for the job at hand —whoever that may be."

"Well said," Shadow replied.

"You're on—at least on a provisional basis. Let's head back, and I'll introduce you."

Shadow followed Turner back to the building beyond ASRI headquarters. There was only one other car in the parking lot. Turner must have called ahead, because when they entered, a stern-looking man was waiting for them. *He doesn't look like a biochemical engineer, not by a long shot.*

Turner introduced him, "Mr. Robertson, this is Dylan Farrell, but he's called Shadow... it's an internet thing."

Callum Robertson grunted, shaking his head at the silliness of these geeks. Shadow held out his hand but Robertson didn't take it, eyeing him up.

For his part, Shadow evaluated the security man. He was tall and muscular, and his countenance was grim with what he imagined was a perpetual scowl. He wore paratrooper-style boots. *Certainly not what I'd expect from a corporate guy, and a programmer would be wearing kicks.* In fact, to Shadow, the man looked more military than corporate.

"He's one of my guys," Turner said, gesturing to Shadow.

"Freelance?" Robertson asked.

"Yes, he is—like everyone else in this town. But he's highly qualified and can step into this job right now. I'd like to rotate with him if it's okay with you."

Robertson stroked his chin and asked Shadow a direct question, "Can you integrate data from multiple sources, compile and transmit it without making your own analysis?"

"Yes, I can process a lot of information without drawing conclusions. I've done plenty of sensitive projects and never knew what they were about. I'll sign an NDA if it'll make you feel better."

Robertson turned to Turner. "What kind of schedule do you have in mind?"

"I was thinking, one week on, one week off. Does that work?"

"I think we can do that. Take him upstairs and show him around. When will he begin?"

"I'll have him shadow me today, then turn it over."

CHAPTER 49

Wednesday, everybody gathered in the suite. Joel took the lead, "I trust everyone had a productive day yesterday... Let's start with SpartanZ."

Davies began, "I used a fabricated AT&T work order to gain entry. Some big guy with a suspicious look stopped me and inspected the document, asking what the problem was. I told him it was routine maintenance, that we come every six months to check the system. That seemed to satisfy him, and he showed me to the utility room in the rear of the building.

"Once inside, I found the T3 drop. It's adjacent to the main telephone terminal box. When I opened it, I found the service nicely separated into twenty-eight bundles. I selected one bundle, and then one line in that bundle."

"Did you cut it?" Hannah asked.

"Heavens, no! Each line has twenty-four channels. Cutting all twenty-four would create a huge problem. I only want a small problem that they'll have to call me back to solve. I didn't terminate a channel, only reversed the connections. That way, an anomaly would show up and, with Shadow's help, will be reported."

Shadow picked up the narrative, "I shadowed Turner, or 'Stre-Greg' as he likes to be called. The setup's straightforward and seems to be ready to begin processing a whole lot of data. We agreed I'd begin tomorrow."

"Great work," Joel said. "How about our other infiltrator?"

Hannah recounted her story, ending with finding the USB drive. She held it up for all to see. "I found this in what I presume is Callum Robertson's room."

"The security guy?" Shadow asked.

"Yes, and I'm sure you two can open it."

"No problem," came the simultaneous answer.

"There's one more thing. One room on the second floor I was told not to clean. It's assigned to Margaret Corbyn."

"Corbyn..." Joel's tone was none too friendly. "You're going to have to get inside that room."

"I know. Our next shift is Tuesday. I'll get inside, and this time, I'll bring a lockpick."

Hannah went to the computer station on the far side of the suite's living room. "I could use your help with this," she said, holding up the USB drive. Davies and Shadow followed her.

Davies put the USB drive into a slot. "Password protected," he said.

"Is that a problem?" Hannah asked.

"Naw," Shadow said. "We'll handle it."

Within five minutes, Davies announced, "Got it open." Joel came over, and they all huddled around the screen.

"Here's a folder named *Corbyn*," Davies said. "Another is ASRI, and a third, Satellite."

"Where do you want to start?" Davies asked.

"With the Satellite folder," Hannah said.

Davies opened the folder, and they all looked at it with varying degrees of interest. There were a number of documents, including the lease agreement. They opened the first one on the list. It was a transcript of a conversation between Callum Robertson and some outfit calling themselves *Snadow Hawks*.

"Robertson's looking for someone to do some dirty work," Hannah said.

"And it looks like their leader, Eric Reid, has agreed," Joel added.

"Look at how much Reid and his crew are asking," Shadow said. "That's an awful lot of dough to pick up homeless people."

"Robertson's not concerned about the money," Hannah said. "Look at his comment, 'I'll get what you need, no problem. Corbyn will clear the way.'"

"I'd say this looks like a conspiracy," Davies said. "Let's take a peek in the Corbyn folder."

Davies opened it. There were many more documents here. Going through them all would take time.

Hannah stood back. "We're going about this all wrong. We need to be methodical. Also, I have to get that thumb drive back before Robertson discovers it's missing. Can we copy the drive?"

"No problem," Davies said. "Let me find a clean one." Davies and Shadow set off in search of a USB drive.

Tuesday came, and it was time for Kimberly Ryan to go back to work. Hannah dressed in what she thought of as her costume: a day dress with a faded floral pattern, solid-looking black shoes, bobby socks, and a pullover smock that looked as if its best days were in the last century. She covered her hair in a wig that gave her a tight bun of faded brown hair. Her only cosmetics was a theatrical makeup kit. With it, she shadowed under her eyes and across her cheekbones, making her look old and weary. Inspecting herself in the mirror, she declared she was officially frumpy and totally forgettable.

Joel had arranged a rental car for her use, an older model Ford Focus. "The perfect disguise," he told her.

She looked over the car in the hotel parking lot. "This is just about as vanilla as you can get... it fits my disguise."

At the satellite building, she parked around back and met up with the crew on the loading dock. Once again, Patty rang the call bell. After a minute or so, the door rumbled up, and they filed inside.

This time, there were no orders given. Everyone knew their jobs and went to them.

Hannah found the second floor once again deserted. *Thank goodness for small favors!* She wanted to get the pilfered USB drive back as soon as possible, so she began with Robertson's room. Knocking first, there was no reply, and she assumed the room was vacant. Opening the door, she stopped in her tracks. A man was stepping out of the bathroom. It was the security man, the one she'd met in the lobby of ASRI-Great Britain. She could only hope he didn't recognize her.

"Who're you?" Robertson demanded, surprised to be interrupted like this.

He was dressed, but had shaving cream on his face. *I hope my disguise works this close...* "I'm Kim. Housekeeping. I'm sorry to disturb you. I'll come back later." She turned to leave.

"Hold it," Robertson ordered. "You're the new girl, right?"

"Yes, sir." *He doesn't recognize me.*

"What time is it?"

"It's a little after nine, sir." *He's hardly paying attention to me. I'm just the hired help.*

"Damn. I'm late. You can go about your chores. I'll just finish up in the bathroom." He returned to the bathroom, shutting the door behind him.

Hannah only had minutes to get the USB drive back in the drawer. *The trick's doing it without making noise.* She went to the desk, sat in the chair, and pulled out the center drawer. She heard noises coming from the bathroom, like something dropped. It was followed by a muffled curse.

She froze, waiting to see what would happen. The bathroom doorknob began turning. She stood, grabbed the feather duster, and hastily closed the center drawer. When the door didn't open, she let out a breath, relieved at not being caught again at the desk.

Laying the feather duster on the desk, she pulled out the center drawer, all the while listening carefully. *It wouldn't do to be caught now.*

It took only a moment to place the drive in the back of the drawer. With relief, she left the desk and walked over to the dresser. As she began dusting, the bathroom door opened.

"Here, that's enough for now." Robertson looked around. "Everything looks fine. You can go."

With Robertson gone and the USB drive successfully replaced, she could concentrate on Corbyn's room. She'd been told the woman had arrived over the weekend. She found the door was locked. This time, however, she'd brought her lockpick set. Setting down her bucket of cleaning cloths and feather duster, she made quick work of opening the door.

The room was larger than Robertson's. It was actually two rooms. *This was surely a senior executive's suite. There's an office in back, and here in the entry was no doubt meant to be for reception.* The back office had been converted into a bedroom. She decided to begin there.

Not a very homey bedroom.

Flanking the queen bed were simple nightstands. An upholstered bench sat at the foot of the bed, and a chest of drawers was placed against the wall. A desk and chair were positioned under a window with what must have been the original curtains. They looked decidedly unfeminine—gray panels flecked with white and hanging to the floor. At the moment, they were closed, creating a bleak environment.

The nightstands yielded nothing. The chest of drawers held underwear, a couple of sweaters, hosiery, and socks. She looked around for anywhere else something might be kept. She gave the closet a try. She found a large suitcase, along with two pairs of leather shoes and a pair of athletic shoes. Above the shoes hung two identical medium gray pant suits along with an empty hanger for a third—*the one she must be wearing.*

On a shelf above the clothing rack, she spotted a small cooler bag. Taking it down, she realized it was the same cooler bag she'd used when the canister was nicked. *She must have taken it along with the canister from my flat.* Zipping it open, a wisp of white smoke came out, and within was a tiny fragment of dry ice. *It looks like she transported the nanites with my dry ice, too.*

Going back to the main living area, there was nothing unusual. Instead of a reception station, a low table with four chairs sat in the middle of the room. A desk similar to the one in the bedroom was off to one side. There were two windows in this room, both treated with the same gray/white patterned drapes. These, however, were open, allowing light to come in.

She wondered if the desk would hold anything of interest like she'd found in Robertson's room. Checking the drawers, she found them empty. *Since she just arrived, it's not surprising.*

She made a point of checking the center desk drawer all the way to the rear but found nothing. *Whatever she's doing, it must be downstairs. Now, how do I get myself assigned down there?*

CHAPTER 50

When everyone left for their respective duties, Joel called Rick Simmons at the FBI. The conversation was cordial. Simmons wasn't exactly a friend, more like a colleague, so he was a bit circumspect.

"Are you and Hannah still working together?" Simmons asked. "I saw her a while back, before all the mess with SIS. I heard they drummed her out of the service."

"That they did, and it wasn't pretty. She took it hard."

"I also heard she disappeared. There was speculation that she might even have committed suicide."

"I'm happy to debunk that rumor. But the circumstances surrounding her dismissal go to the heart of what I want to talk about. Is there any chance we could meet?"

"Are you in Brussels?"

"No, as a matter of fact, I'm in San Francisco—or more precisely, San Mateo."

"That's fortunate for both of us. I flew into San Francisco last night. I can meet you here at the Field Office."

Joel parked at the FBI Field Office building on Polk and Golden Gate. Going up to the agency's floor, he went through visitor processing. A young man escorted him to a small conference room. "You'll find Special Agent Simmons in here," the escort said.

The conference room may have been small, but the large windows on the thirteenth floor offered a spectacular view of San Francisco. Simmons stood as he entered, extending his hand.

"Welcome to San Francisco, Joel. It's good to see you again."

Shaking the agent's hand, Joel responded, "Good to see you, too, Rick."

The pair sat at the conference table, and a woman entered with a tray holding two cups of coffee and some donuts. Joel commented on the service, "This is certainly not necessary on my account."

"Nonsense. It's just common courtesy."

They engaged in small talk about the weather, family, and arcane policing topics. Joel finally steered the conversation to the purpose of his visit. He described the origins of Hannah's inquiry and the subsequent expansion that included ASRI. "This is when we got wind of the Buchanan family's involvement. We divided up, each of us taking a separate line in inquiry. It led us to what seems to be a deeper, more far-reaching conspiracy." He went on to describe the bioengineered nanites, how they'd been corrupted, and the deadly result of their introduction into a human body.

"Whatever is happening is centered in San Mateo," Joel said.

Simmons went to the windows. After a few moments, Simmons turned. "Why haven't we heard anything about this?"

"It's been kept secret. Only a small number of people know about the deadly nanites, and all of them are in that building in San Mateo."

"San Mateo falls into this office's jurisdiction. But as far as I can tell, there's been no criminal activity. Until there's a change, I can't open a case."

"Will you come down, meet with my team and make a first-hand evaluation?"

Simmons drove down to San Mateo the next day, where he was met by Joel in the hotel lobby. Joel escorted his FBI guest to the suite, and when they entered, Davies and Shadow jumped up, shaking Simmons' hand. "It's good to see you again, Agent Simmons!" Their overlapping exclamations humored the FBI man.

Hannah stepped from behind the pair and Simmons started.

"So, you're not dead…"

Hannah laughed lightly. "Whatever gave you that idea?"

"Rumors… strange reports… at the very least, it sounded like you'd run off to a deserted island somewhere to shake off the terrible SIS publicity."

"Let's all sit down," Joel said. "I think Agent Simmons needs a debrief."

Their summary of events was a little disjointed, mostly because the boys tended to jump around in time and place. Joel did his best to keep them on track, only to give up in the end.

"It's okay," Simmons said. "I think I can keep up. What interests me most is what Hannah has to say."

Hannah went through a detailed account of the case. Joel popped in from time to time, mostly to clarify a point from his perspective. When she finished, Simmons sat back and let out a slow breath.

"This is remarkable, Hannah. Even though they disgraced you and now think you're dead, or at least out of the picture, you were still able to get inside their facility." The tone of his statement indicated disbelief—and respect.

Shadow jumped in, "You should see the getup she wears."

"Yeah," added Davies. "You'd never think a woman as beautiful as Hannah could look so plain."

"My hat's off to you, Hannah." Simmons turned to Joel. "I think this is something the FBI should be watching. You mentioned Kurt Buchanan's involvement. Can you elaborate?"

Joel described how he followed Myra Shipman to a compound in Hillsborough. "It turned out the place is owned by Senator Jack Buchanan. After a while, Myra was returned to the lab building."

"And you think she went to meet with Kurt Buchanan?" Simmons asked.

"Yes, I do. He's gotten wind of Corbyn's off-the-books project and wants in."

Simmons turned back to Hannah. "Can you tell me more about this deadly nanotechnology?"

Hannah described, as best she could, nanotechnology and how it has been adapted to the biomedical field.

"So, you're saying these tiny robots can be programmed to kill someone?" Simmons asked.

"In theory, once you've successfully created a biological organism with a programmable nucleus, it will carry out its instructions. Because the nanites are biological, the body reads them as 'natural' cells, and normal defenses aren't activated."

"Do these nanites reproduce?"

"Not in the sense you're asking about," Hannah said. "A single nanite isn't able to do much, like a single stalk of wheat won't make a loaf of bread. But let it fabricate, duplicating in the hundreds, thousands, and millions, then you have a powerful force." She paused for effect. "Corbyn's brought the seed colony here, and they're building an army of new nanites."

Simmons shook his head in confusion. "What's their objective? The endgame?"

Joel answered, "That's what we're here to discover. They're doing this in secret. I don't—we don't—believe corporate ASRI has any idea the program exists. After seeing what happened to Hannah's friend and the subsequent attempts on her own life, I'd guess their purposes aren't humanitarian—or legal."

"I'm sorry," Simmons said. "Until we have credible evidence of criminal activity, we can't act."

CHAPTER 51

The team gathered in the hotel lounge over drinks. Joel said it fostered fellowship. Hannah enjoyed the relaxed atmosphere. The boys were just happy that Joel was buying the drinks.

The lounge had an interesting carpet with overlapping swirls in varying colors, giving it a light, open feel. Mellow jazz music played from ceiling speakers, and uniformed waiters cruised between tables taking orders. It was, in short, a nice place to hang out. They occupied a table at one end of the lounge where they could talk and not be overheard.

The collegial discussion soon moved to the tasks each had been given.

Joel looked at the team. "The FBI is going to need more than theories before raiding that building."

"I guess I can understand," Hannah said. "I don't like it, but I understand."

Davies jumped in, "Trying to kill you isn't action enough?"

"Hold on," Joel said. "Those events took place in the UK, not the USA. Hannah's right, we've got to catch them at least planning to commit a crime. So far, all I can see is that the security guy, Robertson, has been going back and forth to San Francisco. The others stay inside."

"What about the woman, Myra Shipman?" Davies asked.

"She went out."

"Yes, just that one time, and it was to the Buchanan estate."

"What did the FBI think about that?" Davies asked.

"There's no law about visiting someone, even if it is suspicious." Joel took a sip of his drink. "What about you, Shadow? Anything to report?"

"I'm in, but now Davies has to plant the glitch—then we can get him inside."

"Are you ready to go?" Joel asked Davies.

"All set. I'm just waiting for the order."

"Hannah, how about you?"

Shadow gave a laugh while trying to sip his drink and spurt it all over himself. "Sorry!" He grabbed several cocktail napkins and began patting himself down. "It's just, well, I saw you leave the other morning and had to look twice to be certain it was you."

"You like my disguise?" Hannah asked.

"I wouldn't have believed a beautiful woman could be transformed into... well, you just looked really different."

"Thank you, Shadow. That's probably the nicest thing you could say to me." She watched a blush come over Shadow's face. She turned to Joel. "I did manage to get into Corbyn's room but didn't find anything useful. I thought getting closer to the action would be a good idea, so I'm going to ask Fatty to trade work assignments with another girl. When I walk through the main floor, I can see why the cleaning staff finds it creepy. It's the construction they're doing... It's not a renovation exactly—they're building booths and covering them in heavy plastic."

Davies said, "I've been going through the documents we copied from the thumb drive and found some interesting stuff. For example, it seems Corbyn has budget signing authority for the

UK operation. She answers only to the Chief of Operations here in San Francisco."

"Sweet deal," Hannah said.

"There's more..." Davies paused, like a stage actor delivering an important line. "It turns out Callum Robertson, the security man, was a US Special Forces operator. Highly trained. He led a unit called *Shadow Hawks*. Now, he's hired an old teammate, Eric Reid, to help him with what he's calling the 'implementation phase' of the project."

"How soon is this happening?" Joel asked.

Davies gave a troubled look. "Assuming they've got the seed colony of nanites, it could be any day."

After dinner, the team reassembled in the suite's salon. Everyone was concerned about Davies' report, and all wanted a plan of action.

Hannah took the lead, "It seems we need to find out a few things. First, where are they in the process of building more nanite colonies? Second, what volume of nanites are they looking to produce? Third, who are they targeting? And finally, when are they going to begin?"

"All good questions," Joel said. "As I see it, there's only one way to find out: we have to get into the lab."

"I got a look at the lab area," Hannah said. "Well, the door to the lab anyway. It looks like a bank vault, and it's been fitted with a vacuum seal. The door's kept closed, and there's a security keypad to get in."

Joel went to a desk, opened a drawer, and came back with a large, folded document. It was a blueprint. He spread it out on the coffee table.

"The FBI helped me get this floor plan of the building. It was submitted by the previous tenants but should still be valuable." He looked up. "Hannah, where is the lab?"

Hannah leaned over the blueprint, getting her bearings. "A lot's changed. Where this blueprint shows rows of cubicles, there's only open floor." She traced her fingers across the image. "Here. This large area that's labeled as a conference room—that's now the lab."

"I'll guess there's a security system in the building," Joel said.

"Let me take a look," Davies offered. He spun the blueprint around and made marks with a pencil. "The place is pretty well covered. These are all camera positions."

"Are the cameras operational?" Joel asked.

"There's no way to tell, but we should assume they're active."

"Any ideas about getting past the alarms and cameras?" Hannah asked.

Davies and Shadow huddled privately. After a minute of discussion, Davies had an answer, "We have to shut it down."

"That's too simple an answer," Hannah said.

Shadow stepped in, "You're right, it sounds that way, but it's not that simple. It will have to be done in two phases. First, while I'm in the tech area working, I'll access the security system and disable the alarms and cameras—hopefully, without getting caught."

Davies spoke up, "Then, I have to get to the main feed lines, locate and disable the alarm circuits, and deactivate any notification protocols they may have in place."

"That sounds like a daunting task," Joel said

"Daunting, yes... insurmountable, no," Davies said. He glanced at his partner, Shadow.

"Okay," Joel said. "Now, let's talk about our infiltration plan."

"When my crew reports for work," Hannah said, "we enter through the loading dock. I'd say that would be our best bet, too."

"How do you get in?" Joel asked.

"They have to open the overhead door—no controls outside. Only a call bell. Inside is an open area. There's a door in the rear that leads to the main working space."

"Are there any other doors?" Joel asked.

Hannah thought for a moment. "Yes. It's outside, off to the side of the loading dock. I've never seen it open. It must go to another part of the building."

Joel sat forward, chin resting on his fist. "Since everyone's quarters are on the floor above, opening the overhead door isn't a great idea. It would make a lot of noise and raise an alarm, regardless of what Davies and Shadow can do." He looked at Hannah. "What about the front doors?"

"They're alarmed, too. More importantly, they have an electronic key device—like the lab door. It's round with buttons in the middle. It looks like something you'd see on a bank safe."

"That's not good," Davies said. He went to his laptop and pulled up the specs for that type of lock. "The pushbutton access uses a six-digit combination. That means there are one million permutations, something we're not likely to crack in a few minutes. Also, the lock can only be used by designated people."

"The security guy... what's his name?" Joel asked.

"Robertson," Hannah replied.

"He's got to be one of the users. And the second?"

"Has to be Corbyn," Hannah said. "And the technicians—they'd be given access."

"Continue, Davies," Joel said. "Sorry for the interruption."

"As I said, only designated users can control the lock. If we attempt to guess the combination and don't do it within four tries, the lock goes inactive for a period of twenty-four hours."

Joel let out a long breath. "We're back to that rear outside door. It's our only viable option."

CHAPTER 52

The next morning, Hannah set off for work. When she arrived, she asked Patty, her supervisor, if she could swap her upstairs cleaning duties.

"As luck would have it, one of the other women wants to switch," Patty replied. "She said it feels creepy on the main floor and would like to trade duties."

With the switch approved, Hannah moved down to the main floor. She understood how her co-worker felt. *There's a strange vibe in this building, especially around that large room.*

Hannah was told by Patty that the large room was off-limits. She knew what that off-limits room was: a laboratory. Beyond that, she counted six enclosed rooms on the perimeter encircling a large open space.

The central area was something of a construction site, but not the kind normally associated with an office building. Neat piles of two-by-fours, one-by-three furring strips, step ladders, buckets of screws, and large rolls of thick plastic were all stacked against one wall.

A large part of the area had been framed out but in an odd way. Typically, full walls would go up, or perhaps cubicle-height walls. But here, it looked like they were building a series of rooms eight feet square. These rough frames were covered on all sides with thick plastic. Even the floors and tops were enclosed in plastic.

Working her way around the cubes, she wondered what their purpose might be. Her inspection brought her back to the door to the laboratory—the door she was ordered not to enter.

She reached out to touch the door and was startled when it opened. A woman came out. She recognized her as Myra Shipman, the only female on Corbyn's staff. "I'm so sorry, I didn't know you were coming out," Hannah said apologetically.

Myra said nothing and headed toward the building's front doors. Hannah continued to play her part as a cleaning lady, and as she dusted, watched Myra.

Myra looked back. Re-tracing her steps, Myra came up to her. "I haven't seen you before. What's your name?"

"Kimberly, ma'am."

"You know this area's off-limits to you people."

"Sorry, ma'am. I'm new."

She could see Myra was inspecting her closely. "Despite your clothing, you don't look like a cleaning woman. Your eyes are too shiny, too inquisitive."

Hannah made no comment. She was worried her cover was about to be blown.

Myra turned to leave but stopped after a few steps. She watched Myra staring at her. *She's trying to decide about me.* Myra tilted her head toward one of the small rooms on the outer wall. Hannah got the message and followed.

When the room door closed, she felt a pressure wave. *This isn't a regular office door.* She ran her fingers around the seams. *A silicone seal, like you'd find in a testing chamber.* Myra looked at her with a puzzled expression.

"You're not really a cleaning lady, are you?" Myra asked.

Hannah didn't respond.

"You just examined the door seal like an expert. A normal cleaning woman would never do that. I think you're more than you seem."

Hannah moved closer. Dropping the American accent, she spoke in a hushed voice, "You're very perceptive. My name isn't Kimberly, it's Hannah. I get the sense that there's something you want to talk about. Something you can't share with your colleagues."

Myra gave a soft laugh. "You sound British, and you called them 'colleagues.' That language—not to mention the accent—is a little sophisticated for your average cleaning woman." Leading them away from the narrow door window, Myra continued, "You're right. There's something going on and I don't know who to trust... can I trust you?"

"Yes, you can."

Myra looked guilty but obviously had made the decision to confide in her.

"I'll have to make this quick. I'll be missed soon. I'm a biochemical engineer for ASRI, although I actually work in the UK facility. My supervisor recruited three of us to work on what she called a 'special project.' That project turned out to be something another scientist was working on. Somehow, my supervisor got her hands on a sample of the project's assets. That other researcher went missing."

"Would that have been Dr. Amy Perry?" Hannah asked.

Myra's eyes went wide. "How do you know?"

"I know a good deal about this—and Dr. Perry's death."

"Who are you? Are you in law enforcement?" Myra's tone was one of puzzled surprise.

"Let's just say, I'm someone who can help—if you'll let me."

Myra looked around and stiffened. "I need to go."

"When can we talk again?" Hannah asked.

"I don't know. Maybe I've said too much already."

With that, Myra rushed out of the room.

Returning to the hotel, Hannah went directly to the suite. She found everyone busy, but they stopped the moment she entered. Joel could see concern on her face as she went to the couch and dropped down.

"Looks like you had quite a day," Joel said as he joined her.

She related her encounter with Myra Shipman.

Joel listened, and when she was done, he called over to Davies, "Would you bring us that memo you found?" Davies shuffled through some papers and brought a single sheet to Joel. Thanking Davies, he handed the paper to her.

"Oh, my God!" She looked at Joel. "Is this true?"

"We have to assume so."

She read the document again. It was an "eyes only" memo from Corbyn to Callum Robertson detailing her orders regarding the development team. "This says, 'Once the efficacy of the nanites is confirmed, you are to dispatch them all.'" She looked at Joel. "Why?"

"It's pretty simple," Joel said. "She plans to keep the technology all to herself, and she can't leave witnesses."

She looked at the memo again. "Not even Dr. Hughes will be spared, it seems." She placed the memo on the side table. "What's her endgame?"

"Who knows? Set up her own business... sell it to the highest bidder? It could be anything, but the point is, she's going to clean house and get out of there."

"Unless we can stop her," she said. "I need to talk to Myra again. There's more she hasn't told me—I know it." She picked up the paper. "This memo may be just the motivation we need."

CHAPTER 53

The next day, Saturday, meant it would be three days before Hannah could get back in the building. Shadow, however, was on duty. "They work seven days a week there," he told them.

She had a thought: *Shadow might be my way in.*

Hannah set off after her colleague. Unlike her, Shadow was allowed to park in front of the building. She smirked about the prejudicial treatment as she got out of the car.

"You look like Cat Woman," Shadow said. "I hope you can find a way in."

"Don't worry. I've got my ways."

"And I know what to do first," Shadow replied.

They parted ways, Shadow going in through the front door, and she around the building to the loading dock area. Instead of going to the overhead door, she went to the smaller door to the right. The door itself was metal, and because the hinges weren't visible, she knew it opened inward. She was thankful there wasn't one of those fancy electronic locks. The standard doorknob didn't look like it would present much of a problem. Her only concern was whether the door had an alarm. *Can't worry about that now.*

Kneeling down, she took a small wallet-like container from

her cross-body bag, zipped the wallet open, and selected the lockpick tools she wanted. It was quick work to open the door.

She inspected the jamb, looking for alarm leads, spotting a small white plastic box at the door top. *I hope Shadow was able to intercept the alarm. If not, this'll be a short trip.* Looking more closely, she noticed the small light on the box wasn't glowing red. *It's not armed—good going, Shadow!*

Closing the door, she found herself in a long hallway. It looked like it ran parallel to the loading dock wall. Getting mental bearings on the location of the laboratory, she moved down the empty hallway, hoping her plan to lure Myra out of the lab would work.

While Hannah was infiltrating the building, Shadow entered through the front doors and up the stairs to his area. He went straight to the security monitor system and turned off the rear door alarm. Watching a bank of video monitors, he held his breath until he saw Hannah enter the hallway. He released it with a heavy sigh. "Step one complete."

He turned to another workstation. "Time to nudge Miss Myra."

Accessing Tor on the Dark Web, he composed a message that couldn't be traced. Hannah told him it had to be short and to the point. "The purpose is to get Myra out of the lab to meet with me."

There was no way to know how Myra would respond. He could only pray that she would.

Myra's mobile phone made a quiet *ding*. She looked at the device sitting on the edge of her worktable. She'd been thinking about her meeting with the cleaning lady who wasn't a cleaning lady. She opened the messages icon.

Curious, she thought. *There's no sender, not even an originating number*. She looked around to see if the others had been alerted. *Apparently not...*

Oliver, at an adjacent worktable, had his back to her and was busy peering into a microscope. On the other side of the lab, George was helping Dr. Hughes with an apparatus that was critical to conducting the proof of concept.

Keeping the mobile flat on the table, she read the message:

Your new friend wants to meet. She has important information you need to know.
9:30—same place as before.

She quickly closed the message, her thoughts churning. She had no idea who sent the message, but it was clearly a meeting request. What was the "important information" referring to? Her interest was piqued, but a sudden fear gripped her stomach. The wall clock showed it was almost nine-thirty. *What do I do?*

After shuffling around, she came to a decision. She approached Oliver, tapping him on the shoulder. He looked up with a questioning look.

"I'm going to the ladies."

Oliver grunted and turned back to his microscope.

CHAPTER 54

Hannah came to a door that she believed opened onto the central area of the main floor. This door wasn't locked. Opening it a crack, she checked out the floor. It was much the same as the day before: framed rooms, some covered with heavy, opaque plastic, others not covered. No one was in sight. She moved with practiced stealth through the structures to the room of her earlier meeting with Myra.

Shadow's done great so far. The outside door alarm was off—I only hope he was able to get that message to Myra.

Inside her designated meeting room, she peeked through the door window to see if Myra would come. She checked the time on her mobile. It was 9:32.

I'll just have to wait—and hope.

The lab door opened and Myra stepped out. Hannah watched her look around and then head straight toward her. When Myra entered the room, she looked on in amazement.

"Is it you?" Myra was clearly startled by her appearance. She was no longer the frumpy cleaning lady. Instead, she saw a beautiful, dark-clad woman about her own age.

"Yes," she said. "Come in. There's much to talk about."

They moved to a position where they couldn't be seen from the outside.

"The message I received said you have important information," Myra said.

Hannah reached into her cross-body bag, took out a folded piece of paper, and handed it to Myra. "You're in danger. All of you are in danger."

Myra gave a startled look and read the memo. "I don't understand."

"I think you do. Just give it a moment to sink in."

Myra re-read the memo and then handed it back. "I can't believe it. This must be a fake."

"It's not. This came from a USB drive that I found in Robertson's room."

Myra backed up to a wall, wiping her hands on the lab coat. Her face was ashen. "What do I do? How do I get out of this? How can any of us get out?" Panic laced Myra's voice.

"I need you to tell me everything, Myra."

———

Myra, shaken to her core, shut her eyes tightly. "I was coerced into this job and forced to work on this project."

"Who forced you?" Hannah asked.

"It's a bit of a story..."

"I'm here to listen."

She looked into Hannah's eyes. Myra saw understanding. There was also empathy and compassion.

"It began years ago, in graduate school. I got hooked on drugs. I know... it's stupid, but I was just trying to get through school. I was arrested. I couldn't face my parents—I was in a predicament. That's when a complete stranger not only bailed me out but managed to have the charges dropped I was saved from humiliation, not to mention jail. I determined that no one would ever know about the incident. In fact, you're the first person I've ever told."

"Except for that angel," Hannah said.

"Yes. That man knew about my drug problem. I want you to know, from that moment on, I didn't do any more drugs. When I graduated with my MS, I was hired by a new company in the biotech field, ASRI. It was all very exciting, and the drugs and arrest incident sort of faded from memory.

"I progressed quickly in ASRI, becoming a senior technician. I must have caught Corbyn's attention. She approached me. I felt privileged that the operations manager would notice me. Corbyn told me she was conducting a special project and wanted me to be a part of the team. I was honored."

"What was the project?" Hannah asked.

"Corbyn said it was an investigatory analysis. All lab work, she said. It was small, but the potential was nothing short of world-changing. I was hooked and joined. Soon after joining, I received a letter... Who writes letters these days? Anyway, the letter was from my long-forgotten benefactor, back to collect on my debt. It was essentially blackmail. I was to become an informant on the project or my background would be exposed. What choice did I have? If my record were made public, I'd be disgraced. I'd lose my job. I'd lose everything. I had to cooperate."

"Who was the letter from?" Hannah asked.

"Kurt Buchanan. An ASRI board member."

"Why was he interested in Corbyn's project? Did the letter say?"

"Not exactly. All he was interested in was results. I was never fully briefed on the project, none of us were, but I think she's trying to develop some sort of bioweapon."

"Did you send back reports?"

"At first, there wasn't much to report since he was only interested in outcomes. Then there was the incident with Dr. Perry. You said you knew her?"

"Amy Perry was my friend," Hannah said.

"I'm sorry..."

"She died a horrible death," Hannah said. "Then her body disappeared. When I began questioning and searching, I encountered your ASRI friends. Since that time, they've tried to kill me."

"How did you escape? I can't imagine..."

"I have certain 'skills.' Their failure to silence me may be the reason the operation was moved to the US." She saw Myra softening. "I'm in government law enforcement... or, I was, until the Buchanan family mounted a smear campaign and ran me out of the service. So, you see, this is much bigger than any of us can imagine."

"Can you help me get away?" Myra asked.

"I'll need you to stay in place, at least for a little while," Hannah said. "You'll have to act like nothing has changed. Just carry on with your duties. I have some friends working with me, but we need tangible evidence of a crime. Can you find that for us? A solid piece of evidence that we can take to the authorities?"

Myra stood up, straightened her smock, and went to the door.

"May I have that memo? I'll need it to get the others on board. Don't worry, we'll get what you need."

Joel had followed Hannah and Shadow that morning. He was especially interested in Hannah's means of entry. If that worked, it would be their entry for a larger action. He parked in the lot of an adjacent business where he could watch the building's loading dock.

By 10:30, Hannah emerged through the rear door adjacent to

the loading doors. Joel flashed the car's headlights to alert Hannah.

"You're not going to believe what I've found out," Hannah said as she got into the car.

Joel had a questioning look, one prompting her to continue.

"I just need a few minutes to process…"

"No problem."

Joel drove them back to the hotel.

Once in the suite, Hannah was ready to tell him about her meeting with Myra, the revelations and the dilemma all three technicians were in. "I gave her my copy of the memo to prove to the others that Corbyn has a plan for them, and it's not a retirement plan."

Joel took out his mobile. "I'm going to call Simmons and fill him in. This business about Buchanan may be just the thing needed to get the FBI involved."

CHAPTER 55

Myra went back to the lab, but her mind was a million miles away. At first, she wasn't sure what to do with the memo. *How do I casually bring up the subject of our impending deaths?* She thought it was crazy. *In this modern world, who would do something so barbaric?* Her doubts prevented her from running straight to her teammates, George and Oliver.

After sitting on the explosive memo all day, she finally worked up the courage to talk with her colleagues. She waited until Dr. Hughes left the lab before calling them over. As they took chairs and pulled up to Myra's workbench, they sensed something was wrong.

"What is it, Myra?" Oliver asked.

She cleared her throat. "We're in trouble. Deep trouble."

George gave a startled look. "What do you mean?" He waved to encompass the room. "We have a first-class set up, and the development process is moving at a good pace."

"When we signed up to be on Corbyn's team, she spun a story of worldwide impact, of patents and licenses… I don't know about you, but I was dazzled."

George and Oliver nodded in agreement.

"But Corbyn didn't share key details with us, did she?" The pair had to admit that was so. "Despite that, we continued, blindly believing. I met someone yesterday, a woman. She's some kind of government agent. Somehow, she got into Robertson's room and found a thumb drive. She claimed the files on the drive were compromising and she shared one with me. I want to share it with you." She handed them the memo.

After reading the document, Oliver said, "This explains some things I've been wondering about."

George agreed. "This suggests our work is being corrupted."

"It's more than that," she said. "The nanites we're engineering are going to be used as *weapons*."

After initial expressions of shock, they moved to denial.

"No, no, no... that's not right," Oliver said. "This memo is probably a fake. Some competitor's way to get inside and steal this technology."

"I don't think so," she said. "The government woman knew all about Dr. Perry. When she investigated her death, the trail led to ASRI. She told me of attempts on her life. I think that may be why our operation was moved from the UK."

There was discussion, and as they worked through it, they ultimately came around to Myra's point of view.

"There's more, I'm afraid." She took a deep breath. "There's another player in this drama—Kurt Buchanan."

George and Oliver both recognized the name.

"You mean the Buchanan on the Board of Directors?" George asked.

"I don't need to go into detail, but he got his hooks into me years ago. Ever since getting this assignment, he's been pumping me for information about the project. I have a feeling it's Buchanan who wants this technology."

"Why would he want it?" George asked.

"I don't know if you're aware of the Buchanan history."

"They're a political family, right?" George asked.

"Yes, they are. They're powerful and well-connected. From what I hear, they're not shy about trading influence for other 'considerations.' Whatever they're up to, I can't believe it's for the good of mankind—or ASRI."

"What do we do?" There was desperation in George's question.

Myra looked up at the ceiling as if searching for an answer. It was her question, too. "We don't have enough information. Somehow, I need to meet with the government woman again. Meanwhile, we have to slow this process down. Give ourselves time."

"If our work slows, Robertson will know it."

"Then we'll have to be smart about it. Interfere with the data and results in a way that can be explained, or at least understood by Robertson."

"What about Dr. Hughes?" Oliver asked. "He won't be as easy to fool."

She thought on that. "He's also not a hands-on bioengineer like we all are. We'll need to couch the altered data in a way that will convince the good doctor that we're doing our best, and that we don't want to make mistakes."

With the group in agreement, all went back to their workstations.

———

Robertson had been scouting San Francisco's Tenderloin District to identify the best area to gather the first set of test subjects. Dr. Hughes called and reported that all systems were in place and were ready for a preliminary test. "If all goes as we hope," Hughes said, "we'll be able to go into full-scale testing."

Satisfied he'd located a rich hunting ground, Robertson put in a call to Reid.

"Ramp it up. Let's get ready for the first delivery."

When he returned to the facility and told Hughes that everything was now in motion, Hughes corrected him.

"Mr. Robertson, I think you're moving too quickly. I said we'd be ready *if* everything goes as we hope."

"What are you saying?"

"It's just in the last day or so, there've been some unexpected variances."

"What does that mean?"

"It's not catastrophic, so please don't panic. The process of going from a universal contamination to a target-specific contagion isn't like flipping a light switch. We're working at sub-microscopic levels, fusing mechanical and biological materials, and then giving them specific—and differing—tasks."

Robertson was long past being patient with these scientists. "I need you to tell me when we can begin."

Dr. Hughes hemmed and hawed and could give no answer.

"You have one week. Make it happen!"

Margaret Corbyn had set up her base of operations in what had been a boardroom. The room was enormous and meant to impress. Located on the top level, it occupied most of the floor. A wall of windows overlooked a lawn, and, in the distance, a wall of trees outlined the perimeter and shielded it from traffic beyond.

Inside the boardroom, there was a sense of contemporary elegance. The walls were paneled in walnut; lush carpeting covered the floor. A massive table of light oak was polished to a high sheen. Discreet ceiling lights bathed the table in pools of light in a procession that added to the drama of the setting. Dozens of expensive executive chairs sat in ordered rows like a palace guard.

As Robertson entered, he couldn't help but think, *It's a throne room, not a boardroom.*

A single chair was positioned at the end: the CEO's chair. It looked more like a royal seat than a chair. On the "throne" sat Margaret Corbyn, who was deep into something. Corbyn's attention shifted between a yellow pad and a large computer monitor that all but blocked her view of the massive table.

When he cleared his throat, Corbyn looked up, annoyance on her face.

"Callum," she said flatly. He interpreted her greeting as, *Why the hell are you disturbing me?*

"You wanted the first phase to begin tonight," he said. "I'm afraid we're not quite ready."

Corbyn sat back, pushing herself from the table. "You've come to explain this delay?"

"There are technicalities—Dr. Hughes could explain them better. In any event, they need more time. I gave him a week, then they must be ready to begin."

"That damn fool!" Corbyn said. "I'm always cleaning up after him. He also botched that business with Perry... what a mess!"

"I don't know what to say. As you've said yourself, this is cutting edge technology..."

"And you haven't exactly covered yourself in glory," Corbyn retorted. "That SIS woman has eluded you at every turn."

Stung by the accusation, he responded, "She's no longer a factor. The public exposure of her past got her drummed out of the SIS. She's no doubt licking her wounds somewhere private and more concerned with her own future than pursuing us." He paused to look out the windows. "Besides, how would she ever find us here?"

Corbyn glared at her partner. "You have one week. Five days. Make it happen."

CHAPTER 56

Shadow returned to work the next morning. He went directly to his area, checked the time—9:00 a.m.—and closed the door. "It's showtime!"

Sitting at his control console, he entered a string of command lines and hit *Enter*. Wavy chevron shapes appeared on the screen. The shapes moved left to right, disappearing from the screen and then returning.

He picked up the office phone and called Robertson to report the problem.

"What do you mean, 'there's a glitch?'" Robertson asked. Shadow couldn't decide if his tone was angry or suspicious—maybe both.

"I'm not sure what else to call it. I came in, logged into my workstation, and the screen just went crazy."

"I'll be right there." Robertson hung up; rather rudely, Shadow thought.

Moments later, Robertson barged into the computer control room and went directly to Shadow's workspace. Looking at the dancing chevrons, he asked, "Can you fix this?"

"By myself? No, I don't think so. This is going to take more expertise than I have."

"Fine. Don't worry about it, I'll call AT&T. It's their responsibility, after all."

With that, Robertson left.

That worked out better than I hoped.

The team had been prepared to intercept the call to AT&T. It was all part of the plan, of course. Earlier, they'd had a discussion about this very matter.

"How do we create a distraction that's large enough to get their attention but not destructive?" Shadow asked.

"If I can get back in and give a little snip to a wire or two," Davies said, "it should give us the excuse we need." He looked at Joel. "The problem's going to be making it look 'official.'"

"I've got you covered there," Joel said. "Our FBI friend, Agent Simmons, made an AT&T service van available for our use. We just need to pick it up."

"What about a hat, or shirt, or something?" Davies asked.

"That's part of the deal, too."

Joel looked over to Shadow. "What exactly do you need from Davies?"

"We need access to the lab's computer network. I can see it from upstairs, but I can't get in."

Joel looked pleased. "That hack could give us the tangible evidence we need to get the FBI mobilized. Can you do that, Davies?"

"Get me to the T3, and I'll send their entire feed not only up to Shadow but also back here to the hotel."

Davies pulled up to the building in the AT&T service van. He looked very official in his company shirt and ball cap. He even carried a clipboard. Shadow met him at the front doors and took him to Robertson.

"Did you show him the problem?" Robertson asked.

"Not yet," Shadow replied.

Davies handed Robertson the clipboard. "I'll need your authorization before beginning."

Robertson gave an annoyed look and signed the work order. "Do you know what the problem is?"

Davies took back the clipboard. "As I understand it, you're getting static instead of data."

Shadow agreed, "Yeah, nothing but static."

"I'll need to get to the server room," Davies said to Robertson.

"Take him back there," Robertson ordered Shadow. "And let me know when the job's done."

Davies and Shadow went across the main floor to a door that opened into a back hallway. "This is how Hannah got inside yesterday," Shadow said. Instead of turning right toward the loading dock, they went left. The hallway ended at a door. "This is it," Shadow said.

Beyond the door was a room. It was filled with racks of servers with flashing red, green, and amber LED lights. "This looks like the place," Davies said.

"I'll go back upstairs," Shadow said. "You can message me with your mobile."

Davies wasted no time getting to work. He located the T3 feed coming through the back wall. The line went into a splitter terminal, where bundles of lines led out to the server racks. "This looks like a straightforward job," Davies said to himself. "Now, to identify the lab feed…"

His had to be cautious as he probed. Any misstep, and the lab would be alerted. He began with a passive IP "sniffer," a device that reads IP addresses without interference. Once he'd located the lines leading to the lab servers, it was a simple process. He attached a series of small clips to each lead. The clips resembled tiny hair clips—the kind young girls wear as a hair accessory.

Once attached, the clips became operational. Small red lights signaled that the devices were active and transmitting both to Shadow upstairs and to their hotel setup.

When he finished the job, he re-bundled wires to conceal his installation. It wasn't exactly perfect—the tiny clips peeked out here and there—but standing back a few paces, he decided it was concealed enough.

Next, he found Shadow's glitch and disconnected it. "That should make everyone happy." He texted Shadow the job was done.

CHAPTER 57

Shadow returned from work in the early evening, grateful his week would soon be over and Turner would take over. Back in the suite, he found things were humming. Beyond the computer setup processing the data from Davies' hack, he was a little surprised to see something else. He soon understood what all the excitement was about.

"Shadow, you're back—and just in time," Hannah called out.

He went to the main console, where Davies and Joel were deep in a discussion. They hadn't noticed his return. Hannah came to his rescue.

"Hey, guys! Shadow's back."

They turned around, greeted him, and told him to pull up a chair.

"We were just having a discussion about information from Dr. Hughes' computer," Joel said.

"Yeah," Davies chimed in, "Hughes seems to be structuring a series of experiments to alter the nanites' programming. It seems his first attempt resulted in the nanites attacking the entire living being."

"Amy's notes said she was working on a treatment for certain brain traumas," Hannah said.

"That's where Hughes went wrong," Davies replied, "or maybe not, if he was trying to alter the technology to attack not heal. The death of your friend was proof of that. Now, it looks like they're trying to modify the nanites to accept different programming."

"What would be the purpose of that?" Shadow asked.

Davies looked between Hannah and Joel before responding, "The only reason I can see is to create a targeted bioweapon."

Everyone went silent, each playing out scenarios in their minds.

Hannah was the first to speak, "You're saying, once they've worked out the modification bugs, they can use the nanites to attack and kill an individual?"

"Yes," Davies said. "And here's the kicker: Once Corbyn has the biomechanical problems solved, she no longer needs the tech team—including Dr. Hughes. She'll be the sole source of supply for this weapon. Imagine taking an order to assassinate someone and then delivering a custom-made weapon that is undetectable, untraceable, and guaranteed one hundred percent effective.

"And from what I can see, the modification process can include entire groups or ethnicities. It only takes a slight alteration of the basic programming."

"This is unbelievable," Hannah said. "We have to stop this—stop it now."

Joel stepped in, "Easier said than done. We can't get the FBI involved until something tangible happens."

"What does that mean?" Hannah asked.

"I don't know… maybe a series of new deaths."

"Didn't you say the security man, Robertson, was making regular trips into San Francisco?"

"Yes. Usually, three or four times a week."

"Why is he going into the city? I can't believe he's just going to museums like some tourist." Hannah was angry. "To hell with the FBI! We've got to put a stop to this."

"She's right," Davies said.

Joel looked to Shadow. "What do you think?"

"I say we go."

Joel stood. "Then let's make a plan of attack."

Hannah spent the day going through documents copied from Robertson's USB drive. Beyond the memo she'd shared with Myra, there was more. She called Joel over. "Look at this…"

Joel peered over her shoulder. "Looks like a GanttPRO chart. The grid's set up with task headings and dates."

She tapped on the keyboard. "Let me show you… Going down the left, the Y axis, are a series of task identifiers. Along the top, the X axis, are threshold or task completion markers." She clicked on one of the tasks. It opened a drop-down list of previously hidden lines, each with its own heading. Some were names of people, but most were algebraic entries.

"If you follow the flow lines across the X axis, you'll see very specific deliverables and completion dates. This one has to do with production elements. I take that to mean the nanites."

"This whole thing is a roadmap—to what?" Joel asked.

"I'm not sure," she said, "but it's clear Corbyn has been working on this a long time."

"What about Myra and the others?"

"They show up a little farther down. From what I can gather, when Corbyn reached the goal of theoretical possibility, she needed help. That's when she recruited Myra, Oliver, and George."

"What about the doctor?"

"It looks like he was in on this almost from the beginning. While he is a skilled physician, the rigors of microbiology and nanotechnology are beyond him. Corbyn needed specialized help." She clicked on another file.

"There's more. This is some sort of diary or logbook. Corbyn entered all manner of events and contacts, but the interesting part begins about the time of Amy Perry's death. She talks about Robertson's hiring two former London policemen, Walters and Smith. They were the ones who came to my flat. They were convincing, and I guess I wasn't expecting subterfuge from the London Police. When I investigated the following day, it turned out they were phonies, as were the EMTs that took Amy's body.

"Here's another entry. This time it's about Robertson breaking into my flat. Curiously, here he tells Corbyn his belief there was no connection between Amy and myself. That, of course, wasn't true. He just assumed there was no way a white woman and an Arab woman would ever intersect, much less become friends.

"Corbyn finally realizes that Amy and I were friends. Her big shock was finding out that I was a SIS agent. That's when she went on a drive to eliminate me. But get this: After my humiliating exposure and subsequent dismissal from SIS, she seems to have decided I'm no longer a threat, a belief shared by Robertson."

"Is that all there is?" Joel asked.

"Not by a long shot. It's just that I'm no longer the focus of their attention." Closing the GanttPRO document, she opened another file.

"This is a series of memos to Corbyn from Robertson. He talks about contacting someone named Reid. It seems they were in the Army together. Now Reid runs a security consulting firm."

"That can mean only one thing," Joel said. "Gun for hire—a mercenary."

"It certainly seems that way. Looks like he had Corbyn authorize a healthy payment to Reid. Once that was in place, Reid was ready to go to work."

"And what, exactly, is that work?"

"Unspecified. Robertson talks about *orders to come*."

"What about that original memo, the one indicating the three technicians were going to be eliminated?"

"That's here, in another memo. Robertson outlines how the doctor and the other three are to be dealt with."

"Hold on," Joel said. "They can't afford to get rid of the technical staff while they're still working."

"That's right. There's a status quo that will tip decidedly against the three and the doctor once they've completed their job."

"And what is their job?" Joel asked.

"To duplicate and differentiate the nanites. Once that's accomplished, their usefulness ends."

Joel understood. "They can't let them live—they know too much... We've got to get those people out of there."

———

Joel got busy on the phone with Agent Simmons, explaining they'd found Corbyn's master plan. Hannah was huddled with Davies and Shadow, discussing their infiltration plans.

"I sneak in tomorrow and try to talk with Myra again," Hannah said.

"Do you think she took you seriously?" Davies asked.

"She was visibly shaken when I left her... Yes, she understands the seriousness of the situation. Whether or not she's taken any action, like telling her colleagues, I can't know. That's what I need to find out."

Shadow jumped in, "I've been in there every day this week,

and I can tell you that there seems to be a slow-down in the work coming out of the lab."

"Is that normal?" Hannah asked.

"I'm not sure what normal is. I've only been there a week. But looking at the electronic activity on Monday and then again yesterday, something's happening. What do you think that means?"

Hannah thought for a moment. "I think Myra's behind it. And it must be to slow down Robertson's schedule to collect subjects."

"Can you confirm that?" Joel asked.

"Not until I get back there," she said. "Shadow, how about you? Can you get any more information about what's happening in the lab?"

"I'll try," Shadow said.

"Meanwhile," she said, "let's lay out a strategy to stop this before these nanites get loose and do who-knows-how-much damage."

They continued their brainstorming. In the end, the results were inconclusive. There were too many variables they couldn't predict or control. It came down to waiting until test subjects were brought in.

Hannah spun her laptop around for all to see. "The project management software shows almost all milestones have been reached and sub-tasks accomplished. It also indicates the 'proof event,' as it's called, will follow immediately upon completion of the objective—a viable colony of nanites, differentiated and ready to test."

CHAPTER 58

Myra received a summons from Corbyn, ordering her to report to the boardroom on the third floor. She couldn't imagine what Corbyn wanted or what was wrong. She was very nervous.

Knocking quietly and then entering the boardroom timidly, she looked down the long room and was even more intimidated. It was a long walk to Corbyn's place at the head of the huge table. It made her feel like she was approaching a monarch on a throne.

As she came within a few feet of Corbyn, the director looked up as if noticing her for the first time. "Aah, Myra, take a seat."

Pulling a chair from the table, she sat, her hands clasped in her lap. "You asked for me?"

Corbyn pulled off her oversized glasses and placed them on the table. "I'll get right to it. I've known about your connection to the Buchanans from the beginning. In fact, that's why I recruited you for my team. Clearly, you'd been compromised somewhere in the past, something that put you under the Buchanans' control."

"I—you don't understand—" Myra stumbled, trying to explain.

"Quiet! I don't like interruptions. Knowing the Buchanans had you under their thumb meant I could actually trust you to be circumspect about my project. When I received a recommendation from Kurt Buchanan to include you on my special project team, I knew he was putting a spy in my camp, but I also knew I could make it work to my advantage.

"I've intercepted your various communications... No, don't try to deny it. You were using the Dark Web—so was I. I even know about your little meeting with Buchanan at the family compound. I don't imagine you had much to tell Mr. Buchanan. But now, it's time to use your connection to get what I want.

"You are to contact Mr. Buchanan and tell him I wish to meet with him personally. Tell him I have a proposal that I believe will be of interest to him and his father."

Myra looked at Corbyn wide-eyed, stunned that she knew all about her arrangement with Kurt Buchanan.

"Well, what do you say, girl?"

"Yes, ma'am. I'll send the message."

Corbyn watched Myra leave the boardroom, satisfied she'd played her card at just the right time. The proof of concept would take place within days, and the way she saw it was the perfect opportunity to turn Kurt Buchanan from an adversary to an ally.

She called Robertson to the boardroom. Minutes later, he entered and stood before her.

"Callum, we're going to institute the parallel part of our plan. I'm going to meet with Kurt Buchanan."

"Is that a good idea?" Robertson asked.

"Yes. It's time we get the Buchanans on board. We can't complete our task without them. As a matter of fact, I've been planning on using them from the beginning. Once we have a viable product, who better to sell it to than Kurt and his father?"

"How will you do that?"

"I've just dispatched their spy, Myra, to set up a meeting."

"They'll be surprised to know we weren't fooled by Myra's placement on the team," Robertson said.

"All the more reason for Kurt Buchanan to accept a meeting."

"What part do you want me to play?" Robertson asked.

"I want you to go with me for protection, just in case."

CHAPTER 59

Instead of returning to the lab, Myra went to her quarters. She sat on the edge of the bed, not knowing what to do. She'd been blindsided by Corbyn's revelation that she knew of her spy duties for Kurt Buchanan. She was surprised when Corbyn took no disciplinary action, instead asking her to send a message.

She was trapped and she knew it. She'd been found out and now turned into a counter-spy. It felt dirty. After wringing her hands and arguing with herself, she came to the only decision possible: she would have to tell Mr. Buchanan she'd been discovered. She would also have to deliver Corbyn's request for a meeting.

Tor was her only means of communication, so she composed a concise message:

Corbyn discovered my connection to you.
She asks for a meeting—one she says will be of interest to you and your father.
Corbyn awaits your response.

Touching the send button, she hoped she wasn't signing her death warrant.

Kurt Buchanan's operative, Ed Pearson, had been delivering regular reports on Corbyn and her movements. Since her arrival at the San Mateo building, she hadn't emerged. Buchanan was annoyed by the lack of progress. Until now.

> **The security man, Robertson, continues his regular trips to the city.**
> **We followed him today and found he's cruising the Tenderloin District,**
> **apparently interested in out-of-the-way alleys and abandoned buildings.**
> **Objective is unclear.**
> **Next report: tomorrow, 5:00 PM.**

Kurt Buchanan knew what Robertson was doing. *He's looking for places to find, or hold, subjects. It can't be too hard in that sea of derelicts.*

He thought the project must be coming to a head. *It's gonna be time to move.* He thought it best to contact his father and let him know.

That afternoon, Kurt received a Tor message from Myra Shipman.

So, Corbyn's discovered my spy. It had to happen sooner or later, but what's this? She wants to meet... How interesting. I need to think about this.

The next day, he sent a Tor message back, setting the time and place.

I'm interested to hear what she thinks will be so appealing to us.

The next day, Myra performed her usual tasks, but her co-workers noticed she kept checking her phone for messages. A little after noon, George Kraft came to her station.

"Is everything okay?"

She looked at George, blinked twice to hold back the tears, and shook her head.

"What is it?"

Before Myra could respond, her mobile dinged. She looked at the screen and then to George. "I'm sorry, I need to take this."

George shrugged and went back to his station while she stepped out of the lab.

The protocol for contacting Kurt Buchanan meant she had to first access the Dark Web and then get the Tor message. She went to her room where she could use her laptop to retrieve her message.

Sitting on the bed with her laptop, she soon had it pulled up. She let out a sigh of relief. Kurt Buchanan had accepted Corbyn's invitation. She immediately sent a regular text message to Corbyn.

Kurt Buchanan has agreed to meet with you.
He suggests his compound in Hillsborough, tomorrow
at 10:00 a.m.

Myra placed the laptop on the bed and paced as she waited for Corbyn's reply. Ten minutes later, the response came:

Agreed. We will be there at ten o'clock.

As she sent Corbyn's reply back to Kurt Buchanan, she wondered who "we" might be. *Certainly not me.* Completing the transmission, she closed her laptop and thought more about who Corbyn would take to the meeting. *Could it be someone from corporate?* That made no sense. As far as she could tell, Corbyn was keeping knowledge of this project far away from ASRI. *Unless she has someone there—someone watching her back.* That was a valid thought, except the more she thought about it, the less likely it seemed. After all, Corbyn was meeting with a board member.

Unable to come to a satisfactory solution, she put it out of her mind and returned to the lab.

CHAPTER 60

Dr. Hughes was habitually standoffish with Myra and the others. It wasn't that they were bad people; he just considered them beneath him. *After all, I'm a medical doctor with decades of training and experience. They're just glorified mechanics with master's degrees.*

He did have to acknowledge the tech team was doing exceptional work. He smirked. *They think they're working toward life-changing medical cures. If they only knew...* He stopped his musings when one of the computers in his area emitted a soft *ding. Ahhh... it looks like the analysis is complete.*

Keying the computer, he inspected the data. His brows furrowed, and his mouth turned down. "This isn't right," he said aloud. He swung around to look across the room at the technicians. They were all huddled over at their workstations. Inspecting the data more closely, he could see there had been progress, but in certain areas where he expected to see results, it was simply blank. He went over to the technicians.

"All of you! Your attention, please..."

The technicians, startled by his loud order in the normally quiet lab, turned, questions in each of their gazes.

"There are holes in the data. Why? Don't you realize we can't move on to the next phase without complete data?"

Oliver looked at the other two. Hughes could see sheepish looks on their faces. He began to suspect these people were hiding something.

"I'm sorry, Dr. Hughes," Oliver said. "To what data are you referring?"

"The points of functionalized nanomagnetics. They are either incomplete or devoid of data altogether. How do you expect the nanorobots to function as planned? Why is this data missing?"

Oliver again looked at his colleagues. "We've encountered some difficulties. Out of caution, we slowed down."

Exasperated, Hughes glared at the technicians. "Damn your caution. Go back and complete the work right now. We must have fully functioning nanorobots by Friday."

With that declaration, he walked away. He didn't see the defeated look on the technicians' faces.

"What do we do?" Oliver whispered to the others.

George could only shake his head and mutter, "This can't be happening..."

"We're caught in the middle," Myra said.

"And we're going to be killed," Oliver added.

Myra had an idea. Speaking softly, she said, "Hughes has given us a forty-eight-hour reprieve. Let's go back to work and begin filling in some of the gaps, but only some. Tomorrow, I'll find our pseudo-cleaning lady and ask for help."

"How can she help?" George asked, almost whining.

"She's somehow wired in here. She also said she has a team."

"Can we trust her?" Oliver asked.

"What choice do we have?" Myra said. "If we don't do what

Hughes asks, we'll be killed. If we do give him what he wants, we'll still be killed."

Oliver and George looked stricken, like small animals caught in a trap.

"There's only one way out of this," she said. "That woman and her team."

CHAPTER 61

Corbyn marveled at the wealth displayed in Hillsborough. It was neither gaudy nor garish like Beverly Hills. Here, the homes were understated yet elegant. All the homes bespoke wealth and power. *This is a place I deserve to live...* Passing home after beautiful home, her thoughts twisted into intense coveting. *How did these people get here? What have they done to deserve such luxury? I deserve this, too!* She looked at Robertson, knowing he'd never understand. *Very soon, I will have it. This meeting will set me on a course to untold riches.*

These thoughts kept her mind occupied as they drove on, finally reaching the Buchanan compound. When she saw the gate and the long drive up to a massive estate house, her yearning turned to intense desire. *This is what I'm talking about.*

Pulling into the porte cochère, they were met by an older man, clearly a servant, who escorted them inside.

"Mr. Buchanan is waiting for you in the drawing room," the elderly man said, extending his arm toward a door.

Corbyn was uncharacteristically nervous as she rapped on the door before opening it. *What's wrong with me? I called this meet-*

ing. I'm in charge, not him. Robertson entered first, scanning for threats.

Seated comfortably on a leather couch, Kurt Buchanan stood and motioned his guests to sit on the couch opposite. Corbyn took a seat, but Robertson remained standing behind her. Sitting back down, Buchanan said nothing. Corbyn knew this psychological technique. Her initial nervousness disappeared and was replaced by stern resolve.

"Mr. Buchanan. I know you're aware of my 'project.' I've come to brief you more fully than your spy ever could." She paused to watch his reaction. There was a hint of surprise.

"Go on, I'm listening."

"I have developed a means to target individuals, or groups of people, in a way that is undetectable and untraceable."

"Target? What do you mean?"

"Assassination… elimination… purging… Whatever is desired."

Kurt was quiet for a long time, thinking.

———

Kurt Buchanan couldn't believe what he was hearing. As he considered the implications of what Corbyn was not only confirming but expanding on, his thoughts went first to his father and their initial interest in this cutting edge tech.

If what she says is true, how many enemies could be eliminated with this technology? My God! Even whole nations could be subjugated or blackmailed into cooperation, not just pesky individuals. Dad needs to be updated and brought into this fully before I can make any commitments.

———

Corbyn watched carefully as Buchanan churned through the possibilities. After a time, he looked her in the eye. "I'll need to know more about your technology."

She had him!

"I'll provide more details once we've reached an agreement."

"What is it you propose?" Buchanan asked.

"A partnership. I provide the product you provide the distribution."

A wry smile came over Buchanan's face. "Before we can fully agree, I'll need to see a demonstration."

"That's what I've been working toward. I can give you a proof of concept on Saturday. When you see the awesome power and potential, I'm sure you'll agree to my proposal." Standing to leave, she turned back. "One more thing, Mr. Buchanan. No one is to know about Saturday, especially nobody within ASRI."

CHAPTER 62

It was late evening. Myra dropped onto her bed, exhausted. Dr. Hughes had been pushing them, and it was getting harder to slow things down. They had to show something for all the effort being put in. She felt they were in a losing battle. She was anxious to talk with Hannah again, but the cleaning crew wasn't scheduled for work until the next day. It would just have to wait.

As she lay there, a chirping sound came from her laptop sitting on the small side table next to the bed. With a heavy sigh, she rolled over. She knew what the sound was—her computer announcing a new message. Opening the messages app, she saw only numbers listed as the sender. *It's probably junk mail.*

Tapping the app icon, she found it was an encrypted message. She knew what that meant... *Kurt Buchanan.* The message was a link. She tapped on the link and was taken to a Dark Web message board. This was the only way Buchanan would communicate. He was paranoid about being tracked.

Buchanan's message, in its decrypted form, asked her when the trials were to begin. She hesitated before replying. *Do I tell him? If I don't, what will he do?* She knew the answer to her question. *He'll expose my background and have me fired.*

With a heavy heart, she sat on the end of the bed and sent her response.

Final formulation will be complete by Saturday. First test subjects to be delivered that night.

Despite exhaustion, she was unable to go to sleep for a long time. She sensed a conflict was coming.

Kurt Buchanan smiled as he read Myra's reply. "This confirms what Corbyn said." He made an initial report to his father. It was important to keep him in the loop. "Dad, I think you'll agree this is going to be the most lucrative arrangement ever." He explained the meeting with Corbyn, and that he'd garnered confirmation over their earlier speculation, that she claims to have developed a new technology that could be programmed to target individuals or even groups of people.

Senator Jack Buchanan didn't respond immediately. He, too, was digesting the growing implications. "Are you saying this technology can be used more like a terror weapon, not just on an individual basis?"

"It is my understanding that it can," Kurt replied. "And Corbyn claims it's undetectable. Imagine how many people who are in our way could be silently eliminated..."

"No, with this new information, you're thinking too small, son. We need to have a more global view. Let me make some discreet inquiries... political leaders, military commanders, and the like. Before getting ourselves in too deep, we need to know if there is a market."

"Corbyn is giving me a demonstration on Saturday. Would you like to be there?"

"Absolutely not! I need to maintain my distance. I'll rely on you to report back."

Next, Kurt contacted Ed Pearson and informed him the surveillance service was no longer needed. He agreed to pay through the end of the week.

CHAPTER 63

Friday morning came, and Hannah/Kimberly reported for work. She waited at the loading dock door with the rest of the crew. Shadow was already in place, having arrived a half hour earlier. It was a comfort to know an ally was in the building.

Before leaving the hotel, she asked Shadow to ping Myra's phone and ask for a meeting. As the cleaning crew split up to go to their assigned tasks, she made sure to begin in the lab area. As she passed through, she saw that virtually all the cube rooms had been covered in heavy plastic. *It looks like they're ready to go.*

Thirty minutes passed with no activity at the lab door. *I wonder if Shadow got the message to her?* She was worried her standing around on the main floor would be noticed. *I guess I'll have to go to my other assignment.*

As she collected her cleaning supplies in preparation to move on, the lab door opened. It was Myra.

Hannah moved to the room they'd used previously and waited. In a few moments, Myra entered. She saw distress on Myra's face, combined with relief at seeing her.

"I got your message," Myra said.

Hannah moved them out of view from the narrow door window. "I have news for you, but it seems you have something to tell me."

Myra told of their plan to slow down the data, but it was discovered by Dr. Hughes. "Oliver did some quick thinking and fast talking to appease Hughes. It worked, but only temporarily. We have a deadline today to complete the narocomposites for the field tests. Also, I had to tell Kurt Buchanan."

Hannah was startled by the mention of Buchanan, but she'd save that for a discussion with her team.

"It sounds like this first test is going down tomorrow," she said.

Myra nodded. "Yes, and we don't know what to do. The others are sitting on pins and needles."

"How will the field test be conducted?"

"Robertson is going to bring in a number of subjects tomorrow. I'm not sure how many."

Hannah thought for a moment. "You must complete the last phase of the project. But I want you all to be on alert."

That night, Joel's team assembled in the hotel suite. Hannah led the discussion, "Myra tells me they've been ordered to complete their work by tonight. Corbyn will begin the field test tomorrow."

"Do you know what time?" Joel asked.

"I'm afraid not. But if I had to guess, it would make sense to do it under the cover of darkness."

"When no one can see what they're up to," Davies said.

Joel rubbed his chin in thought. "Unless we can establish some legal precedent like kidnapping, there's no way to activate the FBI. We're going to have to be content to watch and listen."

"There's another wrinkle in this," Hannah said. "Kurt Buchanan has been alerted as well. It seems Corbyn has come to some sort of arrangement. I'd guess Buchanan will be in attendance for whatever Corbyn is planning."

"You can bet it won't be legal, whatever it is," Davies said.

CHAPTER 64

The three technicians were frantically putting the finishing touches on the functionalized nanomagnets. This was the last step in preparation for the composite nanorobots. Once complete, the nanites would be ready for introduction into a human host. Dr. Hughes was pacing.

"Hurry it up! The test subjects are on their way."

Myra, not turning from the task at hand, gave a sharp reply, "One moment, please!"

Oliver took a dozen storage containers into the chamber, then exited. A window on the chamber room wall allowed the others to observe as Myra manipulated the hand controls. A mechanical claw moved to a spigot. Above the valve was a small screen indicating which strain of nanocomposites was to be dispensed. The mechanical claw moved a stainless-steel container and placed it beneath the spigot. Myra opened the canister and poured a cloud into the container. After ten seconds, she closed it and placed the tightly sealed container on a rack in the sealed room.

"One down," Myra announced. From the control panel, Oliver selected the next strain.

The process of preparing the nano-cylinders was repeated until all twelve containers were ready to go. Dr. Hughes stepped forward. "Everyone, stay here. I'll collect them." The three technicians gave him looks that were eloquent of disdain.

Inside the chamber, Hughes took a black plastic tray, the type used in grocery stores to hold quart bottles of soft drinks. With the containers in place, Hughes left the chamber.

No sooner was Hughes out of the chamber than the lab door opened. It was Robertson. The technicians all took a small step back. Even though Robertson had never directly threatened any of them, they still had an irrational fear of the security man.

Dr. Hughes had no such reaction. Instead, he stepped up to Robertson. "We're ready to go." The three technicians noted a tone of triumph in Hughes' voice.

Robertson said nothing, motioning for the three to stay where they were.

Reid received Robertson's "go" signal. He sent his team of four to scout the selected alleys and derelict buildings. The orders were to select a sampling of two types: male and female. Reid's team had no trouble finding and subduing a dozen subjects. Most were already passed out or in a drug-induced stupor.

One by one, Reid's team half-carried, half-dragged the drunks and addicts to the waiting trailer. When they reached their quota, Reid said, "That's it for tonight."

One of his team asked, "What exactly are these people for?"

"Some kind of experiment," Reid responded. Then he wondered, "Why is it so secret?"

It was well after midnight when Reid backed the twenty-four-foot trailer up to the loading dock. Robertson was there, waiting. When the trailer's lift gate opened, Robertson noted inert bodies laid out on the trailer floor, like a haul of fish on a trawler's deck.

"Okay, we're in business," he said to Reid.

Reid's crew went to work, carrying the homeless to the loading dock floor. Each "participant" was marked with a number on the left hand. Reid paid attention to the surroundings and again wondered what this was all about.

"I count twelve," Robertson confirmed to Reid. "Leave the truck and trailer. You and your team come inside."

Kurt Buchanan had been notified by Corbyn and arrived at precisely midnight. Robertson met him at the door and escorted him to a prepared waiting area.

"If you wouldn't mind waiting here," Robertson said, "we'll come for you when the subjects are in place. Meanwhile, may I offer you anything?"

"A scotch on the rocks would be good," he said.

"Sorry, we don't have any alcohol in the facility."

"Nothing then. How long will I have to wait?"

Robertson checked his watch. "Not long. The subjects will be delivered soon. When they get here, we'll need to prep them and get ready for the demonstration. Say, fifteen or twenty minutes."

"I don't want to sit around here. Let's go down to the lab and wait."

There was some uncomfortable hemming and hawing, but Robertson agreed, "As you wish. Please follow me."

CHAPTER 65

The team huddled around Shadow, everyone watching the security camera feeds from Corbyn's facility. There was activity in the loading dock.

They watched Robertson activate one of the overhead doors and imagined the sound of rumbling as it opened. When the door reached its full, open position, a trailer backed up to the loading door. Four men got out of the truck, one of them jumping up to the dock and throwing the truck door's lever. They couldn't see inside the trailer, but soon, the other men started carrying out bodies.

"The subjects!" Hannah exclaimed.

"Are they dead?" Shadow asked.

"No," Hannah replied. "The protocol calls for live subjects. My guess is they're drugged."

They watched as the men from the truck finished unloading. "Twelve in all," Joel said. "What happens now?"

None had an answer.

Robertson left and returned with another man. "Definitely not one of the techs," Davies said. "He looks like a suit to me."

"And Corbyn's making nice," Hannah said.

Joel asked, "Is there audio with this feed?"

"Sorry, no. Just video," Shadow replied.

The loading dock door was closed, and Robertson gave orders to the men who offloaded the subjects. They split into teams of two and began moving the inert bodies to the main floor area. The man in the suit stood to one side with Corbyn.

"It looks like the subjects are evenly divided into male and female," Davies said.

"Where are they taking them?" Joel asked.

Shadow tapped on his keyboard and the scene changed. They were no longer looking at the loading dock but the main floor.

"They've sure done a lot of building in there," Joel said. "Can you zoom and pan with this camera?"

"Yes," Shadow said. "These were originally set up to survey the entire floor." Shadow used the up and down arrows on the keyboard to demonstrate.

It didn't take long to place each of the subjects into individual cubes. "The good news," Shadow said, "is that those cubes are encased in plastic. The bad news is, the plastic is thick and opaque, so we can only see forms inside."

Joel grew confused. "Why one to a cube? They look like they could hold many more."

"It makes sense," Hannah replied. "This is meant to test and validate the process. If the nanites are programmed to infect just one individual or one group, this is a good way to start. When you look at the total capacity in there, it's clear Corbyn plans to expand the experiment."

Davies leaned over Shadow's shoulder. "Look! Corbyn and the suit are going into the lab room."

"Unfortunately," Shadow said, "there aren't any cameras in there."

"I guess we wait and see what happens," Joel said.

Robertson took charge of the subjects. Calling over Reid's men, he gave orders to carry each to a separate cube. When they were placed, Robertson made sure each door was properly sealed and bolted.

"I'm going into the lab," Robertson said. "You can return to the truck." He addressed Reid: "You *do* remember the way to the crematorium…"

Reed was seeing his old commander in an entirely new light. During the war, Robertson looked out for his men. Now, he seemed to think they were his slaves. *There's more going on here…* He looked again at the people inert on the floor of the cubes. *I'd say they're into something at least unethical and, at worst, illegal. I wonder if there's more to get out of this.*

Inside the lab room, Kurt Buchanan and Margaret Corbyn waited. Dr. Hughes and the lab workers stood off to one side.

Dr. Hughes stepped forward. "Now that we're all here, I'll start placing the canisters. Myra, you can help me. You two," he said to Buoy and Kraft, "start the exposure sequence." The technicians went to their workstations and began entering computer commands.

Dr. Hughes came into the lab carrying the first canister in both hands as if it were a newborn child. "Get the door for me," he ordered Myra. She followed him out to the main floor where he placed the canister vertically on the floor next to one cube. Hughes took a ribbed hose that was affixed to a port cut into the plastic wall and screwed it onto a receptacle on the canister top. Myra checked for leaks with a handheld device. Hughes was satisfied the installation was correct.

Myra saw motion from inside the cubes and said something about it. Hughes was untroubled. "They're just waking up,"

Hughes said. "Besides, it's important that they be conscious for the test."

The process was repeated eleven more times.

With the placement of the last canister, Corbyn and Buchanan emerged from the lab. They stood in a position that allowed them to observe the twelve occupied cubes.

"There's movement in there," Buchanan said.

"It's all planned," Corbyn said. "The subjects must be conscious for the test." She gave a hand signal, and Hughes went down the line, opening the valve on each of the cylinders. When the task was complete, Hughes turned to Corbyn and gave a thumbs-up.

"Now, Mr. Buchanan, observe… and be amazed."

CHAPTER 66

Inside the first cube, a man began stirring. Sitting up groggily, he surveyed his surroundings. "What the hell is this?" He tried to stand but was unable to get his balance and collapsed back on the floor. He looked at the opaque walls surrounding him. Scrambling over, he touched the odd-looking wall. It gave slightly.

In his drugged state it was difficult to concentrate. That was the point of taking heroin—to make you feel like you're floating. In this state, the man was unable to reason or evaluate. He could only sit and look around.

There was movement in the next cube, although the opaque wall made it look like a ghost image. He called out, "Hey! You there! Can you hear me?"

The figure moved around and, like himself, seemed unable to stand.

"I said, can you hear me?"

The figure managed to reach a sitting position. "Hey, talk to me."

The ghostly figure moved slowly, trying to stand, but then slumped back onto the floor. He watched the figure look around.

Must be tryin' to figure where we are. There was a scream. *A woman!* The man clapped his hands over his ears.

The woman stopped as suddenly as she'd started. Now, she whimpered.

"I don't know what the hell is going on, but it looks like we're in for the full ride," the man said.

He noticed a shadowed figure outside approach his cube, kneel down, doing... something. "Hey! You! Where are we? What do you want?"

There was no response. The person outside completed whatever they were doing and moved on to the next cube, the one with the woman. He listened to her call out to the outsider, just as he had. Again, there was no response. The figure just finished whatever it was they were doing and moved on; he assumed to another enclosure like his own.

Through his drug-induced stupor, the man heard something. "Sounds like hissin'." He still couldn't stand, but he began looking around for the source of the sound. Looking up at the ceiling, he expected to find a hole or tear, but there was nothing. Gazing around, he tried to get a fix on the source of the sound. He bent all his diminished concentration on listening.

"Sounds like it's over there..." He pulled himself to one wall. "Gettin' louder." Sliding up to the plastic wall, at first, he saw nothing, but the sound was louder. Then he saw it: a small patch with a hole. "That's where it's comin' from." He poked an index finger into the hole. It began squelching and he quickly pulled his finger out, inspecting the digit for damage. The move was soon followed by a light mist.

He decided the finger was no worse for the wear. Leaning down to get a closer look, he saw through the plastic wall that there was a hose of some sort attached to a small canister on the other side. Pulling back, he puzzled over what it all meant.

Then he suddenly felt strange. His breathing became labored. He began wheezing with each breath.

The man leaned back, pushing with his feet like he was pedaling a bicycle in an attempt to get away from the mist now filling the room. Wrapping his knees in his arms, he began to whimper, "What's happening to me?"

Each breath was more difficult than the last.

He tried desperately to get up and escape, but his legs still wouldn't respond. All he could do was drag himself to what looked like a doorway.

He almost made it.

By this time, the mist had filled the space, making breathing almost impossible. With a final gasp, the man dropped his chin to his chest and died.

Kurt Buchanan was riveted by what he was witnessing. The person in the first cube moved around, but as the canister filled the cube with a light mist, he slowed and eventually stopped all movement. Turning to Corbyn, he asked, "Is that one dead?"

"Yes," Corbyn replied. "And in under one minute."

"Have you developed your technology into some kind of nerve gas?

"No. It's completely different. It's a biological construct that we've programmed to attack certain portions of the brain and lymphatic system. Completely undetectable, as I mentioned before. Look... the others are succumbing as well."

Kurt looked down the line of cubes, where all of the occupants dropped, one by one. All except the last two. They were moving around, shouting, and looking totally unaffected. "What about them?"

"That's our control. You see, one is male, the other female.

We made our programming for this test specific to gender. The man is getting the female dose, and vice versa."

"There seems to be no effect," Kurt said.

"Just watch." Corbyn motioned to the doctor who went to cubes eleven and twelve, unhooked each, and swapped canisters. Within a minute, the last two dropped into lifeless heaps.

"I'd say this has been a successful demonstration, wouldn't you?"

Kurt was having a hard time digesting what he'd just witnessed. "You're telling me you've truly programmed your nanites to infect and kill *only* certain people?"

"That's correct. We're going to run a more extensive test tomorrow night. You're welcome to watch."

"I've seen enough. I'll be contacting my father to get this deal rolling."

"While you're doing that, I'm going to need some seed money to begin full production."

"How much seed money?" Kurt asked with a note of suspicion.

"I've got a full budget worked out. Come up to my office and I'll give it to you."

Kurt looked at the cubes. "What about them? How will you dispose of the bodies?"

"Don't worry about that," Corbyn said. "That detail has been handled."

As Corbyn escorted Kurt Buchanan to her boardroom office, Robertson returned to the loading dock and lifted the overhead door. Reid and the others were lounging outside, smoking and talking in low tones. As the door came up, Reid approached Robertson.

"Are you done already?" Reid asked.

"Gather your men," Robertson said. "We need to get the bodies loaded and out of here as quickly as possible."

With a sharp whistle, the men were summoned and gathered around Reid. After giving a few short orders, they followed Robertson through the loading dock.

In ten minutes, the bodies had all been loaded back onto the trailer. Before closing it up, Robertson looked in. Unlike the arrival where the subjects had been laid out more or less orderly, they were now piled in stacks on shipping pallets.

"You know where to go?" Robertson asked.

"You told me a dozen times. We take the 92 to 880 past Emeryville. I've got the address for the cremation facility here in the GPS."

"Here's tonight's payment," Robertson said, handing Reid a thick envelope. "There'll be a man waiting for you. He's a City Cremation employee. Give him the envelope."

"Any message you want me to give?" Reid asked.

"Tell him there'll be another shipment tomorrow."

The truck and trailer departed. In Hayward, they pulled up to a free-standing single-story brick building. A number of pipes extended perhaps ten feet up from the roof and marched down the length of the building. Reid figured the pipes were for cremation oven exhaust.

There were no other buildings in the area. There were some in the distance, but for the most part, the crematory was isolated. Reid thought it a good thing.

"Pull around back," Reid ordered as they approached the building. In the rear, they found a loading dock. A single light hung from a metal fixture. It provided no real illumination, only a pool of weak light. A man sat on a metal folding chair in the light and stood as the truck came to a stop. The man was middle-aged, significantly overweight, and dressed in a cheap, outdated suit.

The man gave a few instructions and the trailer backed up to the dock. Once in place, Reid opened the trailer's rear door.

"You ready for us?" Reid asked the crematory man.

"You got my money?"

Reid handed him the envelope. The man opened it greedily and fanned out the bills. "Wait right here."

A moment later, the overhead door lifted, and Reid went inside. The crematory man stood next to a small forklift. "Can you operate one of these?"

Reid nodded and looked at the power cable connected to the forklift. *Electric, not gas. That's unusual.* "Unplug me, please."

The man pulled the cable from the forklift chassis. "You're good to go."

Reid aimed the forks expertly and scooped up the first pallet. Looking down at the crematory man, he asked, "Where to?"

"Follow me," the man said and walked down a wide hallway.

Reid followed with the loaded forklift until they came to a wide hall lined with cremation ovens. He counted ten ovens. "How many to an oven?"

The man scratched his head in thought. "These are large capacity. They'll hold about two dozen. We use these mostly for indigents we pick up. The individual ovens are farther down. You can tell them by the smaller doors."

"We'll only need one oven tonight," Reid said. He dropped the pallet and returned to pick up the second. His men returned with him.

The crematory man opened the large NTD impermeable oven door, and Reid's men loaded the bodies onto the sliding tray. It was an untidy pile of bodies. The heavy door was closed, and the crematory man pushed a large red button.

"You can stay if you like," he offered Reid and his men. Just then, a *woosh* came from deep within the chamber. "That's the ignition. This will take about four hours."

"We'll watch for a few minutes. Make certain all is going as it should."

When the team left, Reid stopped them. "I'm starting to think this whole thing is a little fishy. I also think there's a lot of money in whatever Robertson and those scientists are doing."

One of his men scratched his head and posed a question, "Do we get a piece of the action?"

"No. Only our fee. That doesn't seem fair, does it?"

CHAPTER 67

Kurt Buchanan was anxious to call his father, but looking at his watch, he checked himself. "It's much too late to call Washington. I'll call him first thing in the morning."

He overslept. It was noon before he got up. "Damn! I wanted to call Dad before his day got started. Now it's after three in Washington." He placed a call but, as expected, got voicemail. He left a message asking his father to call him as soon as possible.

It was after five o'clock when the call finally came. After preliminary greetings, Kurt got right into it.

"This nanotechnology thing is going to be big; the best thing we've ever done." Kurt continued with a detailed explanation of the process he'd witnessed. The senator remained silent through his son's soliloquy.

"What do you think?" Kurt asked.

"I think you've uncovered something very useful for our enterprises—and I think others would be willing to pay a great deal of money to have this new weapon."

"Not only that," Kurt said, "it's a weapon that can only be used once. If they want another 'shot,' they'll have to come back to us. We'll own the market on this technology."

"Son, you've done well. But how do we set up production? We'll need a laboratory and people to do the actual work."

"That's the beauty of this... a full lab's already in place. And as far as staff, from what I understand, Corbyn can pretty much run the operation herself."

"Wouldn't she need specialists to program the nanites?"

"All she needs is a sample of the target's DNA. All of the programming is already in place. She just inputs the data and cooks up a new batch of nanites."

"Here's our plan," his father said. "You look into that building. Find out who owns it. I think it would be best if we bought it outright. We don't want a nosy landlord poking around our business. For my part, I'll begin to put out feelers and gauge interest in such a product."

"Perfect!" Kurt exclaimed. "I'll get right on it."

"Also, you'll need to solidify the arrangement with Corbyn. Be certain we can hit the ground running when we're ready to take orders."

Kurt returned to Corbyn's satellite operation and found her in the boardroom. She didn't seem surprised to see him. "Welcome, Mr. Buchanan."

"I'll get right to it," he said. "I've spoken with my father, and we're willing to enter into an arrangement with you." He pulled out the spreadsheet Corbyn had given him. "From this, it looks like you will need one million dollars to set up a new facility."

"Yes, that is my estimate."

"What if we were to purchase this building? Wouldn't that eliminate that line item?"

Corbyn looked as if this were a completely new idea. "Why,

yes, I suppose it would. But the equipment—what about that? It all came from ASRI."

"Equipment breaks, wears out, and diminishes greatly in value. I'm sure I can devise a plan to amortize it all out of existence. After all, a new car's value drops by half when it's driven off the dealer's lot."

"An electron microscope isn't exactly an automobile, Mr. Buchanan."

"But it does diminish in value, does it not? As newer models are introduced, doesn't that impact the value of the older one?"

"I suppose it does…"

"And since I'm on the ASRI board, I can make certain this equipment is written off."

Corbyn gave an uncharacteristic smile. "I guess that addresses the facilities and equipment budget."

"Now, let's discuss what you call 'licensing fees.' You're asking for monthly payments of five hundred thousand dollars or six million dollars a year, is that correct?"

"Yes, it is."

"This document suggests payments are to be made in perpetuity."

"That was my thinking," Corbyn said.

"Perhaps we can discuss some kind of term for this item…"

They entered into a spirited debate. Her point was there would be no product without her. His was there would be no one to sell it without him. Each had their point, but in the end, Corbyn gave in.

"Very well," Corbyn said. "We'll start with a one-year period at this rate. Based on success and continuing demand, we will extend for another five years. If the figures are good, we'll keep the same licensing rate. If not, we'll have to have a discounted rate. If that's acceptable, we will move forward. If not…" She shrugged.

"It's a deal," Buchanan said.

When the door closed as Kurt Buchanan left, Corbyn let out a small cry of victory. "I'm going to be rich! I'll be a multi-millionaire. I can go anywhere, do anything..." She closed her eyes, imagining all that wealth would bring her.

"It turns out to be a good thing that I've got someone on the board. It simplifies everything." She stopped to get control of her emotions. "I must tell Callum." She sent a message to Robertson, summoning him to her office.

Five minutes later, Callum Robertson knocked and entered.

"Have a seat. I've got good news."

Robertson sat and gave her a quizzical look.

"I've just had a meeting with Kurt Buchanan. He's agreed to a partnership."

"What about a new facility? And equipment?" Robertson asked.

"All handled. The Buchanans will purchase this building, and as a member of the ASRI board, Kurt will make certain all our equipment is amortized out of existence." She gave Robertson a serious look. "I made it sound like you and I could provide product on demand. Do you agree?"

Callum pushed back his chair, stood, and began pacing. "If you're willing to do all the lab work, I suppose that's correct. However, it might be good to keep at least one of our lab rats."

"Who are you thinking of?"

"Myra Shipman—our little spy."

"I like that. She's already compromised, so it shouldn't be a stretch to keep her working. Besides, she'll be well-compensated for her work."

"What about me?" Robertson asked.

"How does one million a year sound?"

Robertson stopped pacing and sat back down. "That will suit me fine."

CHAPTER 68

For the first time, Senator Jack Buchanan felt excited. He tilted his high-back leather chair and looked around his Dirksen Senate Office Building suite of rooms. It was adequate, as government offices go, but it was still plain. He'd added his own touches over the years he'd been in office, like the crossed native spears and thatch shield mounted on the wall, a gift from a grateful government official in South Africa. Still, his private office in Hillsborough was much more comfortable and decorated to his liking.

This ASRI development is the opportunity I've been working toward all my life. Imagine, no more bickering with partisan politicians... no more masking deals behind legislation... no more investigative reporters snooping around...

He was already imagining how he would use the nanotechnology. *Maybe we should just keep it for ourselves.* He shrugged off the thought, recognizing the technology involved. *There are so many that would pay anything to eliminate dissidents or detractors or just plain enemies...*

He opened the lower drawer of his desk and lifted an old-style rotary telephone, his private line unconnected to the main switchboard. The senator didn't trust office phones or wireless technology. Too easy to hack, listen into, or subpoena for records. Landlines required a court order to wiretap. Hefting the handset, he admired the feel of the Bakelite. It was sturdy, permanent. He dialed a familiar number, his old friend and confidant, Michael Roark. His expertise as a fixer put him in touch with many people, not only in the United States, but abroad as well. In fact, it was Roark who put together the ASRI deal, not to mention the oil deal in Latvia.

Roark's pretty young secretary answered and put him right through.

"Jack! Good to hear from you," Roark said.

"Mike, there's something I'd like you to do for me."

"Certainly. What is it you need?"

"Discreet inquiries. Test the waters for something new." The senator briefed Roark on the nanotechnology weapon.

"Damn, Jack. Is all that for real?"

"It is."

"Do you realize you have a perfect weapon? Scalable, targeted, undetectable, and completely controlled by you."

"My thoughts exactly. I want you to poke around for me, get a feeling for how such a weapon would be received—and more importantly, how much would they be willing to pay?"

Roark called back that afternoon, "Let's meet for drinks. How about Filomena on K Street?" Jack Buchanan knew the restaurant well. It was a regular hangout for lobbyists and legislators. His presence wouldn't be seen as unusual.

He found Roark at a back table.

After ordering and receiving drinks, Roark began, "I posed a hypothetical question to several of my contacts. They were cautious with their answers, but all of them were interested—more than interested—and wanted to know more."

"Did you suggest a price?" Buchanan asked.

"I threw out a general number—half a billion."

"How did they react?"

"For most of these players, half a billion is chump change."

"No pushback?"

"None. They were all were interested, but want more specifics."

Jack Buchanan took a long sip of his martini. "This is good. Did you tell them more information will be coming?"

"I did. I think you've got a solid market, Jack."

Lifting his glass, he said, "A toast." Roark lifted his glass as well, lightly clinking.

"To a successful next chapter," Buchanan said.

CHAPTER 69

Corbyn called together her team. She could tell they were anxious as they shuffled into the boardroom. "Take a seat. I trust you all had a good night's sleep." Skeptical looks were exchanged between the three technicians.

Robertson, who came in last, watched the lab crew carefully. To Corbyn, he looked almost suspicious. He didn't sit but chose to stand at the door.

"You all performed well yesterday."

"Where is Dr. Hughes?" George Kraft asked.

"Don't worry, he'll be along soon. I would like a post-op briefing from each of you."

Oliver Bouy shifted around in his chair. "Those people... are they all...?"

"Dead? Yes, of course. The preliminary test went perfectly. You are all to be commended. In fact, each of you will receive a bonus."

That news seemed to relax the three technicians.

"Now, tell me what worked and what didn't."

Each, in turn, recounted that all processes and systems operated as expected. As they finished their reports, Dr. Hughes entered. He nodded to Corbyn before moving to a chair somewhat distant from the technicians.

Corbyn leaned forward, hands clasped. "Now we prepare for the final test: a much larger and more diverse group." She looked at Dr. Hughes. "Are you ready, Doctor?"

"As you know, we've been working day and night to get the differentiated strains isolated. I'm happy to report that all canisters are in place and ready for deployment. We only need subjects."

"You will have them." Looking to the door, she asked, "When can we expect delivery, Mr. Robertson?"

"Tonight. As we discussed, based on the results, more can be gathered and delivered for as long as you need subjects."

"How many in this first group?"

"Fifty."

Corbyn dismissed everyone except Robertson. "Come here, Callum." Robertson took the first seat. "Based on yesterday's results, I don't anticipate needing any more than tonight's delivery. Our deal with Buchanan is set. We only need to show data supporting our claim that the nanites can be programmed to attack individuals as well as specified groups. I need you to be certain that we have a wide range of subjects: young, old, black, white, Asian. We'll keep one from each group as a control and hold them in one of the side rooms."

"What do we do with the control group when the experiment is over? Take them back to the Tenderloin District?"

"Good Lord, no. Dr. Hughes will have a canister of the original, undifferentiated nanites. When we have all our data, we'll dose them."

"What about the lab team?"

"You have a pistol, correct?"

Robertson produced a wicked looking Colt Combat Unit pistol. "It came in with our last shipment." He brandished it, admiring the flat black finish and patterned grips. "This .45 is made for US Special Forces—equipped to handle and shoot with the highest levels of control, accuracy, and reliability."

"Very impressive, Callum. You will take care of them after we've disposed of the test subjects… all except Myra Shipman, of course."

CHAPTER 70

Reid and his team returned to their chosen hunting ground in the Tenderloin. His doubts and the concerns of his men regarding compensation were grating on him. He couldn't get it out of his mind. There was the germ of a plan swirling around his subconscious, but it would have to wait. Now it was time to fill Robertson's order.

His men were dressed in military-style fatigues, complete with web belts and pouches. The purpose was to intimidate the drunks and addicts to give themselves up without a fight. Should someone become belligerent or combative, they all carried collapsible steel batons—despite their being illegal in California.

"One rap on the head will quash any resistance in this crowd," Reid said while handing the batons out. He watched his men snap out their batons, wave them around, and collapse them back to the closed position.

"The clip will let you attach them to the web belts," he added.

He then briefed the team on the night's objective: different ethnicities, genders, and ages. "Based on the success of this group, we'll be going for five hundred more—one hundred a night. Try to keep them diverse." He looked over the team. He was proud of his men. "Okay, let's go!"

Initially, there was resistance among the homeless, but the military uniforms, balaclava hoods, and batons were an overwhelming deterrent. Some whimpered as they were taken, others expressed outrage, but that was quickly suppressed. The great percentage, however, was no trouble at all. They were passed out or comatose. The team's biggest problem was carrying them to the trailer.

It took almost three hours to subdue, collect, and load everyone. The mostly inert bodies almost filled the trailer. There was no laying them out neatly; instead, each subject was thrown on top of the pile of bodies. There was no concern or regret.

"After all," Reid rationalized, "they're homeless drunks and crackheads, no good to anybody."

With all subjects loaded, Reid sent a message to Robertson. The reply came back almost immediately:

We'll be ready for you.

Robertson received the message from Reid and went to gather the lab team. Even though he'd sent them to their quarters to get some sleep, he found each still awake. He supposed they were anxious about the coming experiment.

"Get ready, it's time to go to work," he ordered.

He left the group to make its own way down to the lab. He didn't know Myra had earlier sent a message to Hannah telling her that another experiment was to be run that night.

Heading up to Corbyn's boardroom office, he began fantasizing about the rewards Corbyn had promised.

CHAPTER 71

Hannah, Joel, and Davies huddled behind landscape shrubbery. Shadow had remained at the hotel to monitor the parallel feed Davies had set up.

They had a good view of the loading dock and watched a pickup with a large trailer back up to one of the two bays. The overhead door lifted, squeaking and grinding as four men got out of the truck. Robertson appeared from the building and talked to the men. They were too far away to hear what was said. Regardless, it was clear Robertson was in command.

Because of the trailer's position, their view of the loading bay was blocked. Even though they were unable to see what was being unloaded, they knew what the cargo must be.

They heard indistinct shouts and calls, and then the truck and trailer pulled out, clearing their field of view.

"Oh, my God!" Hannah exclaimed.

It looked like hundreds of bodies were laid out on the loading dock floor. The dock door lowered and shut. It was time for them to act. Hustling to the small door to the right of the overhead doors, the group stopped to confer.

"Is everyone ready?" Joel asked. "Do you all have your ears on?"

There were nods from all as they checked the small transmit/receive devices in their ears.

They moved in single file up to the side door. "I hope this door is still unlocked," Joel said.

Shadow, monitoring their transmissions from the hotel suite, replied, "That was the last thing I did before leaving. Only someone with knowledge of the computer systems could override my command."

"Good man. Let's go." Joel twisted the knob and pushed gently.

Hannah cringed, expecting the wail of a klaxon. There was no alarm. They all relaxed and entered.

As they stepped into the hallway, Hannah whispered that she knew this passageway. "It goes the entire length of the building." They moved on, everyone's senses on high alert. At one point, Hannah touched the left-hand wall. "I think we're just about even with the lab. See? There's a boarded-up door frame."

They continued on to a door on the right. Davies said, "This is my exit—the T3 room." He went into the service room and closed the door.

"It's just us now," Joel said. "How do we get onto the main floor?"

"This way." Hannah pointed to the left. "Through there."

Joel saw another door. He gave a questioning look.

"It opens onto the main floor area," she said.

With a careful push, Joel opened the door, peeked in, and then pulled back. "All clear," he said.

Robertson went to Corbyn's boardroom/office and found her surrounded by papers, muttering to herself. When he cleared his throat to make her aware of his presence, she seemed annoyed by the interruption.

"Reid has made his delivery. Do you want to come down to the loading dock area and inspect them before we begin?"

"Has Dr. Hughes completed his work?"

"I believe he has."

"I'll be down in a minute. Make sure everything is ready."

Joel was ready to go. Hannah stopped him. "Once we go in, there's no turning back. We have to complete the mission."

"I know."

"Every minute we wait, the closer those victims are to death."

They entered the main floor area as quietly as possible. They moved in a crouching run. Fortunately, the fabrication of the temporary rooms gave them the cover they needed.

Hannah stopped with a start, grabbing Joel's arm. "Corbyn," she whispered.

The director marched in and looked around as if searching for someone. A moment later, Robertson entered. He was followed by Dr. Hughes and the three technicians. She could see anguish on the technicians' faces, especially Myra's.

She watched the group gather around Corbyn, who was issuing orders. Hannah couldn't make out everything said, just a few words here and there. Myra and her colleagues were hesitating, trying to find a way to disregard Corbyn's orders.

The assembly broke up. Corbyn set off toward the dock area at her typically rapid pace, Myra trying to keep up. The others exchanged looks and went to the laboratory.

Joel watched the assembly with interest. He whispered through his subvocal mic, "Did you see all that?"

"Careful! You may be seen," Hannah said.

Joel asked, "Do we follow them?"

"No," she said. "We lay low and wait."

CHAPTER 72

Kurt Buchanan had been busy negotiating the satellite facility purchase. The owner of the building turned out to be more than happy to unload a property he considered a white elephant. After consulting with his father, an agreement was reached and would be finalized the following week.

"This is all coming together. After tonight, we'll have the world's most significant—and deadly—weapon."

He returned to the satellite facility with dreams of untold wealth and power swirling through his mind.

Corbyn entered the dock area, strutting like a monarch surveying her estate grounds, Buchanan and Robertson following in her wake. As they strode through the neat rows of incapacitated subjects, Kurt made an observation, "It seems your men have done a good job."

"They're organized by gender, race, and age," Robertson said.

Reaching the loading doors, Corbyn turned to Robertson.

"This is a good mix. It should make for an interesting experiment. Did you sedate them?"

"Yes. There won't be any problems."

"You may begin taking each group to their places."

Robertson called over Reid and his team. "Bring the flatbed cart." The team traded looks, ones that could be perceived as almost rebellious—that is, had Robertson seen them.

Meanwhile, Corbyn ordered Myra to her side. "Do you have them logged in?"

"Yes, ma'am. Right here." She held up her iPad.

Corbyn turned back to Robertson. "Start placing them in the designated areas. You'll see a note on each cube. Once they're in place, prepare them for exposure." She turned to Kurt Buchanan. "You may want to observe from over there…" she motioned to the side wall. Buchanan followed her instruction.

The placement work began. It took longer than Corbyn expected and, pacing back and forth, she ordered the men to hurry up. Robertson had to ask her not to distract the team; the men were doing the best they could.

Finally, all subjects were in their cubes. Robertson said, "It looks like we have them positioned well before the sedation wears off."

"Are they tightly secured?" Buchanan asked, coming back to join Corbyn.

"There'll be no trouble. Once they wake up, they'll still be immobilized."

Reid and his men didn't move. They waited until Corbyn and Buchanan had left the area, then gathered around Robertson. "What's this?" Beyond the question, there was a touch of outrage.

Reid looked toward his men. "It's like this: we want a piece of the action."

"You're crazy! You have no idea what's going on; besides, you're being well paid."

Waiving his arm around, Reid responded. "Look at all this... all the equipment... and you have us collecting homeless people to conduct some sort of experiment that kills them in minutes. I think you're working on some kind of weapon, something that'll be sold to the highest bidder. We want in. That's it."

"I don't think I can make that decision..."

"Make it happen, or we collect these people and return them to the city."

Robertson was trapped. He looked at the cubes, now occupied. Then it occurred to him—Corbyn had mentioned they wouldn't need any more subjects after tonight. His need for Reid and his men was over.

"Okay, I see your point. Let me clear it with Corbyn. Meanwhile, why don't you wait in one of the lounge rooms? It'll only take a minute or so to get approval."

Reid looked at his men. "We'll just wait over there," he motioned to the darkened front area.

CHAPTER 73

Hannah saw Kurt Buchanan retreat to a position to observe yet not be in the way. A stream of inert bodies were then delivered to the sealed rooms, each bound hand and foot. She wondered why the outer rooms weren't being used.

Joel used the distraction of moving people into cubes to take a new position.

When all subjects were placed, Corbyn waved her arm. It was a dismissive gesture for Reid's team to stand by.

Robertson remained with Reid while Hughes, Buchanan, and Corbyn went to the lab room.

After fifteen minutes, Corbyn and Hughes reemerged and joined Robertson while Buchanan returned to his previous observation position. Hughes went to each cube, placing a small box on the floor. When the task was complete, Corbyn rechecked to be certain that everything was in place and ready to go.

As Corbyn was conducting her inspection, Dr. Hughes went to a nearby table and picked up a crate of silver canisters. Before Hughes could begin deploying the canisters, he stopped and looked up sharply. "Hey, what's that?"

Out of the darkness, four figures appeared. It was Reid and his team.

"What are you doing here?" Corbyn demanded. "I thought I dismissed you all."

Instead of answering, Reid and his team surrounded them. Each held a weapon. The purpose for drawn sidearms wasn't lost on Callum Robertson.

"You damn fool, Reid… What are you doing?"

"Sorry," Reid said. "I'll take your sidearm…"

Robertson gave an angry look but he had no choice and handed over the Colt. Reid inspected the weapon. "Very nice," Reid said, and put the Colt in his web belt. "As I said earlier, we figure you've got something big going, something we don't want to miss out on."

Robertson glanced around, looking for some way out of this situation.

"You can't do this!" Corbyn shouted.

Reid stepped forward, and with a vicious backhand blow, struck Corbyn's face. The sound of the slap was like a shot echoing in the open space. To her credit, Corbyn didn't scream or let out a cry. Instead, she gave Reid a truly hateful look.

"Bring the other one here," Reid ordered.

Kurt Buchanan was added to the hostage group, and Reid's men began prodding with their weapons, herding the four captives to a side room

One of the men picked up the crate holding the nanite canisters. "Is this what we came for?"

Reid looked at the stainless-steel cylinders and then back to Corbyn, who was nursing a growing bruise on her cheek. He snarled, "Is that all of them?" The menacing tone of his question wasn't lost on Corbyn. She made no reply.

"I'll bet that means, 'no.' You've got more, and I think I know where to look." He turned to his team. "Secure them."

Reid's men carried out the order with harsh efficiency, shoving their captives into a side room. Locking the door as they left, one man was assigned guard duty.

Hannah watched the entire scene, helpless to take any action. Neither she nor Joel were armed, and it would be foolish—no, deadly—to step in. She could only hope Joel was able to reach the FBI. Clearly, they were going to need the help.

Joel, from his position, watched the unfolding drama. It was time to take action. He sent a brief text message to Simmons, asking for the FBI's help. He was confident the message would set the FBI into action. Now, it was only a question of monitoring the activity. He was surprised when one of the men struck Corbyn. *He's asserting his power and control over this situation.*

The four captives were moved at gunpoint to a side room. He wasn't sure if the room was an office or not, but he noticed a hasp had been installed on the door. *That couldn't have been part of the original installation.*

There was a single narrow window in the door. He saw no other windows along the wall and wondered what kind of office that could be. *It must feel like a jail cell in there.*

One man was left outside the door, his weapon held at the ready.

Hannah also observed the handling of Corbyn and the others. Earlier, she'd watched Myra return to the lab, leaving the door slightly ajar. *I guess she must be expecting me.*

She made a call to Joel, "Can you handle the guard at that door?"

She received a single *click*—the signal for *yes*.

Joel was doing his best to keep out of the door guard's line of sight. He spotted a tray holding silver canisters on the floor beside the room holding the captives. *That must be the nanites.* He looked over to the now-occupied clean rooms and had a good idea what was going to happen.

He moved furtively through the cubes. He was glad for the cover. Sitting behind the wood framing of one occupied cube, he looked through the opaque vinyl covering. Bodies were scattered on the floor. All bound hand and foot. Turning back to the guard at the room door, he considered his options.

The guard is armed, and I'm not. That's not insurmountable, but it's a problem. I'll have to disarm or distract him somehow, at least enough to prompt him to leave his post.

As he pondered the situation, something strange happened. The guard stiffened and looked toward the dark shadows in the front of the building. The guard appeared alarmed and checked the room door, then walked away before properly securing the door.

Joel didn't know what act of providence was at work, but he was thankful. Crouching and moving to the room door, he could deal with the simple door lock. Had the guard put the padlock on the hasp, that would have been another situation. It would take much more time to pick or break.

He fished a small lockpick set from the pouch at his waist and opened the door. The looks of astonishment on the captives' faces told the story: they weren't expecting rescue.

"Don't I know you?" Corbyn asked.

CHAPTER 74

Joel closed the door behind him and looked over the prisoners. Corbyn had a hostile look, Dr. Hughes seemed defeated, Buchanan looked afraid, and Robertson was defiant.

"Yes, we've met before. My name is Joel Braithwaite with the UN Terrorism Prevention Bureau."

"We're not terrorists," Corbyn stated emphatically. Dr. Hughes' body language suggested otherwise. Buchanan's face went white.

"I suppose all those people out there, bound and drugged, are volunteers," Joel said.

"What do you want with us?" Robertson asked.

"Who are the men who attacked you?"

Disgust and disdain boiled up in Robertson. "Traitors."

"I'll bet they came to take your nanotechnology. What do you think?"

There was only silence.

"Regardless, they're armed. I assume you don't have any firearms in this building."

"No," Robertson said. "Not anymore. They took my piece."

"Then, against my better judgment, I'd say we all have to get out of here."

There was shouting outside the room. Everyone froze. Joel went to the narrow door window.

"I can't see much from this perspective. Just some movement." Joel looked around within the small room. "From what I can see, there's not much here that could be used as a weapon."

There was noise at the door. "What's that?" Buchanan asked.

Joel leaned against a wall, trying to get a better angle looking through the narrow window. "It's the padlock. The guard came back and set it." Desperation washed over the others' faces.

Robertson said, "I hope you have another way out, hero." The derision in his voice wasn't lost on Joel.

"Give me a minute," Joel said.

They watched as he pressed something on his neck and began talking.

Hannah watched the hasty regrouping of the four men. One of them broke away and went to the lab. Looking back, she saw the room guard leave his post and come to the front area. *Something's got them spooked. I hope it's the FBI.*

After the one man entered the lab, everything went quiet. It seemed even the building held its breath.

The others were paying attention to something outside. She was interrupted by a call from Shadow. Unable to speak, she listened to his report. There wasn't much time. She had to get to the lab.

CHAPTER 75

The room guard joined Reid and the other men at the front of the building. "We've got company," the guard said.
"Yeah, two SUVs," Reid said. "They've just turned onto the approach drive. Time to get out of here."
"What about them?" the guard asked, motioning to the room holding the four hostages.
"We gas 'em, then bug out the rear entrance."
Reid's team acted quickly. The guard returned to the room, secured the padlock, and picked up the tray of canisters. Reid met his man at the room door. "Give me one of those." The guard handed him a canister. Reid attached it to a port on the outside wall, made sure of the connection, and then opened the valve.
"That should do it. Now, let's get out of here."
One of the men unhitched the trailer while Reid put the remaining canisters in the truck bed. "Mount up, and let's go," Reid ordered.
As they rounded the corner of the building, the driver made an abrupt stop. "Looks like company, boss."
Two more black SUVs turned at the ASRI building and extinguished their headlights.

"Hold a moment," Reid said. "Let's see where they go."

They watched the SUVs pull into the car park, taking places at the very back.

"Gotta be Feds," Reid said. The others remained silent, fearful of being discovered.

The driver asked, "How'd they get onto us?"

"I don't know," Reid said, "but we got lucky. They're going inside."

CHAPTER 76

Special Agent Rick Simmons was the operational leader of this offensive; however, tactical control rested with HRT. With a squad of six, the Hostage Rescue Team would take command. They would also be the ones in the line of fire, should there be armed resistance.

The two black SUVs extinguished their headlights and made their way past the ASRI headquarters building, continuing around a curve to the building next door.

"No lights at the front entrance," Simmons announced to the team. "Park away from the building. We'll begin from there."

The SUVs pulled into the last line of parking spaces. The HRT operators gathered in silence, awaiting instructions.

"Check all comms," the HRT leader whispered.

All team members, along with Agent Simmons, checked to be sure their in-ear tactical radios were working. When everyone gave a thumbs-up, the squad leader inspected each man. He wasn't looking for razor-creased uniforms; he was making sure each man's assault rifle and sidearm were in working order. Once the inspection was complete, he issued orders.

"We'll divide and approach from two sides. We're not certain what we'll encounter. Agent Simmons has reported that there are a large number of hostages." The leader turned to Simmons. "Sir, do you have anything more?"

Simmons stepped forward. "I do. Freeing the hostages is the priority, but I want to warn you: there is a deadly virus in there. They're planning to test the virus on human subjects. It's my understanding that any exposure to the virus will result in death."

The squad leader asked, "How do we recognize the virus?"

"It's as deadly to the handlers as it is to the test subjects, so they'll take precautions. Look for small containers, like thermos bottles. When you find them, secure and protect them at all costs."

"Thank you, Agent Simmons," the squad leader said. "Let's move!"

The HRT squad split into two groups, with the leader accompanying one and Simmons the other. Dressed in dark tactical attire, they were practically invisible as they approached the building.

They stopped at either corner. The squad leader motioned, and one of the men moved to the front doors. After a moment of inspection, Simmons waved to the squad leader.

Over the comms, the leader announced, "All clear. Breach with care."

The HRT squad affixed plastic explosives to the door. A muted *wumpf* initiated a practiced tactical entry: one man covering the open door, another moving inside to take up a defensive position. The entire process took less than a minute to get both teams inside. In the darkened lobby, the team leader used hand signals to disperse his men. In pairs, they moved through the lobby to the open main floor. One man was left at the door.

The HRT squad found half of the floor lit, the other half,

where they were positioned, was in the dark. The squad leader lifted a fist, the signal for everyone to hold their positions. He surveyed ahead, dropped back, and keyed the comm link.

"All clear. Team One, move forward and test the perimeter."

The team of two men moved out, crouching as they secured a position a few yards ahead of the main company.

CHAPTER 77

Davies was busy unscrambling bundles of wires while Shadow monitored the team's activity from the hotel. Shadow spoke into the microphone on the desk, "Davies, how're you coming?"

He received a grunt in response.

"I can't do anything more until you get me access," Shadow said.

"Hold your water," Davies said. "This isn't as easy as you think."

"Sorry. Just anxious to get this over with."

While waiting on his partner, Shadow thought it would be a good idea to check on the others. Switching channels, he called Hannah, "Miss Hannah, are you there?"

He received a single *click* in response.

"Can you talk?"

A double-click reply.

"Okay, you can't talk. I'll just give you an update. We're working on installing a worm in the main T3 drop. Once it's ready, someone has to initiate activation. That can only be done at one workstation in the lab—the one used by Dr. Hughes. Can you do that?"

A single *click*.

"Good. Signal when you're ready, and I'll walk you through the activation sequence."

Another single *click*, followed by three *clicks*—understood and over-and-out.

Returning his attention to Davies, Shadow called, "Not to rush you, partner, but we don't have as much time as we thought."

Davies extracted himself from the tangle of wires. "I'm done. We're good to go."

"Are you sure this worm program will destroy everything?"

"It should. It'll search out every instance of this research and eradicate it, whether dealing with functionalized nanomagnetics, nanocomposites, or nanorobots."

"I sure hope so," Shadow said. "We can't let even a scrap of this program get out."

Davies stood back. "Since this feed's connected to ASRI, I've set it up to remove all instances and mentions in all databases company-wide. Once the worm is initiated, it will be as if Dr. Perry's research—and its subsequent hijacking—never existed."

CHAPTER 78

Hannah approached the laboratory door. It had been left ajar. There was no window in the lab door, so there was no way to know what she'd be walking into. She took a deep breath and pushed the door open.

The lab room was a long rectangle. The entry door where she stood crouching was on the end of one long side. She was able to slip in unnoticed and quietly pulled the door closed behind her. The three technicians were huddled together at the far end of the room with their hands raised. Fear was written all over their faces.

Their captor had his back to Hannah at the entry door. She watched as the man rummaged through drawers while keeping the handgun trained in the direction of his prisoners.

"Where are the canisters?" the man demanded. He threatened the trio with his weapon. "Tell me! You had to use something to make those other ones."

Myra spoke up, "You have to understand how this works..."

"I don't need to understand anything. Just tell me where you keep the rest of the canisters."

Hannah could see this standoff was coming to a crisis point. She raised her arm, signaling across the room. Myra's attention was caught by the movement and hope came to her eyes. Hannah gave Myra a circling signal with her finger, hoping she would understand. She did.

"The process is carried out with electron microscopes and extraordinarily fine instruments," Myra said. "We have to operate in a sealed, clean environment..."

Hannah took advantage of Myra's diversionary dialogue to move forward. She grabbed a bookend from one work area as she passed. It was solid, heavy, and appeared to be the bust of a Roman soldier. *This will do nicely.*

Myra was still talking when Hannah came up behind the man and swung the bookend at the back of his head. He collapsed straight down, still gripping the pistol. Hannah scooped up the weapon and put the bookend on the floor.

The three technicians were transfixed by what they'd just witnessed.

Myra recovered first. "Hannah!" Myra turned to her colleagues. "This is the woman I was telling you about."

"We'll carry on with introductions later," Hannah said. "Right now, I'd like to know what this man was looking for."

Oliver, now recovered, responded, "He wanted all our research materials—all the nanites. He rightly surmised that the canisters outside weren't all we had. We were trying to keep him from opening this cabinet..." Oliver stepped to the wall and opened a concealed door that revealed a glass window. "This is where we keep the seed colony."

Hannah looked through the glass. "There's nothing in there."

All three technicians gasped, staring in like kids in a candy shop window.

"What has Hughes done?" Myra asked. "The master seed colony was supposed to remain isolated."

All three looked to the lab door.

Where Hannah had seen fear when facing the intruder with the gun, she now saw horror and disbelief.

"He wouldn't have, would he?" George Kraft asked. "We've got to get those canisters before the subjects are exposed."

Hannah wasted no time. Looking around, she wondered how secure the lab room was. "Does that door lock from inside?" The looks on the technicians' faces gave her the answer. She went back to the door she'd entered by, gave it a tug, and set the inside bolt lock.

"Where is Dr. Hughes' work station?"

Myra pointed to an area separate from the others. Sitting in the task chair before a large computer monitor, she pressed the subvocal mic at her throat.

"Davies, Shadow? Are you there?"

"We copy you," Davies responded.

"I'm in the lab, sitting at Dr. Hughes' computer. Let's get this worm thing going before we're discovered."

"Here's what you do..."

Two minutes of tapping the keyboard and multiple windows opening and closing brought her to the screen she wanted.

Davies said, "Great. You're there. Hold down the Control and Command keys, and then hit Delete." She followed Davies' instruction. The monitor ran the multiple windows again, this time wiping down to reveal the one behind.

"What's happening?" Hannah asked.

"The worm is doing its work. What you're seeing is the complete deletion of data, files, and folders."

"Is it just here, in the lab?"

"It's everywhere in the ASRI system, even in England," Davies said.

"What about our cloned setup in the hotel?"

"There, too."

She sat back, relieved.

The three technicians had been standing back, watching as Hannah conversed with her unseen counterpart. When the files began to disappear, Myra asked, "What's happening?"

Hannah turned. "Everything related to your project is being deleted."

"Do you mean all that work is... gone?" Oliver asked. The look on Hannah's face gave him the answer.

Going back to the group, she changed the subject, "Our next order of business is to get you three out of here. We have to assume the rest of the assault team is outside. Is there any other access to this room?"

"There was," George said. "Dr. Hughes had it covered up during the initial retrofit."

"I thought I remembered seeing a sealed door in the rear hallway," Hannah said.

George moved down the longer wall to a place roughly across from the main entry to the room. "Around here, I think. I don't remember exactly. I only saw it briefly when the work was being done."

"Hand me that bookend, would you?" Hannah asked. Oliver picked it up and gave it to her.

With a series of light raps on the wall, she soon found the spot she was looking for. "This is it. Let's pry off the drywall."

She looked around for anything that could be useful. She spotted a small zippered pouch on one of the workstations. "See what's in there."

Oliver retrieved the item. Inspecting the contents, he said, "This holds some small tools, like you'd use to tighten up a chair."

Taking the pouch, her eyes lit up. She extracted a flathead

screwdriver and a small hammer. Handing the tools to George, she said, "Would you do the honors?"

With a grin, George took the hammer and screwdriver and began working on the wall.

Once a good-sized hole was made, they all pitched in and pulled off the remaining wallboard. Behind the false wall was a door. Hannah activated her subvocal mic.

"Davies? We've found an entrance to that back hallway. Will you meet us?"

Davies, with his head in the tangle of multi-colored wires, put the finishing touches on the sabotage operation. A quick call to Shadow confirmed that all data had been scrubbed. Davies pulled back. "No one's gonna use this T3 for a while."

Davies received Hannah's call and he left the server room. He didn't have to go far. Hannah was emerging from a door that had no knob on the hallway side. When they came together, Davies was surprised to see three people with her.

"Have you heard from Joel?" Hannah asked.

"Not for a while," he said.

Hannah grew concerned. It was a look Davies hadn't seen before.

"Will you escort these people out of the building?"

"Who are they?"

"Technicians. They were working for Corbyn and Dr. Hughes."

"Doesn't that make them part of the conspiracy?"

Hannah looked at the emotionally battered trio. "I don't think so. They were part of it, but I suspect were unwitting participants in Corbyn's mad scheme."

Her answer seemed to satisfy Davies. "Follow me," Davies said.

The three technicians followed Davies to the end of the hallway.

When the group was well on its way, Hannah thumbed her subvocal mic.

"Joel... Joel... are you there?"

There was a single *click* in response.

"I understand... you can't talk. Where are you?"

There was a long pause. She thought he wouldn't—or couldn't—reply. Then, a hushed voice in her ear.

"Small office... far wall... locked in."

She had a good idea which office Joel was talking about. It was the meeting place for she and Myra.

"Hold on, Joel. I'm coming."

CHAPTER 79

The HRT squad moved with circumspection. As they came into the lighted area they stopped, marveling at the makeshift cells. Inspecting the cubes more closely, they found them occupied by people. They huddled to get new orders from their leader.

"It looks like they beat feet outta here. The only other way out is the rear loading dock. Squad One, you head there. Squad Two, you secure this area."

Squad One, with their leader, double-timed it to the rear area. The squad halted just before entering, their leader cautioning against bursting in.

Splitting up, they hugged the walls and crept into the loading dock. It was empty, the loading door was up, and there were no canisters in evidence.

Lifting weapons to port arms, the team relaxed.

The lookout left at the front called the leader, "Sir, a dark truck just drove off. No headlights."

The HRT leader ordered all squads outside. "I'll bet dollars to donuts they've got the canisters."

Agent Simmons ran out the front doors and saw a dark pickup speeding away. He ran to join Squad Two, ordering them to pursue the truck.

With sirens wailing and emergency lights flashing, they set out.

The driver of the pickup must have panicked. He tried turning onto the main road with too much speed. The truck couldn't hold its balance and tilted up on two wheels. Regaining control, the pickup dropped back slowly onto all four tires.

The driver floored it, and the truck leaped forward.

Unfortunately, there was oncoming traffic. The truck swerved to avoid a collision. Still at speed, the maneuver sent the truck into the soft turf alongside the road. The driver was unable to control the vehicle and couldn't avoid the stand of Coast Live Oak trees in his path, plowing into a tree with a loud screeching crash.

The canisters flew out of the truck bed, scattering on the turf.

The HRT vehicles came to a stop behind the ruined pickup. As the squad emerged, they weren't taking any chances. Their assault rifles were locked and loaded. One HRT member went to the driver's side of the ruined pickup and looked in.

"This one's dead," he announced.

Agent Simmons went around to the other side. The door hung open. The interior was empty. "It looks like the others got away. We need to search. They may be carrying very dangerous biological materials. It's important we don't harm the canisters in any way."

The squad re-formed. Simmons assigned two men to retrieve the scattered canisters while the rest moved into the stand of oak trees.

"Movement ahead... two men," announced one. "Ten o'clock."

Everyone moved in that direction.

Their quarry's movements were hampered by the canisters they carried. The HRT squad soon caught up, surrounding the two men. Agent Simmons stepped forward.

"It's over. Give yourselves up."

Their faces suggested panic. One man turned around, searching for any escape.

"You can't get away," Simmons said.

The men exchanged looks like caged animals. One man, it was Reid, laughed, not with humor but despair. He looked at the canisters he'd risked his life for and placed the crate on the ground. But as he stood back up, he grabbed one cylinder and held it up.

"Back off! I think you know what this is If I open it, we all die. Now, back off!"

The squad took a step back but didn't retreat. Simmons was watching carefully as one of the HRT team approached quietly from behind. Reid held the canister high, his attention on the armed men in front. He was unaware of the danger behind him.

The next moments seemed to move in slow motion. Reid waved the canister around wildly. The HRT squad member came up from behind. The man must have felt the other's presence, because he swung around and let out a shout of surprise.

The squad member grabbed Reid's arm below the wrist, immobilizing the canister in his hand. In a practiced martial arts move, the HRT member spun the man around, dropped him to the ground, and grabbed the canister.

With the man on the ground, the rest of the HRT team handcuffed the second man. Simmons went to gather the scattered canisters. With great care, he placed them back in the crate.

CHAPTER 80

Joel tried the door, but the outside hasp lock frustrated his efforts. Turning to the others, he shrugged. "It looks like we're in here for the duration of whatever's happening outside."

"That's just great," Robertson said. "Can't we break the window in the door?"

"It's too narrow and it's wire-reinforced," Joel replied. "None of us would fit, and we'd need a sledgehammer to get through."

Margaret Corbyn got to her feet and looked around.

"What are you searching for?" Robertson asked.

"I hear hissing."

"You're just hearing things," Hughes said. "Sit back down."

"Shut up, you fool! This is all *your* fault." She began searching along the walls. If someone spoke, she barked an order for quiet. Kurt Buchanan, still in shock, slid into a sitting position and wrapped his arms around his knees.

Joel watched in silent amazement. *These people have no idea the trouble they're in.*

Corbyn reached a small vent cover on the outside wall. Stooping down to listen, she suddenly jumped up and away, her face ashen.

"What's wrong?" Robertson asked.

Corbyn couldn't speak, but pointed to the vent cover. A thin, gray mist began flowing into the room.

"That's just a vent to keep the air circulating," Hughes offered, not seeing the mist.

Buchanan remained silent.

Corbyn shook her head.

Robertson understood what was happening. "We're being exposed! Quick, find something to cover that vent!" Other than the clothing they wore, there was nothing else available.

Joel tore his shirt off and went to the vent. "Maybe this will stop the flow," he said and placed the shirt over the vent grid. It did little to stop the mist's flow. He looked back to Corbyn, still ashen-faced. "How long do we have?"

"It's already too late," she said.

"Do you mean we're infected? I don't feel anything."

Corbyn perked up. "Maybe it's one of the variants, one that won't affect us."

"We've got to get out of here," Joel said. He went to the door and began banging. After a minute, he gave up because he was wheezing while taking breaths. Turning away from the door, he saw the mist beginning to engulf the small room. The others, huddled on the floor as far away from the vent as possible, were exhibiting symptoms as well.

"Which variant is this?" Joel asked.

Corbyn could only whisper a reply, "No variant. It's the original, undifferentiated strain."

Kurt Buchanan began to cry.

Robertson said, "I guess this is it."

Hannah watched as Davies led the technicians to freedom. She turned back and passed through the lab, glancing at the still unconscious man on the floor. Hefting the pistol she'd taken from the assailant, she opened the outside door and stepped into the main room.

There was no one in sight. The space was empty.

There was no sound—except for a knocking. Scanning the room for the source of the sound, it stopped before she could pinpoint the location.

Still wary, she moved through the plastic-enclosed structures. *These are more of Corbyn's "subjects."* Looking through the thick plastic wall of one enclosure she saw the people inside were hardly free. Their hands and feet were bound, and they lay on the floor, inert. *Not dead—drugged.*

At the end of the temporary enclosures, she noticed light coming from a door window. It was the very room where she and Myra had met—and where Joel was likely trapped. Walking up to the door, she tried the knob. She shook it, only then noticing the padlocked hasp. *That wasn't here before.*

Joel's face appeared in the window.

"Joel!" she shouted.

She was stunned by what she saw. The universe seemed to tunnel and her mind was trying to grasp the situation. Joel had a look she'd never seen before. It was sadness... and resignation.

She looked at the padlock as if it was some alien artifact. Her thoughts were confused. Breaking out of her momentary paralysis, she grabbed the padlock. She could only rattle it.

Her mind was having difficulty grasping what was happening, although deep down, she knew. It was just like her experience with Amy.

As if in a dream, she found herself looking into the room, past Joel's shoulder. There were four other people propped against the wall. They didn't seem to be moving.

"The others?" Her question sounded like a plea.

"Corbyn, Hughes, the security guy..." Joel turned his head with difficulty, "...and the senator's son, Jack Buchanan." Turning back to the window, Joel saw the stricken look on her face. "I'm afraid we've been infected."

The pronouncement snapped her back to the present. "Hold on. I'll shoot the lock off the hasp."

"No—you can't." Joel coughed a deep rasp, and she knew there would be no hope of rescue. "Right now, this thing is contained. You can't risk letting the virus out."

The mist swirled up and around Joel like a fog on London's streets. Through the growing mist, she looked into Joel's eyes. "This can't be happening!"

A deep sadness fell over her like a weighted blanket. It immobilized her. As a soldier, Joel had faced death many times. This was different. She looked into his eyes that were beginning to cloud over. He'd resigned himself to this final, terrible fate.

Joel Braithwaite would meet death like a soldier.

Like a hero.

She watched in horror as his face turned gray and his body slumped. "Joel—no!"

Memories flashed through her mind as she watched her partner of so many operations slide to the floor. She saw images of Amy Perry falling into her arms, her face ashen... the delirium that gripped her... her warning to *stop the mist*... then Amy's racking cough, just like Joel's, and finally, a tortured death.

She lifted her face upward. "Oh, God, please, no."

Joel lifted his palm to the window. She placed her hand over his. She looked down into his eyes. They were dimming, and she was powerless to stop it.

A terrible emptiness gripped her. The feeling in her chest was like when she lost her father all those years ago. But this was worse. A void was opening in her soul. There was a sense of falling, endlessly falling.

Joel's eyes went vacant.

She watched incredulously as his hand slipped down the glass and disappeared into the mist.

"JOEL!"

Never miss a release! Join our non-spam mailing list by visiting Thriller Books: https://aethonbooks.com/thriller-newsletter/ and never miss out on future releases. You'll also receive five full books completely free as our thanks to you.

THANK YOU FOR READING DEATH MIST

We hope you enjoyed it as much as we enjoyed bringing it to you. We just wanted to take a moment to encourage you to review the book. Follow this link: **Death Mist** to be directed to the book's Amazon product page to leave your review.

Every review helps further the author's reach and, ultimately, helps them continue writing fantastic books for us all to enjoy.

Also by Adam Clayton

HANNAH AHEMD THRILLERS
Shadow Agenda
Janus Curse
Death Mist

You can join our non-spam mailing list by visiting Thriller Books: https://aethonbooks.com/thriller-newsletter/ and never miss out on future releases. You'll also receive five full books completely Free as our thanks to you.

Don't forget to follow us on socials to never miss a new release!
Facebook | Instagram | Twitter | Website

Want to discuss our books with other readers and even the authors?
JOIN THE AETHON DISCORD!

For all our Thrillers, visit our website at www.aethonbooks.com/thriller

ABOUT THE AUTHOR

With a Masters' Degree in Communications Arts, I established a Los Angeles based production company providing a wide range of creative services including script writing, speech writing, film writing, multi-media and live event production.

I developed domestic and international marketing campaigns for many Fortune 500 corporations, delivering strategic business and marketing messages throughout the world. Multi-disciplinary success led to network television writing and production contracts with CBS Television, Discovery Channels, and other international broadcast interests.

A five-year contract with the Organization of American States (OAS) sent me to the West Indies where I consulted with Presidents, Prime Ministers, Premieres, and Ministers of State. I lived within the indigenous communities to learn about the people, their beliefs, customs, and traditions.

My interaction with people from many nations including Great Britain, France, Germany, Canada, Australia, and New Zealand gave me a fresh perspective that has served me well as a fiction writer.

WEBSITE:
www.adamclaytonbooks.com
EMAIL:
aclayton@adamclaytonbooks.com

Made in United States
Cleveland, OH
28 October 2025